HAVERSCROFT

S. A. HARRIS won The Retreat West Crime Writer Competition in 2017, and was shortlisted for The Fresher Prize in 2018. *Haverscroft* is her debut novel, she is now writing her second, a supernatural tale set on the Suffolk coast. She is a family law solicitor and lives in Norwich with her husband and three children.

HAVERSCROFT

S. A. HARRIS

CROMER

PUBLISHED BY SALT PUBLISHING 2019

2 4 6 8 10 9 7 5 3 1

This book is a work of fiction. Any references to historical events, real people or real places are used fictitiously. Other names, characters, places and events are products of the author's imagination, and any resemblance to actual events or places or persons, living or dead, is entirely coincidental.

First published in Great Britain in 2019 by
Salt Publishing Ltd
12 Norwich Road, Cromer NR27 0AX United Kingdom

www.saltpublishing.com

Salt Publishing Limited Reg. No. 5293401

A CIP catalogue record for this book is available from the British Library

ISBN 978 1 78463 200 7 (Paperback edition)
ISBN 978 1 78463 201 4 (Electronic edition)

Typeset in Neacademia by Salt Publishing

Printed and bound in Great Britain by Clays Ltd, Elcograf S.p.A

David,
Morgan, Emily and James.
Love you all.

HAVERSCROFT

CHAPTER 1

SATURDAY, 2ND OCTOBER

WHERE THE HELL are they?

I cross the tiled hall, weaving between packing boxes and several dining chairs and stop at the bottom of the stairs.

'Sophie?'

The landing is gloomy to the point of near darkness. High in the ceiling, at the top of the flight, hangs a filthy glass shade, its light feeble and yellow.

'Tom?'

'Lost them already?' The removal men manoeuvre the sofa up the steep front steps and into the hall.

'You haven't seen them, have you?'

'Place this size, you'll have a job on your hands just keeping track of them.' The older man puffs as he speaks, tries to hoist the sofa higher, spots the two mugs I hold.

'I'll leave the coffee here for you.'

I jolt the mugs onto a packing case, liquid slops out. Where the hell are the kids?

'Sofa going in the kitchen, you say?'

I nod. This man talks for England, I don't have the time.

I peer at the landing. 'Tom?'

Somewhere a door slams. Mark's told the twins off already for chasing from one empty room to another, slamming doors, kicking up dust. I head upstairs.

'Tom! Sophie! Where are you? I've loads to get sorted today and could really do with a bit of help.'

I reach the landing. On my right is the room to be our bedroom, and the office at the far end of the corridor. The doors are open, no sign of the children. Left is the room we found the twins the day we first came here, hiding beneath a high metal bed and covered in dust. The door is shut. The light bulb flickers, a useless thing. It's only half a dozen steps to the door, stupid to be nervous of shadows and dark corners. I suck in a breath and hurry towards the door, grab and turn the tiny brass knob. Locked.

I rap on the door. 'Kids, open up! I don't have time for games right now.'

No response, not a sound. I try the door again and to my surprise the knob turns easily, the door swinging away from me. Old houses. We'd better get used to this sort of thing in a hurry.

The enormous bed is gone, but the gruesome pink carpet and lingering rank odour remains. I snatch dust sheets off a dressing table and chaise longue. Nowhere for the twins to hide. I step across to the French windows, which open outwards onto a narrow Juliet balcony. An empty lawn sweeps down to a clutch of willows dripping naked branches into the black water of a pond. A perfect spot, the estate agent claimed, beside the church, fishing in the river just beyond. A shiver runs across my shoulders. Click. I spin around. The door's shut. No one here. I'm not good on my own, not yet.

'Tom! Sophie!'

Don't get weird. Just be rational, breathe. A draught, most likely. The smell, stale cigarettes and something sour makes the room claustrophobic. It must be the carpet. What are the hideous brown stains beside the hearth? I put my hand across my mouth and nose and head for the door. I try the handle, stuck again. It won't turn at all.

'Shit!'

Just keep calm. The mechanism's so ancient it's clearly temperamental. Please don't be broken.

'Mark!'

I grab the handle with both hands and shake it, try to turn it, but it's solid. I let go and step backwards, tears sting the back of my eyes. I take a breath and scrunch my eyes tight, count in my head, one, two, three. It's just a closed door, Kate.

I open my eyes and reach out, hold the cold brass doorknob.

Breathe.

It turns, opens. I dash onto the landing. Thank God no one saw any of that. The bulb flickers spilling grimy shadows across the ceiling and walls, it hisses, glows brighter. Pop. An electrician is the first thing we need. Are the electrics a fire hazard? I guess Mark had them checked out along with all the usual survey stuff.

The remaining rooms are empty, the twins must be with Mark, wherever he is. More family time, we said, but that depends on us being in the same room at the same time. I take a slow, deep breath and jog downstairs. I'm much better now at keeping the panic at bay.

The removal men are in the hall, sitting on Mum's sofa, drinking coffee. They think it's odd, a sofa in the kitchen, they said so earlier. I'd never thought about it until they mentioned it. In Mum's small flat it marked the space where the kitchen and lounge met.

'You haven't seen the children about, have you?'

Both men smile up at me as I stop at the bottom of the stairs.

'Boo!'

My son leaps from behind a packing case, a huge grin on his face, uneven half-grown front teeth already too big for his features.

'For God's sake, Tom!'

He sees he's startled me, his grin widens. 'This place is so cool for hide and seek.'

Sophie emerges from behind a neighbouring box. 'We've been waiting ages, but we got you, didn't we?'

I take a breath and bite my tongue. It's not the twins' fault my stomach's turning summersaults. Things improved over the summer holidays. Having the twins at home kept me busy and occupied, but total normality is still a little way off. Even the breathing techniques have their limits.

I muster a smile. 'You did, but now's not the time or the place. How do I know you've not got lost or fallen in the pond?'

Tom glances at the removal men as they shuffle the sofa towards the kitchen, both men still smiling. I suspect they knew exactly what the twins had planned.

'You told us: don't go near the pond, don't go out into the back lane,' says Tom. 'You've told us twice already.'

'And you said we can't have a dog,' adds Sophie in a whiney tone.

'Yet,' Tom says.

A crash from upstairs, the sound sharp and clear in the empty house. We all look towards the landing. The bedroom door slamming, I should've closed it.

'Not you this time, kids,' says the older removal man with a wink.

'It wasn't last time. Dad just doesn't believe us,' says Sophie. 'He blames us for everything!'

'That's a bit of an exaggeration, Sophie. Dad's worried it'll damage something. Just be careful, that's all he's saying.'

A bit of cracked paint and plaster are minor concerns with so much to do, but a united front is essential when dealing with the twins.

'Once we get the big stuff in, we'll close the front door,' the older removal man says. 'Causing a bit of a draught, I expect.'

'Where's Daddy?' I ask.

'In the garage having a smoke,' says the younger man. He's got far more idea of what's going on around here than I have. 'Interesting old car you've got there. Needs a ton of work.'

Mark mentioned the Armstrong Siddeley more than once over the summer. He seems to think Mrs Havers' rusting, immovable wreck, abandoned in the only garage is a positive. I suspect it's going to be an added expense when it eventually gets hauled off to the scrapyard.

'Let's take coffee to Dad then, shall we, kids?'

'Come on, Tom. We'll ask about getting a dog,' says Sophie.

The twins head down the front steps and run off around the side of the house. I feel bad they've been shouted at so much today. Four months is a lifetime when you're only nine, bottled up excitement has to come out some way.

By the time I get to the garage, Tom is sitting behind the wheel of the old cream and navy car. It makes me think of black and white gangster movies, with its elegant front wheel arches sweeping down to narrow running boards. Sophie's in the passenger seat beside Tom. No sign of my husband.

'Mark?'

I squeeze between the car and the junk piled inside the garage. The tailgate is open, Mark peers around it, sees I have a coffee mug in each hand. 'I'm on my way back to the house,' he says, crushing a cigarette butt beneath the heel of his deck shoe.

'Looks like it.' I pass him a mug, raise my eyebrows and smile. 'A grand car once.'

'It needs quite a lot of work – it's a long-term project.'

'Once the house is under some sort of control, maybe? We've only today and tomorrow to get sorted before you're back to London for the week.'

He grins. 'It might be worth a bit once it's restored.'

Sophie slaps the flat of her hand on the inside of the passenger window and yanks the door handle, her lips moving and voice muffled. What she's yelling about?

'Stop that, Sophie!' Mark shouts. I jolt coffee over the rim of my mug.

'Mark, let her out! She can't get out!'

Panic surges through my voice as my chest tightens. Mark jabs his finger towards the car. 'Get out Tom's side. Don't damage anything, either of you.'

Tom's out of the car in an instant. 'We weren't doing anything,' he says, glancing at his sister as she stands beside him.

'It's disgusting,' she says, her skinny arms tense and straight. 'It stinks in there!'

Mark's looking at me, the crinkle between his dark eyebrows deepening. I overreacted. The panic comes so fast.

'Have you sorted out who's having which bedroom?' I ask before Mark has a chance to say anything. My voice is steady, but my cheeks burn. Mark won't miss a thing.

'Mine's next to the bathroom,' says Tom, looking again at Sophie who nods. At least that potential drama isn't happening.

'Go and ask the removal men, *politely*, if they've unloaded the vacuum cleaner. I'll clean the rooms so you can bring your stuff in from the car.'

The twins head back towards the house. I try to keep my breathing steady.

'Can you check out the landing light bulb? It blew just now. It needs something a lot more powerful. Someone'll be head-over-heels down the stairs in the dark otherwise.'

'Have we found the essentials box? It's got a light bulb or two in it.'

'It's in the boot of the Audi where you put it so we wouldn't lose it amongst all the other essential stuff,' I say, smiling. I've been so good lately, almost back to normal most days.

'Cut the kids a bit of slack, Kate. They're so excited to finally move in.' Mark's hazel eyes are on my face as he drinks his coffee.

'I just worry about them, you know? If something should happen . . .' I say.

Mark steps towards me, he hears the wobble in my voice. 'Nothing's going to happen, Kate. No-one said this was going to be easy.'

'And what about you?' I say, making my tone light, teasing. 'I thought you'd given up?'

He knows I hate him smoking, particularly around the kids.

'That young removal guy dobbed you in,' I say and scrunch my face into a mock frown, but he knows I mean it.

'Last one in the packet. I'm out of gum too, so starting from now.' He grins, the cheeky one Tom so often pulls on.

'It's just so bad for you. I worry, you know?'

'Now we're finally here, life will settle down, so will the stress levels.'

After the last few months, it's no wonder Mark returned to the nicotine sticks.

'You'll fall in love with this place, Kate, just give it a little time.'

He said this when we first looked around, then both times we visited over the summer, his heart set on the old house. Maybe he thinks, if he says it enough, it will become true? But I'd no option but to agree to move here, to this creepy old place that makes my skin crawl.

The lie rolls off my tongue, silky smooth, I hope it's convincing: 'I already am.'

CHAPTER 2

'LET'S HOPE IT doesn't go out too often.' Mark straightens up, regards the kitchen stove. 'You'll need to be able to light it in case it happens again while I'm away.'

'Show me tomorrow. Come and relax while we can. I bet we haven't heard the last from the twins tonight.'

I tuck my feet beneath me on Mum's sofa, my sketch pad on my knees. It seems more like a week than a few hours since we left London. Everyone's tired, tempers frayed.

'Bring the bottle of wine with you. I've sketched out a few ideas for a kitchen refurb.'

The shriek is sharp and primeval, we both start and turn to the black window, nothing but darkness. I need to fix up blinds as soon as possible.

'What the hell was that? A fox?' Mark asks as he crosses the kitchen and slumps onto the sofa beside me. 'They're a hell of a lot louder out here than in the city. It's why people in the sticks have dogs.' Mark's smile is flat as he tops up our wine glasses.

'We've enough on our plates right now without adding a dog into the mix,' I say.

Again, I wonder why he was so determined to come here. Every other place we'd looked at was in London. Urban and familiar. Why the complete change of plan? I'd wickedly wondered if he wanted a bit of space between him and his mother. Jennifer's been about a lot since his father died.

'Any luck?' Mark asks, peering into the battered old shoebox on the floor. I'd discovered it under the kitchen sink, full of odds and sods of old coins, washers and keys.

'I'll try these ones when we go up to bed,' I reply, nodding to a couple of keys I'd put to one side on the arm of the sofa. 'See if they fit.'

I want the bedroom with the smelly pink carpet locked. The catch is so worn the slightest draught cutting along the landing reopens it. Quite what happened earlier, when I'd got stuck in there, I don't know. Stupid it alarmed me. In the long term, I'll redecorate it for Mark and me, fix the catch. It's by far the largest, brightest bedroom. Until then, I'll feel more comfortable if we lock it.

Mark looks at the keys and pulls a face. 'They don't look too promising, but worth a try. You're picking up the attic keys from Lovett and Lyle's on Monday, aren't you?'

Mark was furious when we arrived to find a note from Mr Whittle, the estate agent, on the stove top saying the attic key was at the solicitor's office for collection. Closed at weekends, it was either wait until Monday or break the attic door down.

'Mrs Havers has a bloody nerve keeping the key after completion, as if it wasn't bad enough with the attic off limits when we were buying the place. The surveyor reckons there's nothing but junk up there anyway.'

'It'll be an icebreaker at my interview, if nothing else,' I say, trying to steer Mark away from the topic that's irritated him all summer.

'Lovett and Lyle's might be just what you need, Kate.'

I resigned my London post months ago, shortly after I was ill. I've not regretted the decision for a second. When Mr

Lovett said his firm needed a part-time solicitor working from the Weldon office, it seemed too good to pass up.

'I'll take a look and see what I think.'

I miss my financial independence, it sticks in my throat each time I've asked for money, although Mark's never once questioned or refused. A job would give me a routine, show I really am on the mend.

'I'll get on with other things to keep busy: find an electrician, order a skip, contact local builders to sort out quotes for the essential work.'

'Leave it for now. I'll sort it out next weekend with you,' Mark says.

I can't help but feel irritated. When we renovated our London home we'd worked on it jointly every free moment we had, but I'd been the one to book tradesmen, source and order materials, project-manage. Haverscroft is on a different scale, but I'm not an invalid. Something Mark keeps forgetting.

'Take a breath, Kate. Don't go charging in and knock yourself back again.' He's looking at my sketch pad, doodles of what we might do to the kitchen.

'I won't,' I say, hearing my voice rise a notch. 'It's pointless decorating until the basics are done.'

'Let the money settle down. We've only just completed. I need to clear the bills, sort things out.'

Mark sips his wine, stares straight ahead at the stove. He's not wanting a discussion on any of this right now. I shift across the sofa towards him.

'You know me, I have to be doing something.'

'My little control freak returns,' he says, putting an arm around my shoulders.

We're easier together again, a cuddle on the sofa isn't

awkward as it once was. If we put the last few months behind us I could even perhaps grow to like this strange old house.

'Mummy!'

Running footsteps, the twins on the landing.

'Mum!'

Mark groans. 'Bloody kids! Will they ever settle down?' He hauls himself from the sofa.

'What did we really expect the first night here?' I say.

Mark takes my hand, yanks me to my feet. We head into the hall and find the twins at the top of the stairs. Sophie clutches her blanket to her face, only her wide eyes visible above it. Tom clings to her arm with one hand, Blue Duck in the other.

'It's scary here,' Tom says as Mark reaches the top of the flight.

'Don't be daft, Tom. What's there to be scared of?' Mark says.

'The locked door,' says Sophie. 'Something's knocking in there. What if it gets out?'

I get the twins' unease about the attic. In this big old place shadows bounce off walls, floorboards creak and the heating pipes gurgle and ping. Every weird sound spells aliens to Tom and spooks to Sophie.

'It's locked, Sophie. Nothing's in there and nothing's coming out,' says Mark. He's tired and his patience is running thin, exasperation clear in his voice.

'Jump into our bed, Dad'll check around. We'll soon get used to it here. I'll lock up and come and give you a cuddle.'

'Tom's wheezy,' I say, climbing into bed beside our son. The twins fill the centre of our bed, Mark lies on the far side next to Sophie.

'There's enough dust to make anyone wheezy. If I told them once I told them a dozen times to stop chasing around, slamming doors.'

'I think he'll be okay.' I recall seeing his inhaler beside his bed.

'Those old keys you sorted, nothing fits the office, but one locked the spare bedroom. It should help keep the draughts down if you keep it locked, Kate. I can't find where that knocking's coming from, but it's probably in the attic. A window left open, rattling in the wind maybe. Nothing to worry about, I'll sort it next weekend.'

I haven't heard the noises stressing Mark and the twins, only the spare room concerns me. If it's locked it's one less thing to worry about.

'Now they're finally asleep, how about we sneak off to Tom's room?' I say.

Mark lies with his eyes closed looking just like our daughter tucked in close beside him. Both have semi-circles of curling dark eyelashes resting on cheeks flushed pink with the heat of us pressed close together. For a moment, as he doesn't respond, I wonder if he's already asleep.

'You go off if you want, Kate. It's been a long day.'

CHAPTER 3

MONDAY, 4TH OCTOBER

THE TAXI WAITS, headlights streaming in the early morning mist. Mark snaps his case shut and picks up his laptop, phone and keys from the glass bowl on the hall table.

'I'll try and call tonight once I've got myself settled at Charles's place so that I can speak to the twins before they get to bed.'

His lips brush my cheek, he buttons his coat. 'Are you going back to bed?'

I nod. What else would I do a 5:45am? I'm silently willing him to go, my feet so cold on the grimy Victorian tiles they hurt. Frigid damp air flows over the threshold, across the floor and encircles my ankles and knees. I tug my robe tighter about my waist and wrap my arms across my chest. I'd been determined to get up and make Mark some tea before he heads off.

'Re-set the alarm so you don't sleep in.'

I nod, smile. 'I'm sure I can manage to get the twins to school. It's not rocket science.'

We stand close together. He's taller than me by almost six inches and for a moment I focus on the weave of his white cotton shirt, the stripes in his dark blue tie, breath in the familiar citrus cologne. I don't know how to say goodbye. It's not something we've really ever had to do. Seeing Mark off to London with no hint he's planning to move to something more local isn't something I want. Will he enjoy the freedom of Charles's flat? No constraints, no twins or wife to make demands on his time, free to come and go as he pleases? Charles is a good person. I've known him for more than a decade, but he's Mark's old university buddy, not mine.

'Don't get stressed about the interview, okay?' He kisses the top of my head and I look up into tired and strained hazel eyes. 'And make sure you take the meds, keep things on an even keel, yeah?'

Don't let everything get a bit crazy's what he means. Not a great time to mention I've dropped the medication. See how you go, our London GP had said. I've taken an occasional sleeping tablet lately, only if I really need it, nothing more.

'I won't. I need something to do now my brain's back or I'll lose it.'

Mark thinks I'll never be sharp enough for legal work again, always a little slower, duller than before. Months ago I was terrified he might be right, now I'm determined to prove him wrong. I trace my thumb along the dark channel beneath his eye. 'Get some rest when you can, you look so tired.'

'That bloody knocking drove me nuts last night. It's loud at times. I could've done with a couple of your sleeping pills to knock me out if I'm honest. We're full on with this fraud case; Blackstone's not going to cut me any slack just because I'm knackered.'

I stand on tiptoe, pull on the lapels of his jacket, we kiss briefly as the taxi engine revs. His mobile buzzes, the shrill sound wavers, the signal weak. We move apart as he gropes in his pocket for the phone.

'Pick up the attic keys, but don't go up there on your own. We'll take a look next weekend.'

'As if I would!'

I laugh and shake my head. I'm shivering, can't stop. It's just too cold.

He grabs his case. 'I have to get this, the signal's better outside,' he says, waving the phone between us and heads toward the taxi. Who the hell calls him at this time in the morning?

'Don't forget to chase up the position at the local chambers,' I call at his back.

He raises his hand. 'I will, Kate, don't worry.'

He stopped speaking about moving chambers weeks ago. Once we exchanged contracts and were certain of moving here he's made no effort to get the ball rolling. Why hasn't he? Am I over analysing everything, in too much of a hurry, too much at once? Probably.

'Go in, Kate, don't freeze on the doorstep,' he calls back over his shoulder as he jogs down the front steps. 'I'll see you at the weekend. Good luck with the interview.' His tone is distracted, his attention no longer here, moved on already, back to the life I understand.

I'm somewhere between awake and sleep. That soft, fuzzy phase before life butts in. In the distance, a sharp, persistent sound. I can't quite grasp it. I slip away. Sink back into the haze.

'Mummy! Mrs Cooper is here. She wants to know should she do the cleaning.'

Sophie's voice is loud, close to my ear.

'Mummy? What should I tell her?'

My daughter's bony fingers press into my shoulder as she shakes me, her voice ringing with anxiety, thin nails like razors against my skin.

'Mummy!'

Sunlight illuminates the still-closed curtains surrounding my daughter in a halo of soft blue light. I screw my eyes to look into her face. She kneels beside the bed, her face so close to mine I smell chocolate breath, another pre-breakfast raid on the kitchen cupboard top shelf.

'She made me come up here to ask you.'

'Mrs Cooper?'

'She's that cleaning lady.'

We'd met Mrs Cooper when we looked around the house during the summer. I'd forgotten we'd agreed she would do a Monday morning for us. She came in three days a week she'd said for Mrs Havers.

'She wouldn't come with me, neither would Tom. He's too chicken, but I don't like the scary noises either. It's not fair.'

The room begins to come into focus: the hulking dark wardrobe, packing boxes, my clothes heaped over the back of one of the chairs we brought here from London.

'What have you heard this time?' I say.

'The knocking noises, just now, when I came upstairs. She's in the kitchen and wants to know about the cleaning. Her fifteen pounds isn't under the kettle she says, so do you want her?'

I prop myself up on an elbow. Had I heard the sounds when I was dozing? I run a hand through my hair and remember . . .

The interview.

'Bugger!'

I throw back the duvet and sit up on the edge of the bed.

'Mummy!'

'Sorry, Sophie, but what's the time?'

'I don't know. Late, cos I'm starving.'

I fumble for my mobile on the bedside table as Sophie opens the curtains.

9:25am.

'You should've been at school half an hour ago! Quickly, go and get dressed. Tell Tom as well and we do need Mrs Cooper to clean.'

'Tom's watching telly. So was I until *Mrs Cooper* turned up.'

'Both of you get dressed, now! I'll phone the school and say you'll be late.'

'I don't want to go downstairs on my own!'

"It's fine, Sophie. I don't hear anything, do you?' I put an arm around my daughter's shoulders. We walk to the bedroom door.

'It's going to take us a little while to get used to living here. Once we know the house it won't seem so strange.'

Sophie and I peep around my bedroom door jamb like a couple of thieves. The doors at either end of the landing, to the office and spare room, are shut.

'There, all quiet, no weird sounds. I'll watch you run down the downstairs,' I say, hugging my daughter close.

Sophie dashes off along the landing, glancing back at me as she grabs the mahogany handrail at the top of the flight. The ends of her long brown hair fly as she hurtles down to the hall. I head for the bathroom. The twins' rooms are a mess already. The tiny door to the attic, locked. The bathroom door stands open, nothing lurks in the bath or hides in the shower.

I look in the heavy-framed mirror and wonder for the umpteenth time: who is this woman? On the outside she looks pretty normal, someone to pass on the street without a second glance. My light brown bed-head hair is a tousled mess, a disturbed night despite the sleeping pill, and I'm giving Mark a run for his money as far as eye bags are concerned. The haunted look, the blank stare that clouded my blue eyes for weeks is gone, much more my normal self. On the inside though, someone different, different from before. China clatters downstairs and I remember the half-loaded dishwasher, the kitchen table covered in silver foil food cartons and plates of half-eaten Chinese.

'Shit!' Not a great first impression.

I wash and apply make-up for the first time since the Chambers summer drinks do back in July. Socialising isn't something I've done much lately. I straighten my hair into the shiny jaw-length bob I've always worn to the office. The transformation is startling. I instantly look like a woman worth listening to. How looks can be deceiving.

My navy suit hangs next to two of Mark's on the picture rail in our bedroom. I dig in my underwear drawer until I find a snag-free pair of tights. I've worn casual stuff, jeans, tee-shirts and sweatpants since the breakdown. The suit feels alien, the skirt, boxy jacket and heels, as though I'm wearing someone else's clothes. Mark's stuck a forest of Post-it notes on the mirrors of the old dressing table. He left fewer messages through August and September due to his confidence in my ability to cope with the day-to-day again. I hope we're not going backwards.

I snatch one up. *Cleaner coming 9am.*

Then another: *DON'T go in the attic alone. Weekend is soon enough.*

The rest are about minor things: what's in the freezer, where my car keys are, one about the torch needing batteries is handy. Anger and frustration mingle as I stare into the foxed mirror. Why is he doing this again now, after weeks of trusting me with routine stuff? Panic starts to curl in my stomach, a fist slowly tightening. Stop it.

Breathe.

I can do this now.

Breathe.

Even if Mark can't see it.

Breathe.

Keep breathing, take my time.

I count shuddering, deep breaths; count silently in my head, one, two, three . . .

Not bad. Eight is a massive improvement, it took over thirty to escape the ladies' loo in Tesco three weeks ago. I could take a diazepam with me just in case. What was worse? A brain numbed by pills, or running out of the interview sweating like a pig and jabbering nonsense as panic engulfs me? I don't want to go backwards. I won't go back to them now.

The landing is gloomy, the house silent as if it also holds its breath. The icy draught whips along the corridor, even with the doors closed. It sneaks under floorboards, between the gap under doors making showering a total misery, duvets freezing and clothes damp and heavy. Tom's asthma cough returned over the weekend, a result of the damp chill and constantly invading dust.

Our torch, Mark's box of essentials, an empty light bulb box and several blackened spent ones lie on the grimy green runner at the top of the stairs. The last one from the box hangs black from the ceiling. I'd washed the fluted shade when Mark changed a blown bulb, it glistened briefly before the replacement bulb burnt out.

I head downstairs, an enticing smell of buttered toast drifts toward me. Book bags, black school shoes and Sophie's violin case line up beside the front door. A taster day went well at the end of last term. I was supposed to drop them off this morning just after nine when the other pupils had settled. Now we're late. Another not-so-good first impression. I reach the hall and glance back up the stairs. A movement, so fleeting, in the corner of my eye, sunlight and shadows. How long before this old house begins to feel familiar?

The kitchen is already under Mrs Cooper's control. All signs of Chinese swept away, children dressed and eating scrambled eggs on toast to the churn of the dishwasher.

'Morning! Cuppa in the pot if you fancy one, dear.'

Mrs Cooper has what Mum called a comfortable figure. Her large and rather angular backside being its most notable feature, although her bosom is hard to ignore. Her brown hair is threaded with grey and looped in a scrunchy at the back of her head. It must be quite long when loose; I can't imagine her with her hair down. Her yellow sweater has a long thin paisley-patterned scarf in various shades of blue tied at the neck. She smiles, waves a J-cloth towards the teapot, jangling a mass of thin silver bangles on her wrist.

'I called the school and spoke with the secretary. I said the children would be along as soon as they'd eaten. Full stomachs are better than grumbling ones, especially on a first day.' Her eyes flick over my attire, she looks surprised. She'd not expected the suit. 'I can walk them over to the school when they're done if you like?'

The twins look up from their eggs, Sophie pulls a face which I ignore. How dare she phone the school!

'I'll take them,' I say.

A bunch of my drawings are scattered on the table top along with Mark's file for his father's estate. I scoop them into a pile. The rough sketch for a new kitchen has a Post-it stuck to it: *Looks good, discuss at w/end.* I drop the pile of papers onto the sofa, head toward the teapot and put milk into a mug. The tea is dark, almost orange, as I pour it.

'I brought some tea leaves with me, dear. Hope you don't mind none. I can't abide that wishy-washy stuff.' She means the breakfast blend. 'I need a gallon of tea when I'm cleaning. Gives me a right old thirst, and I like to look at my leaves and see what's in store. This morning they reckoned a storm's brewing.'

The liquid is thick, coating my tongue as I sip it. Mrs Cooper wipes the counter with a vigour I have to admire and I wonder from her tone if she means well. I'm just edgy, the twins' first day at school, the interview less than an hour away. I'm not sure I'll get myself to it. My leaves, perhaps, would tell our cleaner if I'll make it.

'You alright, love?'

Mrs Cooper holds the J-cloth in one hand as she peers at me. I stare at her for a second. I've missed a bit. The zoning out hasn't happened in a while. Stress of the interview. Mustn't let it get to me.

'That tea,' the J-cloth waves, bangles rattle, 'will be stone cold if you don't drink it now.'

I glance at the kitchen wall clock. 'Actually, we'd better go, kids,' I say, standing the mug on the kitchen worktop.

CHAPTER 4

THE TWINS DON'T cast a backwards glance as they head off with their new class teacher, but I'm still more than ten minutes late for the interview with Mr Lyle of Lovett and Lyle Solicitors. I tear down the long, wide bend of the village main street, past traditional family businesses tucked into buildings packed cheek by jowl, roofs higgledy-piggledy jostling for light and space. The post office window is plastered with small ads and faded posters for National Savings, a cafe has a Wi-Fi sticker curling off the glass. Several people openly stare at me, my heels clickety-clack on the narrow pavement. I've no idea where the solicitor's office is, my eyes search both sides of the narrow street, a prickle of sweat starts beneath my fitted blouse.

'Mrs Keeling, good morning!'

The booming voice makes me jump, but I recognise it before the tweed suit comes into view. A puffing Mr Whittle smiles and waves a rolled-up sheaf of sales particulars to catch my attention as he jogs down steep steps outside an adjacent building. I stop and wait for him to reach me.

'How have you settled into Haverscroft?'

'Just fine, thanks. Packing boxes everywhere, but we're getting there, I think.'

'No problems at all?' He peers closely at me, lowers the glasses perched on the front of his bald head and studies my face.

'Problems? None we didn't expect from the ancient heating and electrics. They're all a bit temperamental, as you know.'

'Good, good!' He stands back and shoves the glasses back to his forehead. 'It takes a while to get the feel of a big old place. How's Mrs Cooper? I mean, is she coming in for you? She did for old Mrs Havers and a little bit here and there when the place was empty, you know.'

He taps the roll of particulars on the palm of his hand and seems a little nervous stepping from one foot to the other. Perhaps it's me. Colour rushes to my cheeks at the recollection of the first day we met: me, mute on Haverscroft's weed-strewn drive; Mr Whittle gazing down from the top step, the front door wide open at his back. Mark coaxed me inside, but I'd barely managed to string two words together all afternoon. He's dealt with Mark ever since.

'She's at the house today, as a matter of fact. I don't want to be rude, but I'm terribly late for an appointment.'

'Of course! Your meeting with Oliver Lyle's this morning, is it?'

The surprise he knows must show on my face. He catches my expression and smiles, extends his hand towards the building he just came from. Lovett and Lyle Solicitors has a gleaming brass knob, knocker and plate fixed to a glossy black door.

'I've known Oliver for years. He's been needing help with wills ever since Miss Dyer retired. Must be over a year ago now.'

He dashes to the door and holds it open for me.

'Let me know what old Mrs Havers has stashed away in those attic rooms, won't you now!' His eyes shine with mischief as he beams at me. 'Poor old girl. Alzheimer's, you know. She really didn't want to sell up, but with the cost of care-home fees these days.' He shakes his head. 'Be warned, Oliver can be a crotchety old bugger at times. I'll wish you good luck!'

'Come in, Mrs Keeling, come in! It is Mrs Keeling?'

'Yes,' I say, unsure how to respond to the man opening an enormous pile of post at reception. A woman sits at the desk answering incoming calls. He stops slitting envelopes long enough to extend his hand. I shake it, cool and bony, fingernails digging into my skin.

'Oliver Lyle.'

The whole of him is pencil-thin and angular, grey suit hanging with excess fabric about shoulders and knees. The top of his domed head is balding, dark grey eyes sharp beneath greying bushy eyebrows. A thin man grown thinner, shrunken in on himself as the years advanced.

'How are you finding Haverscroft?'

Today's hot topic of conversation.

'Fine, thank you. Still unpacking.'

I try to place a relaxed smile on my face, but it feels stiff, like cold plastic, I doubt very much it fools the solicitor into thinking I feel calm and confident. I had no time to collect myself after Mr Whittle ushered me in. The solicitor stares at me. Does he expect me to speak? I swallow, try to squash the panic down.

'I've called Haverscroft several times this morning. I must have missed you.'

'Oh?'

'There's been a bit of a mix-up. Lovett, my partner, misunderstood what I'm needing in terms of help here. I'm sorry, but we're wasting your time today.'

I hardly know what to say. I have no qualifications or experience with wills, probate or trusts, but assumed I'd learn on the job. My CV makes it clear how my career has run so far.

'With your background, I'm sure you'll be better placed in Ipswich, Colchester, or Cambridge perhaps.' He smiles, the expression as cold as his skin.

'But we do have these ready for you.' He reaches across to a shelf behind the young woman and picks up a thick brown envelope. 'Pre-registration deeds for Haverscroft. I'm not sure what good they are to you, but Whittle tells me you require them.'

'Thank you,' I say, taking the envelope. It's quite heavy with thick black writing across the front: *For Collection.*

'I'm intending to research the history of the house: who built it, who's lived there and when.'

Again, the man stares. The woman is off the phone, I feel her eyes on my face. My face that has grown hot, and is getting hotter.

'I should've made more progress before we moved. We've no internet at present, so I can't do much, not without the internet . . .'

Nervous gabbling, he isn't interested in hearing this. I stop. Shut up.

'Will you visit her, Mrs Havers, I mean?'

'Should I?' This conversation is going places I don't understand. Why would I visit a woman I've never met just because we bought her house?

'We wondered if you'd keep that part of the bargain. An odd term and quite unenforceable, as you'll be aware. I'd caution you against visiting if you're considering it. She's unwell and has been for some time; she's not in her right mind. Whittle's had a torrid time dealing with her, as I'm sure he'll confirm. I understand you have agreed to keep on her domestic and gardener though.'

He scrutinises my features as he speaks, his grey eyes dart about my face. I can't think with him looking at me all the time. My mouth is dry, my chest tightening. These must be things Mark's dealt with. More stuff he's held back so as not to worry me.

'There's a second letter in there, I'm afraid, along with the attic keys.' He's looking at the envelope I'm holding. No wonder it has some weight to it.

'Second letter?'

'In addition to the one Mrs Havers sent you and your husband during the summer. Rather prolific, her correspondence, I'm afraid. We're merely obliged to pass these things on, you understand; nothing to do with this firm.'

'I don't know about any letter.'

I need to get out of here, get some air. I don't remember any letter from Mrs Havers.

'I hope it didn't trouble you? She sent letters to all prospective buyers. Some of them were quite nasty, so Lovett tells me.'

'I'm sorry, Mr Lyle, I've never received any letters from Mrs Havers.'

'I really wouldn't trouble yourself about it. Whatever nonsense she was peddling is hardly relevant, not now you've moved into the house.'

CHAPTER 5

I PICK MY way along Haverscroft's weed-choked driveway, court shoes pinching my toes. The red-brick house hunches into a hollow, brooding under a black canopy of beech and yew. Ivy clambers up the side of the building, claims a chimney stack, smothers a dormer window. Pustules of green moss scatter the roof, a slipped grey slate here and there. A tall man, slightly stooping, is deep in conversation at the foot of the front steps with Mrs Cooper.

She leans on a bicycle, glances my way as I near them. A hurried exchange, furtive glances in my direction. A conversation about the new inhabitants of Haverscroft House.

'Back already, love? You've met Richard Denning?'

The man holds an axe in one hand, raises his other to his flat woven cap and touches its brim. A hazy recollection of him deadheading roses, the dark red climber on the back terrace, his check shirt sleeves rolled to his elbows on a stifling hot day in June when we looked over the house.

'Hello,' I say, aware Mrs Cooper misses nothing, her eyes scanning the heavy brown envelope I'm holding.

'Richard's wanting to know if you'll be needing logs. Mrs Havers always did, didn't she now?' The man nods. Mrs Cooper runs on, 'Said I couldn't think why you wouldn't, for the stove and the other rooms.'

Something in me wants to say she's wrong. We won't want any such thing.

'That would be great, thank you.'

Richard Denning touches his cap again and heads away towards the rear of the house.

'Don't mind Richard, none, love. Never has too much to say, but he'll see you're alright if you have any problems. I left you a note on the kitchen table. The new reverend called, he said he'd try to catch you at home another day. You can't miss him, he comes over on that great motorbike of his. Terrible racket it makes.'

'I bumped into Mr Whittle on the high street. He was asking after you.'

She doesn't respond, continues to look steadily at me. Friendly conversation seems a good idea after our rather bumpy start this morning. I'm hoping I haven't offended her. I try again, 'I said you were in today. He's the estate agent who dealt with the Haverscroft sale.'

'I know Mr Whittle.'

Her tone is flat. Not her easy-rolling chatter. She pulls her bike onto the drive.

'Did you get the children off alright?'

'A bit late, but it didn't seem to bother them.'

'Such lovely children, aren't they. So excited about getting a little dog.'

She mounts the bike, sets the peddle ready to head off.

'Same time then, next week?'

'That would be great, thanks. We'll be a bit more organised for you by then. Would you do the bedrooms? I'll start decorating downstairs this week.'

'I don't go upstairs, love, didn't you know? Mrs Havers suffered terribly with her knees. She kept herself to the kitchen and morning room, so she did.'

She pushes off before I can respond, I step back to let her pass. 'Don't worry waiting in for me, I've still got the keys Mrs Havers gave me. See you next week!'

I watch her peddle up the drive and wonder who else has keys I know nothing about.

The deeds spread across the kitchen table, my mug of coffee stone cold at my elbow. Oliver Lyle is right, these give me little information other than a few old Havers family names and rough dates when they lived here. They owned quite a bit of land, running from the back lane down to the river. All sold off over the years. Somewhere to start, at least. And I feel calmer now. The interview had shaken me. So stupid. The solicitor made up his mind before he met me. Did he know something about me? Has he spoken with Mark? Perhaps Mr Whittle told him how I was in the summer, odd, vacant, strung out on stress and pills. Or was I over-analysing things, making something out of nothing? Mark would say I am.

The small, black attic key is beside Mrs Havers' letter. Was I really not going up there until the weekend? I pick up the letter, read it again for the umpteenth time.

Fairfields
Weldon

1st October

Dear Mr And Mrs Keeling

You will have purchased Haverscroft and most likely moved in by the time you read this correspondence. You have chosen to ignore my earlier communication; I very much hope it is not to your cost. You are aware of the reasons I resisted selling the house to you or indeed anyone else. They made me sell as you know. I shall not trouble you with a repetition of my concerns.

I reside at the above address; call upon me at your very earliest convenience. I would discuss with you the business of the attic.

Yours truly
Mrs Alice Havers

I don't know what to make of her letter. I'll be none the wiser if I read it a dozen more times. What happened to her earlier letter? Did her solicitor send it to us? I'm inclined to think he would. My memory had been non-existent in the days and weeks after the breakdown. By the summer though, it was back, confused and muddled, but I'm confident I'd remember a letter from Mrs Havers. I was desperate to hang on to any reason not to come here. Was that why Mark, perhaps, kept it from me?

I pick up the attic key and turn it between my fingers. Does Mark know what's up there? Wouldn't he have spoken to our surveyor, even if he hadn't had access himself? He'll never know if I take a look.

The staircase is opposite the front door on the left side of the hall. At the top it sweeps right to a dingy, galleried landing. I've forgotten to buy batteries for Mark's torch. Mrs Cooper's leaves are correct about the weather. Clouds scud past beyond the tall casement windows either side of the front door. Light and shadow flicker across the floor tiles, wind puffs and whistles into the fireplace beneath the stairs. My breath is short and shallow. I'm being absurd. At this rate

I'll be like Mrs Cooper, never going upstairs in my own home.

My fingers tighten around the cool, polished bannister. The tiles drain the warmth from my stockinged feet as I listen. No creaking floorboards. No unexplained noises. No doors slamming. Only the occasional tick and gurgle in the ancient radiators. The landing, the entire house, is silent. I have to get used to this place, being alone here. I head up the stairs.

The doors to the spare bedroom and office remain closed, the peculiar odour, faint. We need to strip out all the upstairs carpets, get rid of the smell. I don't try the light. Our final bulb blew last night. Even Mark's running out of motivation to replace them. The torch from his box of essential stuff stands at the top of the stairs, useless without fresh batteries. I'll shop in Weldon before I collect the twins tonight.

I head in the half-light past our room, past the twins' rooms, the bathroom and stop just before the office. To my left is the narrow attic door. I'd assumed it was a cupboard when we first looked around Haverscroft. Set flush with the wall, the paint, yellowed and chipped, it blends into the grimy paper and is close to invisible.

My hands fumble with the tiny metal key. It rattles in the lock. There isn't absolute silence in London like there is here. Always the murmur of traffic, a siren or the bustle and voices of neighbours through partition walls. I'd failed to understand how comforting sounds of life are until there are none. I jiggle the key, it lodges into place, turns effortlessly. The door swings open towards me.

A narrow space, no more than a shoulder's width. Deep wooden stairs rise and curve to the left, a black metal handrail spirals upward out of sight. My feet slither into hollows worn in the centre of each tread as I climb. Mrs Havers' knees wouldn't have managed these in years if Mrs Cooper's to be believed. Cramped, steep and twisting, they must be a nightmare to descend. A short stretch of handrail and half a dozen spindles guard the room against the drop to the stairs. I stop on the third from top step, peep between the spindles at a long, low room.

A narrow section of ceiling runs centrally between two sides of steeply sloping roof, striped green and cream blinds sag at four dormer windows. Two single beds, tucked under the eaves, tumbles of covers and sheets on them as if their occupants had just left. A washstand, a low chest of drawers between the small beds.

I clear the stairs and duck my head as I step into the room. The bare floorboards are covered in dust, a grittiness between my toes, a snag in the foot of my tights running for my ankle. I should have kept my shoes on. At the furthest end of the room is a small grate, the mantel crammed with trophies and photographs.

The first bed has a golly lying across the jumble of sheets, his red felt smile peeling at the edges, black button eyes fixed on the ceiling. Most of his curly hair has worn away, his sailor-blue jacket and striped red and black trousers are grimy. I can't imagine a child playing with such a sinister rag doll.

I pass the first bed, a sock abandoned on the floor, a cream Airtex shirt pushed under the second bed. Next to the fireplace, a chair in faded chintz, a book in the well of its seat. I pick up the book, its pages are dead and lank between my fingers. I don't recognise the title and drop it back onto the chair.

The row of framed photographs on the mantel are

interspersed with cricket trophies. I pick up the nearest photograph and rub my forefinger through the dust on the glass. A woman leans against the terrace outside the morning room, her arms around two blond boys. A young Mrs Havers with her children? I replace the photo, look along the length of the mantel. Another of the same woman, again, standing on the terrace, a summer's evening. Fair and slim in an evening gown, she looks frail beside her taller, dark-haired companion. He leans on a cane, very dapper, smoking a cigarette, he has a bored look about him, perhaps the photographer is taking too long. I replace the photograph on the mantel.

I'm like a thief in the night trespassing on other people's lives. I glance toward the stairs and at the room. Mrs Havers' children's things. Their room. Two little boys of eight or nine years old, I'd guess. Tom's age or thereabouts. What happened to them? Something so dreadful their mother kept this room, never altered or cleared it? I can't contemplate losing the twins. How does a parent deal with it, whatever the circumstances. The anxiety when Tom struggles to breathe is unbearable. I can't sleep, sit beside his bed listening to each struggling intake of air, willing them to continue and never stop. The attic is disturbing, creepy, a little ghoulish. More than anything, desperately sad. I've seen enough, time to head back to the warmth of the kitchen.

The tap, tap is soft and barely audible.

I spin around, a turn in the pit of my stomach. Nothing is here to make a sound. Is this the noise that so concerned the children, annoyed Mark? He said sometimes it's loud, sometimes soft. It seems to be in this room, close behind me, but at the same time coming eerily distant from another part of the house.

I wait, straining my ears although there is no need, the noise was clear. I don't move a muscle as I hold my breath, seconds then minutes pass, certainty ebbs away. My eyes roam the attic, the golly grins its lopsided grin, clothes still scatter the floor, nothing that's a likely culprit is here.

Two slim doors are set flush into the alcove beside the fireplace and behind the armchair. I hadn't noticed them before. Painted the same pale green as the room, their only give-a-way are two brass knobs, no larger than a fifty-pence coin and just visible above the chair back. The doors stand the height of the room. Cupboards, perhaps?

I focus on them and wait, hear nothing. I could stand here for hours and not hear anything. There was nothing yesterday, although Sophie says she heard the knocking this morning. Open the doors, how hard can it be?

The chair is heavy as I drag it away from the cupboard, its feet scrape against the floorboards. Nothing's been here. No footprints have disturbed the floorboard's coating of dust until my feet did earlier. I reach out my hand and grip one of the knobs, ball-shaped, with grooves running around it like ripples in water. The cold metal sinks into the palm of my hand.

I tug.

It's a half-hearted movement with little strength in it. The door doesn't shift. Stepping back, my arm almost fully outstretched, I pull hard. The door jerks open, I stumble backwards and collide with the chair. I hadn't intended to scream. I glance over my shoulder, an empty room, no one to hear me. I look back at the cupboard, a stink of mould leaches into the air. A rail runs across the top of the space, packed tight with jackets, shirts and blazers. Children's clothes, similar in size to the twins'.

Below the rail is a series of shelves neatly piled with folded jumpers and shirts. I pull the second door towards me. Something on the edge of my vision moves, flies at my face. I hold up my hands, scream again. A shoebox clatters to rest in the dust near my feet.

A pair of white cricket shoes have spilt across the floor. A black metal box lies beside the shoes. I thank goodness it didn't hit me on the head. Other boxes are piled behind the door and look precarious, the cardboard failing, collapsing in the dampness. I've been screaming at a pair of cricket shoes. The metal box is the type lawyers kept deeds and documents secure in years ago. It has handles at each end. I pick it up.

Tap, tap.

Twice. Much louder than before.

I stare at the cupboard, the packed space. The mouldering smell, thick with damp. The chimney breast is to my right, the sound seems to come from there, although from above me too. My eyes scan the crease where the ceiling meets the wall. A great patch of black spore-filled stain spreads like canker across the ceiling. Triangles of cobwebs in corners, strands of them hang lankly down the walls. I put the metal box on the chair and reach out my hand to the chimney breast. The painted plaster is blistered and crumbles under my touch. The noise comes again, more faintly but this time I feel it too, the vibration under my hand as though the dankness tries to shiver itself under my skin.

I snatch my hand away. My palm, peppered with green flakes, looks deceased and rotting. Still staring at the chimney breast I press my hands together, rubbing, trying to remove the slivers of paint. They stick to my skin. I rub them against my hips, snatch-up the metal box and head back through the room. I can't think what can be making the noises. I glance over my shoulder at the fireplace, no sound, just the thud of my stockinged feet on the boards as I run for the stairs.

CHAPTER 6

SUNDAY, 10TH OCTOBER

'I'VE GONE THROUGH the shoebox, none of the keys fit,' I say. Mark grins hearing the frustration in my voice.

'Let me try a screwdriver,' he says, opening the garage door. 'I've a small one that might just spring the lock.'

I place the box on the bench beside the Armstrong Siddeley. Mark tries wiggling a couple of screwdrivers in the lock.

'You knew about the attic, didn't you? Is that what Mrs Havers' letter was about?'

Mark rattles a tiny screwdriver in the lock and tugs at the handle on the box lid.

'There's all sorts in this garage,' he says, ignoring me. 'A bit of wire and some WD40 might shift it.'

'If you knew about the stuff in the attic, why didn't you say something?'

He's trying another screwdriver, bent over the box, all I see is the top of his head, his short dark hair.

'The surveyor told me about it and emailed some photos across.' Mark stands, drops the screwdriver onto the bench. 'It'll have to be cut open, I think. Bit of a shame, it's a nice old box.'

He knows I'm not interested in the box right this second so I wait.

'The plan was to get a skip and a couple of local guys to clear it before we moved in. I didn't want you freaking out about it. The hassle the surveyor had getting access was absurd. Even then, Mrs Havers had us both sworn to secrecy.' Mark grins, like Tom when he's been up to no good. 'It's killing the estate agent, not knowing what's up there.'

I quash my anger. Weekends are precious and a row would ruin the short time we have before he heads off tomorrow morning.

'Why has she left the room that way? Did something happen to her children?'

Mark shrugs. 'She's nuts is all I know. Kids died of measles, all sorts of things back then, didn't they?'

'Enough to drive anyone insane, losing their children,' I say.

'Hey,' he says, stepping towards me. 'This is just why I didn't say anything.' I look up into his face. 'For God's sake, don't go in the attic again, Kate. If you fall down those stairs when you're home alone it won't be good. At least we know where the knocking's coming from. I'll skip the lot when the builders are here to give me a hand. Until then, keep out of the attic.'

My shoulders shake, a shiver creeping through my chest. 'Someone walked over my grave. It's damp out here.' I try to smile, to cover my dread of this house. This last week's seemed like a lifetime. Mark wraps his arms around me. He's warm and safe, I wish he was here more often.

'It's been a tough few days, what with the move, the weird interview, all the upheaval. It'll take time for everything to settle down. Let me take the kids to the supermarket, give you a breather. Before we go, though,' he says taking my hand, 'have a look at this.'

He pulls me towards the rear of the Armstrong Siddeley and opens the boot.

'I was keeping it secret until I got it going, but it'll cheer you up after the Lovett and Lyle episode. See what you think.'

Mark delves into the boot and pulls out a cardboard box. His excited tone suggests he's found something he thinks I'll like. He flips back the lid. A record deck nestles amongst white polystyrene beads.

'Hey!' I say, leaning closer.

'I found it in a charity shop one lunchtime. It needs a stylus and a new belt, then it should be good to go. The speakers are in the Audi. Bang and Olufsen. Even your mum's old vinyl should sound great.'

He lifts the deck from the box. The same model I'd owned years ago. I lift the lid and spin the turntable gently with my forefinger.

'It needs a bit of a clean.'

'It's perfect,' I say.

Mark lowers the deck back into the polystyrene and puts it on the bench beside the metal box. He's understood better about Mum since his father died. I'll never be able to part with her records; like the sofa, they travel with me. I reach up and grab hold of the collar of his wax jacket, he pulls me close, his lips hot on mine. I think things will be okay.

Shrieks and mischievous laughter, running feet, scrunching gravel. We step apart and move towards the front of the garage. First Tom, then Sophie sprint towards us. Tom pulls up beside me and I see from the satisfied grin on his face something's up.

'What's going on?' I say.

'He threw that at me! It's dirty and creepy and he did it

on purpose!' says Sophie, jabbing a finger towards her brother. My son holds the balding golly in one hand. The knees of Tom's jeans are grey with dust, both hands filthy.

'Have you been in the attic?' Mark's tone is angry.

'No, no we haven't, have we Tom?'

'It was your idea!' Tom slings the golly towards his sister. Sophie throws up her arms, bats the golly away. It falls limply to the ground, one eye staring up at us.

'Can't you keep them under control, Kate?' says Mark, kicking the golly to one side as he heads off towards the house. 'It's not appropriate for them to be around something like that.'

The twins stare up at me, Tom's mischievous grin and Sophie's anger, gone.

'Come on, kids, if you're coming to the supermarket,' says Mark as he vanishes around the corner of the building. Sophie glances at me and runs after Mark.

'Sorry,' says Tom as he heads after his sister.

I like this room. Sunlight streams through the open French windows from the terrace. Maybe it's the hours spent in here this week, wallpaper stripping, Mrs Cooper's radio on, the space more familiar than the rest of the house. She says Mrs Havers spent her time here, calls it the morning room. The bedroom with the smelly pink carpet is just above. Once stripped and redecorated, it too will be a bright, airy room.

I put the record deck on the paste table and grab a clean paintbrush, flick dust from the turntable. I plug it in, lift the arm and watch the deck spin. Just a stylus then. Mum's LPs are in their case in the dining room with the rest of our stuff yet to be unpacked. I'm smiling, I realise.

I cross the room and close the windows. The gardener keeps the long border immaculate, spectacular, Mark says, in June and July, but I can't remember any of it. I turn back to the room, an hour or so, enough time to finish stripping the old paper. It's like it's embedded in the walls. I smile again at the twins' graffiti, a boy throwing a ball for a small scruffy dog on one wall is Sophie's, Tom's stickmen battling aliens on another.

I pick up the stripping knife and start scraping. Mark reckons I'm reading too much into the interview, miscommunication between busy partners, maybe he's right, he usually is. Does he think I've failed, let him down, again? The record deck's perfect, a replica of what I had before, no bland box of chocolates, or limp forecourt flowers. So why isn't he here, moving chambers? Has he a reason to be in London? He kept the attic secret, Mrs Havers' letter, what else?

I bump my forefinger along the slimy edge of the stripping knife, flick gluey shreds to the floor. She'd been attentive to Mark all afternoon, it wasn't me being paranoid, other guests noticed, side glances at Mark laughing too quickly, too loudly. I wipe the blade between my fingers. I won't go to a chambers do again, no need for me to be there, wives don't usually go. It makes no difference I'm a lawyer too. I dig at the wall. Layer upon layer upon layer of old paper. Why insist I go, though? Rub my nose in it? Cassie's attractive, ash-blond hair, like mine before it darkened after the twins. I could lighten it, grow it again.

I'm staring at a wall of ripped old paper, not moving a muscle. It's absurd, if anything's going on with Cassie he wouldn't have taken me, made it so obvious. His mother would love her, even her name's just right, Cassandra Lewis-Brown.

Thump thump.

The sound makes me jump.

Thump thump.

It's coming from above me. I stare at the ceiling, grey strands of cobweb stir in the draught from the hall. Something, someone is in the spare room. I clench the stripping knife. This is unlike the sharp crack and knock from the attic. What then? I hear only my breathing. Had I imagined it?

Thump.

My ears strain for every sound. Silence hisses in the cold air. I wait. The room above here is empty and locked. No one is in the house. No one is upstairs. The hall door is open. I'm glad of my trainers as I tiptoe across piles of shredded and soggy paper and stop on the threshold and listen.

Nothing. My mobile's on the hall table beside the bowl, next to the box and Bakelite phone where I'd dumped everything in my rush to inspect the record deck. I creep across the tiles to the table and scan the landing and stairs. Not a sound, not even the plink of the radiators. I grab my mobile and dash back to the morning room, slam the door and turn the key. I twist the brass knob, shake it, check the door's locked.

I could call Mark. No signal. I stand still, listening again for what seems like hours but can only be two, three minutes at most. Nothing more.

I step across to the French windows. One bar of signal, maybe enough to connect? What do I say to Mark? I heard a strange noise? I'm thirty-eight years old. A grown woman, for goodness' sakes. I push the mobile into the back pocket of my jeans.

Whatever it was isn't making a sound now. Something

isn't right though, something niggles at the back of my mind. This room is cluttered with decorating paraphernalia, buckets, step ladders and paint tins. Not in here, in the hall. The stuff I dumped on the table, everything's there, except the golly. I dropped the hideous thing beside the metal box after I waved goodbye to the twins. I'm sure I did. It wasn't on the table just now. Or was it? I stare at the door to the hall. I can't go out there again.

I turn back to the room and pick my way through sticky shreds of paper to the fireplace. I hit the power button on Mrs Cooper's radio, turn up the volume and start scraping the wall.

CHAPTER 7

THE DOOR TO the morning room rattles and bangs in its frame. I freeze, stripping knife in hand and stare at the door. The doorknob is twisting, light glinting off metal.

'Mummy! Mummy! Come and look, we've got a dog!' Sophie yelling through the door, her voice competing with the newsreader's voice on the radio. The whole of me sags with relief. I switch off the radio, dash across the room and unlock the door.

Tom bounces with excitement behind his sister. 'Come and look!'

The twins turn and run back through the hall, too manically excited to see they scared their stupid mother half to death. I drop the stripping knife on the floor amongst the mess of ripped paper, take a breath and follow them as far as the front door. I stand on the bristling mat. Mark roots around in the boot of the car, only scruffy jeans and old deck shoes visible.

'A dog?'

'Yes!' Tom pulls the sleeve of my old sweatshirt, urging me down the steps.

'Only a little one. Dad said it won't need walking too far. I'm going to feed him in the mornings, Sophie will after school.'

'We're calling him Riley,' says Sophie as she runs towards the car.

Mark struggles with a large cardboard box which declares it holds washing powder. I'm guessing, not any longer. He hauls it to the edge of the boot and lifts a dirty, some might say creamy, white dog out of it. He straightens up, the twins at his feet, their hands stretch up to pat the furry body.

'We thought we'd surprise you! This is Riley, we think anyway.' Mark looks at the twins and I guess there's been some 'discussion' over the name.

'Riley, like the other dog,' Sophie declares in her 'I'll have my way' tone.

The dog is small, terrier in size and some features. Short tufty fur and ears suggest some Scottie's got in there too.

'Other dog?' I say. I'm entirely out of the loop with this whole dog thing.

Mark walks towards me holding the dog in his arms above the twins' heads, his smile, wide, until he takes in my expression. My face feels stiff, my arms, crossed against my chest, clench tight. Anger boils, I can't speak. I turn on my heel and stride back into the hall. Why doesn't anyone ever listen to me? Why doesn't Mark value any opinion I hold?

The hush behind me is palpable. Furtive whispering, Mark to the twins, it enrages me further. I stop beside the stairs, turn around and face the three of them. Mark stands just feet from me, uncertainty written into his features. The twins watch at his side.

'We thought you'd like him,' says Mark.

'Why? Why would I? Haven't I made myself clear? Why turn up with that when you know I don't want a dog?' I jab a finger at the furry bundle he holds.

'Don't you like him, Mummy?' Tom's voice is quiet and tremulous. I keep my eyes firmly on Mark's face.

'You'll be off back to London in the morning. Not taking it with you, are you? So it's down to me to look after it as the twins won't be here either, will they?'

Sophie starts to cry and the boys look astonished. All I feel is gathering, boiling rage. I push past them and run up the stairs.

I reach the top of the flight and flick the landing light switch. The replacement bulb's glare exposes every chip in the thick cream paintwork, the grey trail in the centre of the sickly-green runner. The spare room door is wide open, the twins presumably exploring there as well as the attic. Mark will go nuts if he finds out. Someone, most likely Mark, will try to find me, the spare room's the last place he'll look. I've absolutely nothing to say to him.

The light bulb flickers, buzzes like an angry insect. I screw my eyes against its naked glare. Shadows bounce off filthy ceiling and walls, light flares blindingly bright. I hurry towards the spare room. The bulb plinks, grey gloom falls across the landing.

I stop on the threshold of the room. Cigarettes, as if someone finished one moments ago. Mark's nipped in here for a sneaky smoke, why lie about quitting? Does he lie about other stuff too? No sign of what made the thumping noises. Only the space where the huge metal bed used to be. Whose room was this? Who slept here? The dressing table, tucked in the alcove beside the hearth, is an ugly thing, its heavy wood so dark it's all but black. I see me, times three, in the tall foxed old mirrors. My cheeks are red, my eyes glassy. The chaise longue in front of the French windows is elegant, the silk and brocade faded to a soft powder blue. I can't hear anything from downstairs. Perhaps Mark and the kids went outside. I over-reacted, especially in front of the twins. What the hell came over me?

I step into the room. I can't bear to shut the door, not after last time. I must calm down, think how to apologise to my family, make things right before Mark heads back to London in an hour or so. But I stand by what I said. I don't want the tie or the hassle of a dog.

A scratching sound comes from behind the chaise, the window frames bump and rattle. I can't see anything, only the willows way beyond the house, branches tangling in the wind. I take a step towards the chaise. The carpet is thin, a floorboard dips, creaks underfoot. The windows shake again, could it be the wind gusting against the glass? The chaise stands on small brass casters. I can pull it away from the doors, towards me, see what, if anything is behind it. I take another step forward.

I throw up my hands to shield my head, a reflex reaction. I duck down, crouch low, banging, flapping greyness coming at me. A scream, my voice. It flies from behind the chaise longue, bangs into the chimney breast, lands in the hearth, pressing close to the empty grate. A few white feathers and splats of shit trail across the carpet. A bird, more terrified than I am, watches, its pebble black eyes fixed on my face. I'm so relieved I laugh out loud. How stupid, how jumpy can I be?

The bedroom door slams. The sound is terrific in the silent house. I spin around in panic. I rush at the door, grab the brass knob. Solid. Locked. I kick at the door, trainers bouncing off the wood. 'Mark!' The knob is so tiny it's hard to get a proper grip, my hands sliding round the metal. Stop it. Stop it. Take a breath.

Breathe.

I let go. Step back, see light glint off the metal as the knob turns. The door opens.

'What the hell's going on, Kate?'

For a moment Mark and I stare at each other. The look on his face changes from astonishment to concern. I need to be normal, normal now. I manage a short laugh, a humourless sound. A smile.

'Just a bird. I was trying to get away from a bird. It came down the chimney, I expect.'

Mark's looking over my shoulder into the room. I turn around, see a jagged crack in the glass of one of the window panes.

'A collared dove. It's gone back behind the chaise longue, I think.'

I take a breath as Mark steps past me into the room, my eyes sting hot, don't lose it, don't have a total melt down, not now, not after so long. Another breath as I watch Mark haul the chaise away from the windows.

'It's cracked the glass,' I say, my voice is level and calm. Keep breathing.

'I'll open this. It'll fly out if we leave it here.'

'I heard something while you and the kids were out.'

I sound okay, my heart's stopped racing. Mark's wrestling with the ancient metal catch on the windows, the dove twitches its neck, jutting back and forth, back and forth. How it isn't injured I don't know.

'Bloody catch. Hasn't moved in years!' It gives way in a shower of dust and cobwebs and the windows open. Mark takes a step forwards, then jerks backwards into the room.

'Fuck me! That balcony's a death trap, Kate.' He's glancing

at me, we look at the rusting metal, the terrace and garden below, dank from last night's rain.

'Let's get out of here, let the bird find its way out. I'll close up before I leave later.'

I'm nodding, heading for the landing.

'Don't open these windows again, not until we get a builder in to take a look, okay? That balcony won't stand any weight at all.'

'Sure,' I say. 'The twins need telling to stay out of this room. I'll find somewhere to keep the key out of their reach.'

Mark shuts and locks the door, drops the metal key into my palm.

'Look, Kate, I really came to speak about Riley.'

He's annoyed, trying to appear calm. He shoves his hands into his jeans pockets and spreads a tolerant smile across his face. I can't blame him.

'I don't want a dog.'

'We said the twins could have one when we moved here.'

'*You* said they could,' I say, stopping just before the top of the stairs. I see the hall is empty, no twins listening in.

'I assumed you wouldn't mind. You've said nothing against the idea every time the twins go on about it, and let's face it, it's a daily mantra with them both. You're the only one who doesn't want him.'

'And my opinion doesn't count?'

Mark runs his hand through his hair and half turns away. His words rush at me. I can't grasp them. Breathe.

'You ignore what I say, my opinion isn't worth a jot. It undermines me in the kids' eyes. I'm sorry I exploded. I shouldn't have gone off like that, but you should've cleared it with me first.'

'You're here alone a lot. I thought it would be company for you.'

'I'm alone because you make no effort to move to local chambers.'

My words stumble out, jerky and unsure.

'If you object so much, the dog can go back to the rescue place.'

'I don't want the bloody dog! I don't want this house. I only agreed to move here for us and you're hardly here!'

I turn away, wrap my arms across my chest. I hadn't meant the last comment to fly out.

'I hate the attic. You keep stuff back and you shouldn't. I can cope with Mrs Havers' letter without going nuts, really I can. I'm not fragile, not precious. Treat me like an equal, like you used to.'

'We've been here just over a week, Kate. If you really hate the place we can sell up and move, but I think you need to calm down, give the place a chance, let us all settle in before making any rash decisions.'

'It's not about the house or the dog,' I say. 'Not even the bloody letter. You know it's not about any of that . . .'

I can't speak anymore. My voice is wavering and unsteady, my throat thick, my eyes hot. The affair is like an unspoken whisper. I dare not ask if he's seeing anyone. Cassy? Someone else? Is it a tit-for-tat thing that will eventually peter out, or more serious?

'I don't know how to make it any better,' I say. 'I can't do it alone. We're going round in circles.'

'You said you didn't want to talk about it, remember?'

Mark's tone is hard, cold, accusing. If we even try to discuss it now the result will be another bitter, soul-destroying row. And he's better at this than me. He has the moral high-ground, I'm always on the back foot. I pull in a deep breath and close my eyes. Mark's right, I don't want to discuss it now. The silence is deafening, my ear drums fit to burst with the pressure of it. I don't even dare say I love him, I'm too scared of his response. Does he still love me? I just can't tell.

'Kate? Are you listening?'

'What?' I say. Shit, I'm zoning out, he mustn't think I'm doing any of that stuff, not any more.

'I said it's better if I take the dog back, before the twins get too attached. If that's what you really want.'

Mark's voice is flat and quiet. He stands for several seconds waiting for a reply. I nod, willing him to go, leave me alone. His footsteps thud along the landing and fade down the stairs. I listen as he crosses the hall tiles, angry quick steps returning to the kitchen. The door slams.

CHAPTER 8

MONDAY, 11TH OCTOBER

MARK LEFT FOR London before I awoke. A forest of Post-it notes has sprung up around the kitchen. I pull them off the fridge, kettle, backdoor, scrunch them in my fist, bin them. Mark's concerned. I need to be back on track before this situation gets out of control. I read one stuck to the middle of the kitchen table.

Stove gone out. Can't relight. Will phone tonight.

The kitchen's stone cold. Half an hour spent trying to relight the stove's got me nowhere. Last night was dreadful. The twins and Mark hung out in the kitchen, cooking dinner, doing homework, while I finished stripping the morning room. Mark put the twins to bed for the first time in weeks, then worked in the office. I curled up on Mum's sofa and tried drawing to settle my anxiety, the pencil like lead between my fingers. Maybe dropping the pills entirely is a mistake. But I can't shake off the feeling I'd be fine at home, in London. I was doing so well back there.

'Dad promised we could have a dog,' says Tom.

Two sullen children have barely spoken over breakfast other than to whinge, moan or complain about the dog. All my cheery attempts at conversation failed. Suggestions of a trip to the cinema or bowling, usually guaranteed crowd pleasers, rebuffed. Nothing but the dog will do. Sophie, possibly Tom too, know I feel on the back foot about the whole damned dog affair.

'If they put him down, it'll be all your fault.' Sophie, slinging back her chair, storms out of the kitchen. Tom looks horrified.

'They won't do that, Tom. It's an animal rescue centre. It's not what they do.'

Tom shoves his cereal bowl across the table, the spoon tips out and clatters to the floor. We look at it, at each other.

'I hate you, Mummy.'

I'm relieved to drop the children at school. I settle on a bench just off the high street next to the church, make calls to builders, electricians and a phone company. A decent landline and internet are essential, Mark might work from home once we have broadband. I head back to Haverscroft.

Mrs Cooper's bicycle leans against one of the pair of massive urns at the foot of the front steps. With all the drama over the dog, I'd forgotten it's cleaning day. The kitchen's warm and welcoming with our cleaner in it.

'Cuppa?'

Mrs Cooper's red and blue striped scarf is knotted at her throat. She stops wiping the surface as she speaks and turns her broad smile in my direction, J-cloth flapping towards the teapot. No bangles today.

'I lit the stove. Hope that was the right thing to do?'

'Thanks. I tried earlier but couldn't do it. One problem solved, at least.'

She gives me a long stare. I smile, determined to be friendly.

'It does go out sometimes. Mrs Havers never did know why. There's a bit of a knack lighting it.'

She bustles with mugs and milk.

'I thought you might like your leaves read.' She nods toward the tea pot. 'See what they have to tell you. What do you want me to do with these?' She points to some sketches I'd swept into a pile on a corner of the table.

'Don't bother about those. Just scribbles for recycling.'

'Recycling! You can't be doing that, love. This one for instance, of the church, it's very good.'

She looks aghast, her brown eyes wide, eyebrows raised. I've roughed out dozens of sketches of Weldon high street, the shops and church with its strange round tower.

'Richard Denning would love this one if you're throwing them away.' She holds a sketch towards me. 'You've caught his houseboat to a tee.'

My cheeks burn, doodles for my eyes only, I don't even show them to Mark as a rule.

'I didn't know he lived on the river.'

'Why would you, love.' She glances at me, then the sketch. 'He likes his own company. He was ill once, all a long time ago now. We don't talk about that.'

'Please, take what you want.'

I should stop her nosing through my stuff, but for some reason I can't.

'This one's so lifelike. Someone you know?'

I take the sketch she holds out. A dark-haired woman, high cheekbones, wide-eyes, striking rather than beautiful. I've never seen her before. Did I draw this last night? I look up, shake my head. 'Just a study,' I say. 'I don't often draw people.'

'Well, you should, judging by that,' she says, pouring the tea.

She's right, the sketch is by far the best of the bunch. As

hard as I stare at the page, no recognition, no memory of her returns. I drop the picture onto the table, my mouth dry, knees buckling. I sink onto Mum's sofa. Am I zoning out to this degree? Chunks of time vanishing?

'A cosy idea, a sofa in here,' says Mrs Cooper, handing me a mug and sitting beside me.

'It was my mum's,' I say, trying to gather my thoughts. My hands are trembling making the surface of the tea, shiver. 'It's a bit knackered. We'll get something smarter for the morning room.'

Mrs Cooper watches me a moment, smiles. 'You wouldn't want this reupholstered, would you? It wouldn't be your mum's then, would it?'

She's right but I don't reply, my mind still on the sketch. Mark suggested we clean the sofa, I'd been uncertain but it came up well. The seats just sag a lot.

'My husband, Nicholas, died five years ago now. I keep little things, you know, his things. Keepsakes. Reminders.'

How did she guess Mum's gone? Simpler though, not having to explain.

'I'm sorry,' I say trying to concentrate on her conversation.

'Doesn't get any easier, does it? Just what we get used to.'

There's strain in her eyes. Small lines either side of her mouth make her seem older, sterner. I want to tell her about Mum, how ill she was and for so long, how it terrifies me I might be the same. Mrs Cooper's looking at me, raises her eyebrows quizzically.

'I was just saying, love, I thought you'd have the little dog with you.'

She pulls the ends of her scarf tighter before patting it into place. How can she know, has she seen it in my horoscope or her tea leaves? All of yesterday's drama. She must see my puzzlement as she continues.

'My niece volunteers at weekends at the animal rescue centre. She said the twins were thrilled with a little dog.'

She continues to look at me. I'm getting the idea nothing happens around here without the entire locality knowing every detail. Astonishingly, it seems she only knows half this story.

'I don't see how we are going to look after a dog. At some point I'll be back at work. They're such a tie, aren't they?' My words splutter out. 'Mark took the dog back yesterday evening.'

'Oh, I expect the children were disappointed! My Amelia reckoned they were over the moon with it.'

She sips her tea and views me over the rim of her mug. Her brown eyes give nothing away. Does she think I'm a bad parent?

'Maybe have it here a little while, see how you get on with it? This place might seem a bit friendlier with a dog running about.'

We're silent for a moment.

'A big old house like this needs a dog, if you ask me.' She nods as she speaks, as though this will convince me for sure. 'I'd certainly be less nervous about the stairs. If the dog's happy, you can be sure all's well.'

'Maybe you're right. I flew off the handle yesterday, I feel terrible about it. If I fetch it back, you realise we'll be stuck with it? For good, I mean.'

She smiles, I continue: 'Mud on the floor, dog hairs on the furniture. You'll be cleaning up and I'll be walking the damned thing.'

'I'm under no illusions there, dear. It's worth the effort,

though. A bit of company for you and the children. I've bought a little green lead for it.' She glances towards a brown paper bag on the work surface. 'Shame to waste it.'

The sky darkens with rain, the treetops blurring when I leave the rescue centre and head for the towpath and river. Riley's an engaging little mutt. His short legs scamper along nineteen to the dozen, nose snuffling under hedges, shaggy Dennis Healey eyebrows twitching up and down each time he looks at me. No wonder the twins were besotted.

Sophie's odd comment, *like the other dog*, unsettles me. Her imaginary friend left us, to Tom's great relief, when the twins started school. Is this another one? Sophie's way of coping with all the upheaval of the last few months. It'll drive Tom nuts. I'd wanted to ask her about it this morning but she was barely speaking. It's probably nothing. My mind wanders back to the woman in the sketch. She turns my guts to jelly. Am I relapsing? Is my anxiety rushing back so fast I'm again doing things I've no recollection of? How had I drawn her so well? I usually draw open spaces, landscapes and buildings, the park near our London home full of stick people. Portraits don't work well for me.

Riley and I pass the church on the way back to Haverscroft. If we hurry, a stomp around the graveyard might reveal a few snippets about the Havers before the heavens open. If I know about the house and concentrate on making the place a home, if I find out what happened to the children, my mind will be calm, the anxiety will settle down. The weird zone-outs will stop.

Ploughed fields stretch to the horizon either side of scraggy bare hedges. According to the deeds, this is land sold off by

Mrs Havers years ago. We turn right and head along the towpath, the river is black and slow beneath an arching tunnel of dank trees. I pull my mobile from my pocket, text Mark to say I'd had second thoughts about the dog. Sorry for yesterday's outburst.

It's almost a year since the chambers Christmas drinks reception. I don't think about that night often now. How Stephen swore me to secrecy, his wife must never know. Mark need never know. Too much to lose, why would either of us whisper a word? But I'm not Stephen Blackstone with years of infidelity behind me. The guilt of one night grew like an aggressive tumour, worming its way into every aspect of my waking hours, depriving me of sleep, driving me insane until one evening, more than three months later, I blurted out to Mark the sordid details of how I'd fucked his head of chambers. The man he works with and juniors for every day of the working week. Could he forgive me? In those few words, our lives changed. What had I thought my husband would say? Offer me absolution, trust and love me as he always had just because I'd come clean.

Mark had known I hated those events. Another evening waiting for him to show up, making polite conversation with his colleagues, getting steadily more drunk and angry as the evening wore on, as texts from Mark rolled in, still working, always working, running late, too late, going straight home. Would someone give me a lift, he asked? I even know the precise time everything changed, Big Ben chiming way off in the distance as my nails dug into the yielding cream leather of the Bentley's back seat.

Riley barks, yanking on the lead, impatient to move on from the spot I've been frozen to. The church tower rises into view above the yews crowding the churchyard. The river arcs left here, widens, heads towards the North Sea. Tucked inside the bend, moored to the bank, is a single houseboat. A row of narrow windows, coloured light spilling through drawn curtains onto the towpath. On deck is a fraying wicker chair, but no sign of Richard Denning.

I turn right, tug on the lead and drag Riley up the steep muddy track past the church. The first heavy spots of rain patter my face. I glance back along the lane. No sign of anyone. The wind whips rain in my face and spins leaves across the path. The sluggish sense of nothingness creeps over me as it so often does when Stephen and that night shoves its way to the forefront of my thoughts. Perhaps I don't deserve the absolution I've craved all these months? The lych gate is set in the brick and flint wall surrounding the graveyard. I turn the metal ring and push it open.

Rain bounces off the path that leads to a black church door. Riley tugs his lead as I shelter beneath the heavy boughs of a yew. The gravestones here are recent, I'm looking for something much older. Wind shakes the tree, shadows rock and deepen, the light fading. The graveyard isn't somewhere I want to be in a downpour. I'll come back with pen and notebook, research things another day.

Mrs Cooper flings open the front door as Riley and I dash up the front steps.

'Oh, look at the pair of you, soaked to the skin!'

She slams the front door on a flurry of wet leaves and driving rain. Riley shakes, water droplets spray across the tiles.

'I thought we'd be back before the clouds burst, but it's so slow walking a dog.' I'm laughing, stripping off my wet coat and scarf, see her concerned expression, her eyes focused on the landing.

'Are you okay, Mrs Cooper?'

'There's been something banging, like the devil knocking to come in. It's stopped now, but it's been right loud. I heard it in the kitchen when I turned the radio off.'

'We've had a weekend of weird noises. I've called a couple of builders in case there was something loose in the attic or the roof. A dove was thumping around in the spare room, frightened the life out of me.'

'Oh, my Lord!' Mrs Cooper covers her mouth with her hands, her eyes wide. 'Foretells a death, so it does, a bird in the house.'

I can't help laughing, but stop myself short, she's quite serious.

'I'm sure it'll be fine. Mark put it out. There was no harm done.'

She watches as I shake out my coat. Riley yaps and wags his tail.

'You're a happy little fella so I guess there's nothing too much to worry over. Let's see what we have for you, shall we?'

I follow them across the hall to the kitchen.

'I was going to walk around the churchyard before the weather closed in. Are the Havers buried there?'

'Come through to the kitchen. Have a warm up while I see what we have for this little dog.'

The kitchen is cosy, spotlessly tidy and smelling of something spicy. A cinnamon cake cools on a wire rack on the kitchen table. Mrs Cooper must have heard my question. She knows something, she usually does. She puts a plate of meat scraps in front of a frantic Riley. I can only think she brought these with her along with the lead this morning, nothing looks like it came from our fridge.

'Riley, you say?'

'According to Sophie. I must ask her where she got the name.'

She joins me beside the stove as I warm my hands around the oven rail. A cardboard box on the floor, just beyond the stove, has an old blue blanket in it. She's anticipated Riley's arrival for sure.

.'So why are you looking for the Havers' graves?' A frown draws her eyebrows closer.

'Just curiosity really. It would be interesting to see who's lived here, what they did, where they came from. It's a bit daft, but I'll feel better about the house if I get to know who was here before us.'

'The family plot's towards the rear of the churchyard . There's great black railings round it so you can't miss them. Mrs Havers' late husband, Edward, he's there. She's the one to tell you about the house.' She nods towards the worktop. 'Letter came while you were out.'

An envelope is propped up in front of the kettle. Even at this distance I recognise the thick cream paper, blue ink, precise looping handwriting.

'She'll be wanting you to visit's my guess.'

I cross the kitchen, pick up the letter and open it.

Fairfields
Weldon

8th October

Dear Mrs Keeling,

Further to my letter of 1st October, I understand you

have ventured into the attic. You have been good enough to retain Mrs Cooper and Mr Denning. I must insist you honour the rest of our bargain and call upon me.

I will expect you 2pm sharp this coming Friday afternoon.

Yours truly,
Mrs Alice Havers

I look at Mrs Cooper and raise my eyebrows. 'She's very direct,' I say, although blunt and rude might be more accurate. 'Do you visit her?'

'When I can. Richard's regular, he visits every week, come rain or shine. They go way back.'

'Maybe I should go?' I say more to myself than to our cleaner.

'I'd go, love. Ask all the questions you want then.'

'I understand she has Alzheimer's.' I tell her about Mr Whittle and Mr Lyle.

'Nothing wrong with her other than her temper and a pair of arthritic old knees.'

'Why would they say that then?'

She's quiet for a moment, watching me as though deciding what to say.

'Lyle's father was a lovely old gentleman. He started up the firm with Mr Lovett and was as honest as the day is long. His son's a different kettle of fish, I can't take to him at all. Makes me feel right uncomfortable, he does.' She's frowning as she speaks. 'Nasty piece of work, he is. Whittle's a fool, running about doing his bidding. He should know better at his time of life.' Mrs Cooper stops speaking, her eyes all the time on my face. 'You go visit Mrs Havers and see for yourself.'

She's annoyed, loyal, I'm guessing, to the lady she's known and worked for, for years. I explain about my trip into the attic. Laugh about my fright over the knocking sounds, the metal box that's so frustrated our attempts to open it.

'It looks like nothing's moved up there in decades. It seems so terribly sad. What happened to her children?'

'I did wonder if the children's things were up there. She doesn't speak about them, two little boys they were. I only know it was a terrible accident a year or two before I was born. I saw your metal box on the telephone table – you're not meant to get in there in a hurry.'

'It'll probably be full of nothing. Why else would it get left behind?'

I drop the letter onto the table beside the cake and look back at Mrs Cooper. Riley's curled up at her feet. I wait, hoping the usual chatter will spill out a little more detail.

'Mrs Havers will tell you what she wants you to know. She's a very private woman, very proper. She always wrote her correspondence in the morning room each day while I was here cleaning. She did her garden in the afternoons.' She watches Riley for a moment. 'My parents used to talk about her husband. He was a drinker, liked the women. Happy to chuck tenants out if they fell on hard times and couldn't pay the rent. Not much fun to be married to, I wouldn't think.'

'And to lose their children,' I say. 'Did they drown? In the pond? It's just that Mr Whittle told us when we looked around that it's very deep and has steep sides. Such a big expanse of water worries me. Mark says I fret too much, so do the twins. But I get a bad feeling there.'

'A car accident, love. Not many back in those days. The

children were playing out and something happened. It was a terrible tragedy.'

'Are they buried at the church?'

'Towards the front beside the path as you come off the lane. I don't think she ever came to terms with what happened, poor woman. She put flowers on the children's graves, very regular about it she was. Richard Denning does that for her now, keeps them tidy.'

She's silent, her eyes focused on the row of faded tea towels drying on the stove rail. I prod one last time.

'Did her husband die after the children?'

'Less than a year later.' She looks at me across the kitchen. 'I wouldn't let it worry you, love. All ancient history now.'

She pushes a smile onto her face, not her usual easy expression. 'I've not made this cake recipe before. Why don't we try a slice with a hot cup of tea. You look frozen half to death.'

I return her smile, she moves from the stove and heads for the kettle. I pick up Mrs Havers' letter and read it again.

'I've often thought it strange she didn't bury her husband with the children.' Mrs Cooper puts on the kettle, picks up the teapot and looks across the kitchen at me. 'Something not right about that, I'd say, wouldn't you, Kate?'

CHAPTER 9

TUESDAY, 12TH OCTOBER

I'VE NEVER KNOWN a storm like this one. Wind whistles between door frames and rattles the old sash-windows. Our London terrace was sheltered on all sides by other buildings. Here the house stands alone. The clicks and pings from the old Bakelite phone chatter away in the hall all of their own accord, the sound amplified in the high empty space of the stairwell. Tom presses close as we sit on Mum's sofa in the kitchen, Riley on his lap.

'It's only the wind rocking the phone lines, Tom,' I say.

'You don't know that,' says my son in a quiet little voice.

'She does, don't you Mummy? There aren't any aliens. You're just being a baby, Tom.'

'That's enough, Sophie. Finish your homework. Daddy'll call soon then I'll unplug the phone.'

I picked up the handset earlier, the sounds echoing down the line were surreal, not helped by the peculiar amplification.

'Should you give Riley something to eat before we head up to bed, Tom?' We bought a ton of dog stuff after school, all necessary according to the twins.

'Dogs need instruction manuals, don't they? Like TVs have,' says Sophie as she sits with her back to the stove. The twins both had homework this evening. Tom's was finished in under ten minutes so he could play with Riley. Sophie still pores over hers, looping her letters perfectly and sprinkling illustrations throughout.

'Can we take Riley upstairs?' asks Tom as he takes a can of dog food from me.

'His basket is here and he'll be warm by the fire. No dogs upstairs,' I say. The twins exchange a glance, Sophie pulls a face but neither pushes their luck any further.

'If you get ready for bed, no messing about, I'll bank the stove and come up too.'

Sophie's happy in her room reading in the rosy glow of her lava lamp. Tom's impossible to settle. I leave him tucked up with Blue Duck who had been abandoned on the bookcase for months back in London.

The gale gusts down the chimney spilling cold air across the bedroom floor. I jump into the thickest pair of pyjamas I own and get into bed. With no Mark and no hot water bottle the sheets are so cold they feel damp. Mark hasn't called. It's getting late, maybe he's engrossed in some prep for tomorrow. I pick up my sketchbook, footsteps patter along the landing, Tom peeps around the doorframe. Tearfully, clutching Blue Duck to his chest, he steps into the room.

'Can I sleep in your bed, Mummy?'

I pull back the corner of my duvet, Tom springs onto the bed and burrows down beside me sprawling an arm and skinny leg across my belly. I'm glad of his warmth. I return to the sketch pad, turning through pages of half-drawn scenes. I'd binned the portrait of the woman, but I see her, every line and pencil stroke as if the pages are full of her.

I glance up, aware of someone watching me.

'For goodness' sakes! You scared me half to death sneaking about like that.'

My daughter stands at the end of my bed, spots her brother's tousled sleeping head and tunnels her way under my duvet.

Sophie's arm is thrown across my chest, her hot sticky hand rests on my neck, her nose pressed to the side of my head. I can barely hear her snuffled snoring above the howling gale. Attempts at drawing failed, the sketch pad lies on the duvet beside my sleeping daughter. I'm too alert to the complaining, groaning house, the storm driving it crazy, and, beneath the commotion of the storm, it's there, unmistakably there. The knocking answers each gusting surge of wind and rain like an eerie echo.

But another sound slides under the noise of the gale. Something I haven't heard before. Something I can't quite place. A tap tap, creak, a floorboard underfoot? The bedroom door is ajar, I can't tear my eyes away from the narrow slice of landing. The house is empty, the attic and office closed and the spare room locked, but it bothers me. Impossible to ignore. I strain my ears, listening, waiting, there's no way of getting off to sleep. I could take a sleeping tablet, smother everything for the next eight hours.

2:36am

Too risky, if I don't wake to the alarm the twins will be late for school again. And I don't want the pills. I don't want to take a backwards step. I glance at the alarm clock hoping time has leapt forward to morning when the world will seem a far more rational place.

2:38am.

My mobile lies beside the alarm clock. No signal. If

anything happens, the landline in the hall, its muffled and crackling old line, is my only option. Mark will be asleep at this hour anyway. Why did he say he'd call then not bother? Was everything alright? I don't let my mind dwell on the various possibilities, they'll turn into monsters at this time in the morning.

Beside my mobile is our shiny new torch. I dump the sketch pad on the floor, tuck Sophie's arm under the duvet and sit up, swing my feet onto the floorboards. I'll take a look, check there's nothing to worry about. I'll drop off to sleep if I can put my mind to rest. Cold air smothers my bare feet. I push on my old pumps and pick up the torch.

The landing is dark, just a hazy glimmer of coloured light seeping along the runner from the twins' rooms. I glance back at my bed, the children both asleep, Tom's face buried in Blue Duck's sagging stomach. Wind gusts another shower of grit down the chimney, it spills like sand through the empty grate and across the green hearth tiles. I can't stand here, I'll lose my nerve if I don't freeze to death first. I grab the small brass knob and pull the door towards me.

The torch's white beam cuts through the black space, picks out the stair spindles, the deep chips in the yellowing paint like pockmarks in diseased skin. I step onto the landing. To my left are the twins' rooms, the family bathroom and office. I closed the office door yesterday. Now though, it's ajar. Its hinges creek, swaying back and forth in the draught. The attic door is locked, nothing's getting out of there in a hurry. I turn the torch beam towards the spare room. Thank goodness it's closed.

I lean over the bannister and peer into the well of the hall. Only buffeting wind and the occasional tring of the phone. I strain my ears and wait. Scratching, urgent and sharp, interspersed with pitiful whining. I hope Riley's just woken and heard me moving around, not been distressed since we came upstairs hours ago. Somewhere, sometime, I've read or maybe someone told me, dogs often fear a storm, hate the thunder and lightning. I knew the bloody dog would be down to me.

I head towards the top of the stairs. The torch beam catches the blackened bulb hanging like a dead thing, beyond it, the locked door of the spare room. At least the bulb won't spook me with its buzzing threat of random darkness. The odd odour of stale cigarettes is here, faint but indelible. The cold deepens, no longer draughts nipping at my ankles but a stillness as though the air has become too heavy to move, solidified, it folds around me.

The whole building shudders as the storm tightens its grip and shakes it. The force of the wind drops and eddies away. Twice, more loudly than before, the knocking.

Riley whimpers and scratches at the kitchen door. I need to check the office and shut the door, deaden the knocking. I ignore the dog and head back along the landing. The twins' rooms are a tumble of duvets, yesterday's clothes heaped on chairs, and in Tom's case, piled on the precise spot where he changed into his pyjamas. An image of the attic with the children's clothes on the floor invades my mind. Not a good place to go right now. Decades ago, as Mark says. Nothing to do with our family.

I stand, torch in hand, facing the office door waiting for the next huge howl of wind. My chest's contracting, breathe. I stare at the grey layers of dust on top of the decorative moulding panels. Has the storm begun to blow over? The house groans, shifts and settles, the wind sinks away. One sharp knock, like a single strike of a fist on wood. It's entirely random. I stand still, several seconds stretch out like minutes. I put out my hand and push the door.

I keep the torch beam trained on the slowly widening gap as the door swings open. Like a searchlight over a black ocean, it picks out Sophie's pink beanbag, dented from when Mark sat there working at the weekend. Two towers of books lean against the wall, large reference works, *The Criminal Procedure Rules*, paperbacks for the charity shop. I remain on the landing runner, push the door fully open and flash the torch around the room, stacks of papers, an angle lamp, bent and twisted like an old man in the alcove beside the chimney breast. The air is cold, thick and damp, an acrid smell of soot washed out onto the hearth. The fireplace shares the same run of chimney, the same sour odour, as the attic. Maybe a roaring fire is all that's needed to dry out the flue.

Satisfied nothing is here, I venture across the threshold and take a closer look at the window catch, caked in paint, it hasn't moved in years. The glass is black, streaked with silver rivulets of water. Torch light rebounds off the window panes as I stand, listening. Nothing but the storm, quieter now, just the occasional buffeting at the windows. No sound, nothing so much as rattles. I close the office door and retreat along the landing.

In my room, the twins sleep under an umbrella of yellow light from the bedside lamp. The storm is turning away, the lightning has stopped, the thunder more distant. The house is freezing and weirdly quiet. I shiver, unexpectedly anxious again for no apparent reason. Riley claws at the kitchen door. The piteous muffled whining starts again. I'll have to fetch the dog and come back to the warmth of my bed as soon as possible. I reach the top of the stairs, the torch picks out the far end of the landing. The spare room door stands ajar. It can't be a draught, I locked it, I'm sure I did. I'm nervous of approaching the room, of closing the door. If I leave it until daylight we'll freeze, the ancient heating system takes an age to restore the temperature, and besides, I won't sleep unless it's shut. I take a deep breath and sprint the half dozen steps to the door. I grab the handle, pull it closed with a bang so sharp I jump. I pull the knob, check the door is properly closed. The key is tucked into the inside pocket of my handbag. Would the twins go there, take the key? Did they unlock the door?

I hurry down the stairs. Poor Riley is overjoyed to see me, tail wagging to a blur, leaping up at me like a jack-in-a-box. Mark was right, I am glad of his company. The hall is alive with shadows, rain splats at the windows. The dog starts to whine again as we head up the stairs following the torch beam. He presses at my shins, his body shivering, my feet so cold, they seem shrivelled in their pumps. Riley gets worse, whimpers more loudly, entangling himself about my ankles. I've no option but to stop, he'll trip me up if we continue.

'Shush, boy, keep still!'

I struggle to find his collar, to pull him away from my feet. The torch slips from my fingers, crashes down the stairs.

'For Christ's sake!'

My voice echoes up the stairwell. The torch beam ricochets off walls and ceiling. Riley shoots upstairs at the sound of my voice, his claws clattering on the floorboards. The torch crashes on the tiles. Darkness.

Damn the dog!

I'm a third of the way up the stairs, horribly aware of how unfamiliar I am with this house. Can I navigate my way from here in the dark? I hesitate, my heart thudding as if I'd run a marathon. My eyes adjust, the glow from the bedroom door just enough to pick out the landing. A white patch of light spreads across the hall floor. Oddly shaped, I can't quite fathom what it is. The torch, not broken but rolled under the telephone table, only a sliver of light escaping. I head down-stairs, glad the phone's stopped its continual tringing at last.

The table is actually a long side cupboard; dark wood, almost black, heavily carved in the Victorian Gothic style. I fumble trying to haul it away from the wall, it's incredibly heavy. I randomly think of Mr Whittle, his recommendations about well-made furniture. Unable to move it, I wonder if it's become embedded in the tiles over the decades. I kneel on the floor and grope underneath it. The tiles chill my already cold hands and knees. Heinous thoughts of unseen horrors lurking in the dust and silky cobwebs beneath the table make me shudder. Just as I can't bear to continue, my fingertips find the barrel of the torch.

'Mummy, where are you?'

Sophie's on the landing, her face, pale and sleepy, chin resting on the bannister, looking down at me.

'Here, Sophie. On my way back to bed.'

I stand, the beam from the torch illuminates my daughter. There's something I can't make out, something black, moving along the landing from the direction of the office. Something dark and tall, swiftly heading to where Sophie stands.

'Sophie!'

Astonishment wipes across Sophie's features. I run towards the stairs, all the while staring up at the landing. A darkness moves behind her, double her height, it will engulf her. What the hell is it?

'What's wrong, Mummy?'

I bound up the stairs, near the top of the flight the torchlight flickers. I shake it, clear the top step. It dies completely as I make it onto the landing runner.

'Mummy?'

Tom's face appears from around my bedroom door. Sophie stands in the triangle of yellow light seeping from the bedroom. She's visibly shivering. There's nothing here. Did I see a shadow, torchlight bouncing them off the high ceilings?

'Quickly now, back into bed, both of you!'

I hurry towards the twins, wrap an arm about Sophie and herd them into the bedroom. I glance towards the spare room. The door stands wide open, the room filled with moonlight. A liquid darkness moves across the space as the door swings shut. Even though I watch it moving, the slam makes me flinch. I hurry after the twins, bang the door behind me. So many of these old doors lost their tiny brass keys over the years but not this one. I turn it now, hear the soft click as the mechanism moves into place. I step back, stare at the locked door as if it might somehow spring open. I'd spooked myself. So stupid, convinced I seen something. But what the hell is going on with the spare bedroom door? I throw my heap of clothes off the dressing-table chair and carry it to the door. I wedge it beneath the handle.

'Mummy, what are you doing?'

I turn around, look at the twins sitting side by side on the bed. Riley, next to Tom, my son's arm around the dog. I'm startled to see them there, utterly ridiculous. It's as if, in my panic, I've forgotten their existence. They stare back at me, waiting for my explanation.

'What's out there?'

Tom sounds terrified. His face is pale, clutching Blue Duck to his chest.

Don't get weird. They're not used to weird anymore. Normal, be normal.

I crease my face into a smile.

'Nothing. Nothing's out there, Tom. Just the wind. It keeps slamming the doors. This'll keep it shut. Come on, get some sleep now.'

I move away from the door, try very hard not to look back at it, to maintain a smile which I pray looks vaguely relaxed and reassuring.

'Why were you downstairs?'

I don't need Sophie's usual barrage of questions right now. Only a plausible explanation will prevent several more following.

'Riley was scared by the storm, so I went to fetch him. He nearly tripped me up on the stairs and I dropped the torch. I had to go back and get it, okay?'

I'm tucking cold limbs into bed, shooing Riley to the floor. Tom's nodding, desperate for good news. Sophie watches and waits for more. I hurry on.

'I must've damaged the torch when I dropped it. I'll have to buy a new one tomorrow. Come on, snuggle down, you've school in the morning.'

I make much of straightening the duvet and am grateful for the warmth in the bed as I slip in next to Sophie. I can see the door from here. Nothing moves. In the safety of the bedroom, my fright already begins to seem ridiculous.

'Can we keep the light on?'

Tom's voice is already heavy with sleep.

'Just for tonight, Tom.'

I've no intention of switching off the lamp.

'Sing our song to us, Mummy?'

Normally I'd laugh, say they're too big now for nursery rhymes and baby things.

' "Sing-a-song of Sixpence"?'

Sophie nods, burrows deeper into the bed. I mumble the song into my daughter's warm hair. Riley sneaks back onto the bed and settles himself at the bottom near our feet. I can't help but strain my ears for every sound the house makes as I sing.

3:29am.

Less than an hour since I went looking for the knocking sounds. I try and think rationally. No one's in the house. Just shadows, wind and my overactive imagination. That's all. It'll seem absurd in the morning, in the daylight.

I'm exhausted. Warmth seeps into my cold limbs as I cuddle up to Sophie's back. Tom's steady breathing suggests he's sound asleep already. Riley makes small whistling sounds from the end of the bed. The pressure of him on my feet is surprisingly reassuring. I'm doubtful though, that he'll be much of a guard dog, judging by his behaviour so far. I let the song fade to nothing and hope sleep will come quickly. Sophie mumbles, her words blurring into sleep.

'Who are the people in the empty bedroom, Mummy?'

CHAPTER 10

WEDNESDAY, 13TH OCTOBER

MRS COOPER AND I stand on Haverscroft's top front step.

'Always sticks in bad weather,' she says, shouldering the door.

'I never imagined trying to break in here,' I reply, pulling a face.

She hefts the door again.

'What made you buy the place, if you don't mind my asking?'

'Mark and the twins fell in love with it. The kids might have changed their minds after last night though. We can always sell up and move on if it doesn't work out.'

The door gives way, Mrs Cooper staggers into the hall as Riley shoots between our feet.

'Lift the handle as you open it, love. Bit of a knack when it's wet. It would've been the rain driving against it last night, I shouldn't wonder, that made it swell. Mrs Havers lit the hall fire to keep the damp out. Let's get this baking unloaded before it rains again.'

Both panniers on Mrs Cooper's bike bulge, the front basket, stuffed. We unload tins and Tupperware, take it all through to the kitchen.

'It's a shame last night's AGM got cancelled, it was such

filthy weather. WI baking isn't to be missed! Here you are – keep some for yourself and the twins and take the rest with you when you go to Fairfields. We can't have it go to waste. Mrs Havers is partial to a cheese scone; it might improve her mood.'

'I used to cook for Mum, but she wasn't interested in eating much really.'

Why I tell Mrs Cooper this I don't know. Mum was bone thin, always cold so she didn't want to leave the flat. I thought if I could cook something she really fancied things might change. Mrs Cooper gives me one of her long stares and smiles. 'Not a problem with the children though, is it? Good eaters, both of them.'

'Can I make you some tea, Mrs Cooper?' She looks so surprised. Have I been that unfriendly? Probably. Her company in this big old house is so warm and companionable I don't want her to leave right now. I might volunteer to have my leaves read if she needs persuading to stay. She starts taking off her coat, stupidly I feel relieved.

'Call me Shirley, love, everyone does.'

We settle on Mum's sofa, Riley curled between us as the kettle boils.

'Not got that old box open yet, then?' She's eyeing the metal document box on the kitchen table.

'I'm taking it to show Mrs Havers, to see if she remembers it. If not, I'm off to the ironmongers to ask if they'll break it open.'

'Probably be full of nothing after all this anticipation.'

'The twins will be disappointed,' I say.

'So will I!' she says, smiling.

The knocking is clear, sharp and unmistakable. Shirley's

expression flashes with concern. The door from the kitchen to the hall is shut, even so, the sound is loud, quite distinct. It comes again, twice, as we dumbly stare at one another. Riley gives a low throaty growl, jumps from the sofa and runs to the door, scratching and scrabbling at its base.

'Good Lord! What in heaven's name is it?'

Shirley Cooper's voice wavers as she clutches the blue and cream scarf at her neck. The sound comes again, three, four times. I stand and head for the door. Riley barks non-stop, leaping at the door handle.

'It was loud last night. What with the storm, I couldn't locate it. It could have come from Mark's office or the attic. Maybe in daylight it'll be easier to find.'

'You're not going out there, surely?'

I glance back at Shirley. Her dark brown eyes bulge with horror.

'I can't just leave it,' I say. I reach for the handle, but Shirley is swift, grabs my forearm so tightly I gasp.

'Leave it, love, please.'

The shock of her face thrust into mine stuns me to stillness. A huge sound, a splitting noise as if a massive whip cracked deep within the building seems to shift the house. For a crazy instant it's as if the entire property has been blasted from its foundations. Splintering, smashing sounds. The thunderous rumble of something heavy falling. The house vibrates as the pounding goes on and on. Shirley grips my arm tighter, her fingers pressing into my flesh through layers of clothing.

Riley sniffs urgently at the gap beneath the door, his claws scratching against the painted wood and floor tiles. He resumes barking. I'm staring at Shirley, her eyes, ringed in dark clumpy mascara, are huge in her face.

'I have to open the door,' I say, as much for my benefit as Shirley's. 'I can't hear anything now, can you?'

She turns to stare at the door, still hanging onto my arm. 'No, love.' She looks back at me. 'We can't stand here all day, can we?'

I'm not a tactile person, not someone to walk down the street arm in arm with a girlfriend or tightly hug people I've only just met, but I find Shirley's firm grip reassuring for no logical reason other than she shares my fear. I reach over Riley's excited pacing body and grab the doorknob. His nose wedges between the door and the frame as I peep into the hall. We stand and listen.

'Only the wind,' I say. Shirley nods. I pull the door fully open, Riley tears into the hall. He barks at the bottom of the stairs, his eyes fixed on the landing. Dust drifts over the mahogany bannister, heavy and thick it's moving in gusting waves.

A further thump, as though something has fallen, but it's hard to tell through the whistling and howling of the wind. Riley's not stopped barking. Should I mention last night? The shadow I thought I saw, Sophie's people in the spare room? It's not going to help, I keep quiet. Shirley and I exchange a glance.

'I'll have to go and see what that was. It sounded like the ceiling falling in.'

I don't want to go upstairs, it's the last thing I want to do, but what choice is there? I hope Shirley's coming, I can hardly blame her if she goes home right now.

'I could go and get George.' Shirley's grip on my arm tightens again.

'George?'

'George Cooper, my brother-in-law. He's working at the far end of the high street on the old post office. Most of its roof got ripped off last night.' We study one another, my stomach's jittering, mouth dry. 'Let's take a peek and if it looks too bad I'll run and fetch him. We'll take the dog with us, you know, in case, there's something up there.'

'What the hell do you think's up here, Shirley?' I ask as we head towards the stairs. A dog of Riley's size isn't likely to scare off a burglar, and he was pretty useless last night. Shirley doesn't reply, maybe it's better not knowing. Dust coats the bannister, grainy thick stuff that gets into the back of my throat. We climb the stairs, eyes trained on the landing.

Riley bounds up the flight and barks in the direction of Mark's office. The spare-room door is closed, thank goodness. To my right the dust is thick, difficult to see the far end of the corridor. The office is open, Riley barks in the doorway but hasn't ventured in.

We head towards the office. I close doors to the bedrooms and bathroom in a vain attempt to contain the spread of dust. The attic door is locked. I glance back over my shoulder, Shirley's still with me, dust fading her brown hair. We reach the threshold of the office. Riley scampers inside, barking, scrabbling paws, I can't see him.

The door's caught on something. I push, lean on it, widen it enough for us to see past it. Wind gusts at my face. I glimpse the top third of the fireplace rising above a pile of rubble stretching across most of the floor. A hole gapes in the ceiling exposing the attic space, fractured roof-rafters and beyond it, a dark and stormy sky.

'Good Lord!' whispers Shirley. She stands close enough

to brush my back. We try to push the door again, it gives a fraction more. We step into the edge of the room.

'The chimney's blown down and come right through the roof,' Shirley says, taking a step further into the chaos and pointing to a smashed section of chimney pot. She stumbles on a bit of brick.

'Careful,' I say, grabbing her arm. 'I don't think we should go any further in case it's damaged the floor. It's probably not safe.'

Black strands of ivy trail from the roof through the attic and into the room. They shake and shiver in the wind, driving Riley to distraction. He's scaled the pile of broken brick and plaster and is barking himself into a frenzy. My face is wet. Rain's coming in.

'The wind might blow more down. We should get out of here.' I back out of the door, hanging on to Shirley's arm. I pull her behind me as she stares at the gaping hole above us.

'Riley, come on, boy!'

To my amazement, the dog shoots through the door, I tug it shut. I can't lock it, no key. I fetch the bathroom chair and ram it under the door handle.

'What the hell am I going to do about that?' I say.

CHAPTER 11

LOUD HAMMERING BOOMS through the hall. Shirley stops beside me at the top of the stairs and grabs my arm.

'Good Lord, Kate! Do you think there's someone at the front door?'

Riley barks and tears downstairs. Dust clogs my nose and throat. The various rooms still have their doors shut and with the office door closed, the wind, at least, is kept at bay. The thumps on the door are louder, slower and very deliberate. We hurry down the stairs.

'Hold your horses, we're on our way,' Shirley says as she sprints across the short space of tiles to the front door.

Mr Whittle stands in agitated fashion on the top step. He stares at Shirley covered from head to toe in dust, then past her to me. I must look the same. His thin hair's caught in the wind, a wild ring of it surrounds the base of a bald dome. He holds his glasses and a check cap in his hands as if about to pray. He waves his cap towards the end of the house.

'I saw the chimney collapse just now as I was coming from the loke. Are you alright? The whole damn thing's disappeared through the roof there. Made a terrific sound.'

'We're alright, just abouts, aren't we, Kate?' Shirley turns to me as she speaks. I see the dazed shock in her expression as she coughs. 'I should've read your leaves yesterday, love. Really I should!'

I stare at Shirley, then the estate agent.

'The room upstairs is covered in rubble,' I tell him. 'We don't keep much in there, my husband uses it as an office. We thought the room would be quiet, away from the kitchen. He'll have papers and books in there, and his laptop unless he's taken it with him . . .'

I'm rambling. They're waiting for something sensible, constructive. The bottom of Mr Whittle's coat flaps around his knees in the wind. My mind feels like it's been stuffed with cotton wool.

'Your roof, it's got a bloody great hole in it.' Whittle waves his cap. 'Something temporary needs sorting out to keep the weather out. You don't want the wind getting under the rest of it and ripping the whole lot off.'

I must look alarmed, horrified; certainly, I feel it.

'That's your phone gone too.' He turns and looks towards the side of the house. The gravel is strewn with twigs, leaves, bits of roof tile and broken bricks. Amid the mess lies a bundle of cables. The phone, presumably, and also the TV aerial, both had been attached to the chimney. The twins will be bored out of their minds.

'How's George fixed, Shirley? Would he be able to do something temporary?'

'I can run and fetch him. I did suggest that dear, didn't I?'

They're looking at me again. I nod.

'I'll take my bike, it'll be quicker.'

Mr Whittle stays to give me a hand, moves my car out of danger from falling debris. I stand in the lane and try my mobile. A weak signal, better than nothing. Mark doesn't answer. I leave two voicemails, both sounding slightly crazed, a text bounces straight back unsent. There's nothing he can do. I just need him to know. To say it will be all right, it can be fixed. Not to worry. On the off chance, I try his mother's number, leave a message on Jennifer's answerphone. Eventually, I call chambers.

'He's not here, Kate. Stephen's been doing his nut most of the morning,' says the clerk. 'Let me double check for you, though.'

I'm put on hold, classical music drones on. From here the roof looks frightening, a quarter vanished into a black hole at one end of the house. I'm soaked through and shivering. Finally, the music stops.

'Kate, how are you?'

Stephen's deep voice. I'm so shocked I hear myself gasp. We had a strained exchange at the summer drinks do and haven't spoken properly since that night. He doesn't wait for a reply, which is good, I can't immediately think of anything to say. I grip the mobile tight.

'Bit of a crisis your end, I hear. London's a mess too. Look, I know now's not a great time, but we've no idea where Mark is. The Jenner fraud starts Friday so we're up to our eyeballs here.' I can imagine. The trial is listed for seven weeks with numerous witness for both sides. 'I've nearly picked the phone up to speak with you a dozen times since the summer. Thought you might not appreciate hearing from me.'

Why would Stephen call? We were clear, that time was the only time, a drunken mistake on both sides.

'The thing is, what the fuck's wrong with him, Kate? He's been all over the place for months.'

Silly but I feel so relieved. It's not only me. Mark has been evasive, absent for periods of time he just doesn't explain. I wasn't imagining it all.

'He lost his father, Stephen. I don't think we've helped either.'

Do I ask about Cassie? Or anyone else? A van bumps along the lane towards me.

'Have a word with him, Kate, when he surfaces. He's the best junior in chambers, but not if he isn't here. I'll let you go as you're busy, but keep me posted.'

I watch the van slow, put the mobile in my pocket. Where the hell's Mark? Would Stephen say if he knew Mark played away?

A man lowers the van window and pulls alongside me on the puddle-strewn lane. He looks towards Haverscroft, back at me.

'Shirley's explained what happened. I'm George Cooper, her brother-in-law. I've got some tarpaulins in the back that'll do for you as a temporary fix.'

I'm so grateful for his can-do-smile.

'Shirley's stayed in the village,' he explains. 'The school's closing due to the weather. She says to let you know that she's taking your two to the cafe while we sort things out here.'

He bumps his van into Haverscroft's drive and heads towards the house. A wave of exhaustion comes over me to such an extent I could happily lie down on the muddy wet verge and close my eyes.

I pull out my phone and press the home-key. My hand is shaking, my fingers clumsy. No service. I could walk to the high street, maybe pick-up a signal. Who was I calling? I turn and walk along the lane towards the village, perhaps I'll remember when I get there. The twins need collecting from school anyway. Mustn't be late. Never late. I'm trembling, tears running down my face, dripping off my chin onto the phone screen streaking the bright colours. I've no idea why I'm crying, why I can't stop.

I must collect the twins. I'm shaking and shaking. It's getting worse, I can't stop it. Am I just cold? Where's my coat, it won't stop raining. Where did I leave my coat?

I turn the bend in the lane, there they are, tucked under umbrellas. The twins. How are they here, not at school? Tom waves, so does the lady walking with them. Do I know her? I feel I should but there's nothing. All those scarves.

'Where's Riley?' Tom says running up to me.

'Riley?' I see from my son's excited face I should know this. Know who this Riley is.

'Are you all right, love?' I nod at the lady. A blue and cream scarf, wool, home-knitted. 'You look terribly pale, so you do. It'll be the shock, I reckon.'

'Have you lost him, Mummy?'

'Lost who, Tom?'

He's confusing me. Why is he confusing me? I look at my phone, the screen dark and wet, no signal. Why are the twins wearing those clothes? Where are their usual uniforms? Something's not right.

'You have, haven't you?' Tom stomps past me.

'Don't leave us, Mummy. You need to come back, remember?'

Sophie holds my hand. Hers is warm. Mine is cold.

'Do your counting and breathing thing.'

I nod at my daughter.

'We'll look after you, Mummy, won't we, Tom?'

We start to walk towards my son. Why is he so furiously cross, his face red and crying? Breathe. Sophie's right.

Breathe.

'What we need is a hot cup of tea.' I look at the lady as she speaks. And remember. Remember Mrs Cooper. Scarves but no bangles today. Shirley Cooper.

We walk through muddy puddles, Sophie and Shirley chatter away, their voices float above me, I can't take in what they say. I need to get back. Catch up. Breathe. Sophie looks so worried and I know it's because of me. Breathe.

'Here's Haverscroft, love.'

Across the lawn is a house, half the roof gone, a van parked to one side.

'I remember this place,' I say. 'The house where the children died.'

Shirley drops mittens and school bags onto the kitchen counter.

'What a day it's been!' That falsely bright tone again, like Mark uses when things aren't going too well. The twins stand in the doorway looking at me with worried expressions. I suck in a deep breath and count slowly in my head. I can get back. It would help to sit quietly and sketch for a bit. Probably look rather odd just now.

'Riley,' I say. 'Riley's in the morning room.'

Recollection drips back. More will follow if I take my time.

The twins turn on their heels and run across the hall. Excited voices and barking.

'Sit down, love. I'll make you a hot drink. You're soaked to the skin.'

Shirley's pulling me towards Mum's sofa, handing me a towel. 'For your hair, love.'

'I can't keep doing this,' I say.

'No, love.'

'You don't understand what I mean.'

It all tumbles out. About being ill for so long. 'It'd been coming on for years, since Mum died really, so why I was ill just then, right before the Easter holidays . . .' I shrug. 'I've had months of counselling and more pills than I knew what to do with. Six months of it before we came here.'

'If you don't deal with these things, they get all bottled up and confused. I've still not come to terms with losing my Nick, not properly. That's the thing, when you don't expect to lose someone, when they go at the wrong time.'

How can Shirley know that? Perhaps I've said something, let it slip.

'Mum had been ill for years and years. She was first bad when I was about eight or nine years old. I'd just met Mark when she died.'

I'd like to tell her right now, but the words gather, crowd, muddle in my head. I can't do it, too much, too weird. She hands me a mug of tea and sits on the sofa beside me.

'I often think,' Shirley stops speaking, her lips press into a thin, straight line, 'if I'd done a bit more, seen he'd not been himself for a day or two, perhaps things would have been different, you know what I mean, love?'

I nod, watch the steam rise and curl from my mug.

'You can't dwell on thoughts like that, they trap you in the past so they do. What's done's done.'

I nod again. 'You're right, Shirley. It's just this creepy old house, being stuck here freezing to death and being left to manage on my own too much.'

I stop. The bit about Mark, about Stephen, stays with me. I don't want Shirley to think badly of me. 'I've hung onto the idea we can move back to London if we don't settle here.

That's not likely now, is it? We can't sell Haverscroft in this state.'

'Drink your tea, love.'

We sit in silence. I drink the tea.

'Why don't you like going upstairs? I'm not imagining things, am I?'

Shirley swallows, her eyes shift to the stove then back to me.

'I need to know,' I say in a low voice.

She nods, purses her lips. 'I can't put my finger on it, love. All I can say is when I've been upstairs, on the landing, I feel something dreadful. Like a bad thing is going to happen.' She looks me straight in the face. 'How do you explain such a thing without sounding fanciful? It's so bad it makes me feel right queer, I can tell you.'

'How did Mrs Havers manage here all those years?'

She smiles, raises dusty eyebrows. This morning, the crashing, the roof all seep back into my mind. 'You'll need to ask her. I don't suppose you'll get over there today now. She didn't go upstairs on account of her knees and that's true as far as it goes. But she didn't go upstairs for years before then when she was as spritely as you and I are now. As far as I know, once her husband passed away, she lived downstairs. My aunt cleaned for her back then and she never went up those stairs.'

Which explains the attic. I'd wondered why, if she couldn't possibly part with any of her children's things, she hadn't gone there or kept the place clean.

'Are the twins, okay?' I ask. I just don't know how odd my behaviour has been.

'The bit about the children dying might be something they mention.'

'Oh, god! As we turned into the drive!' More memory drips back. 'I put Riley in the morning room. I was worried he'd get the cakes in here,' I say, rising to my feet.

'You stay there, love. I'll go and check what they're up too. Drink your tea.'

Shirley's footsteps recede cross the hall. I sip the tea, my memory clicks into place. Mark. Stephen. No gaps as far as I can tell. I look at my phone. No signal.

'Will the roof get mended, Mummy?'

Tom's face is pale, anxious as he stands in the doorway. I manage a nod, stand up and start to help him out of his coat, although both the twins have been perfectly capable of this activity for years. Be normal, don't distress them. No more stupid comments. Breathe.

'You're very dirty, Mummy. Can we go and see the hole?'

Sophie drops her coat to the floor, turning towards the hall. Sounds of hammering come from upstairs. I remember George Cooper is up there.

'Shall we have some tea first, Sophie?' Shirley's concerned. Sophie glances between Shirley and me.

'Let's go and see how bad the damage is. We'll have no peace until Sophie's satisfied her curiosity, and the men might like something to drink.'

I need to know what we're dealing with. How bad things are, the unknown is far more frightening than reality. I'm also aware I'm in no fit state to take on my determined daughter, nor pass muster in conversation with Shirley, not yet.

'You go up then, dear. I'll sort out here, get the kettle on.'

Still reluctant to go upstairs, but after this morning, who can blame her? We leave Shirley to the warmth of the kitchen and head up.

Dust coats every surface, the stairs tracked with footprints. Mr Whittle was here at some point. Did he go home? The hammering stops as we near the top of the stairs.

'It's always too dark, Mummy.' Tom's cold hand slips into my mine, his fingers curl tightly.

'I'll ask if the builder can fix the light. I remembered to buy new torches this morning.'

My memory's definitely returning, but I can't recall where I've left the torches. The kitchen, most likely. We reach the top of the stairs. I glance towards the spare bedroom, the door is closed.

More hammering. Sophie stops in front of the office, Riley beside her. Men's voices muffle behind the door.

'Knock, Sophie. In case they're just inside.'

Sophie's small fist doesn't make much sound but the hammering stops and the door opens a crack. Mr Whittle peers out.

'We've come to see the hole and Mrs Cooper wants to know if you want tea,' Sophie says.

Mr Whittle pulls the door a little wider. He's covered in pale pink-grey dust. Just behind him, George Cooper smiles broadly showing nicotine teeth and a wave of dust-encrusted wrinkles ripple across his face.

'Come in, young lady, but mind where you put your feet,' says the estate agent.

Sophie darts into the room behind Riley.

'Careful, Sophie!' I rush to catch her up, but George Cooper continues to smile whilst brushing dust from his short grey hair.

'It's perfectly safe, Mrs Keeling. I've checked out the floor, and as long as no one's daft enough to climb this pile of rubble, everything's sound for now.'

The air in the room is hazy but clear enough to see just what's happened.

'I understand you've been bothered by some knocking noises.' The builder grins, glances at Mr Whittle who shuffles his feet and brushes at his trousers.

'Ghostly sounds, so I've been told.' His grin widens. 'I'm afraid I've got to disappoint you. I hope you didn't buy the place hoping for a spirit or two. There's nothing going on here other than a split in your chimneystack. It's probably been there for some time, years even. It would've made a good old spooky knocking when the wind picked up enough. It couldn't hold out against this weather.'

Dark green tarpaulin undulates and crackles with the wind where a chunk of roof should be. The room feels like it's under a great mass of shifting water. Sophie's on her hands and knees in the filth burrowing in the piles of debris. Tom presses close, holding my hand tightly as he peers at the room trying to see what his sister is doing.

'Come out of that, Sophie!' I tell her. 'Before you hurt yourself!'

My daughter's narrow back is towards me, her body rigid. She stops scrabbling through the mound of tile and brick, is utterly motionless.

'Sophie? Are you okay?'

Something's wrong. She's on her feet screaming, fear palpable in the high-pitch screech. Tom jerks back towards the landing still clutching my hand as Riley growls and scratches amongst the smashed bricks and tiles. Sophie steps backwards, catches her heel against a broken chunk of brick and stumbles.

'Steady, girl!' says George Cooper, grabbing her arm. He pulls her upwards, breaking her fall. Sophie looks stunned, moves sideways towards me, keeping her eyes on the mound as the dog growls, his snout stuck in the pile of debris. She points to where Riley digs.

'There's a face in there!'

Riley has his teeth sunk into something. He strains backwards, growling, shaking his head back and forth. Bricks shift and rubble trickles down the side of the heap. He drags something free, shakes it, dust exploding in all directions. The dog's growl is deep in the back of his throat. Sophie presses into me, I put my arm around her shoulders. Riley flings the thing towards us. It lands between Sophie's shoes and the builder's boots. Both jump backwards as filth puffs up.

How did he get here? Surely it isn't possible? My stomach turns over, the golly's torn red smile grins up at us.

CHAPTER 12

THURSDAY, 14TH OCTOBER

'I'M PUTTING IT all in here.'

George Cooper made an early start this morning. We stop on the threshold of the spare room, the door wedged open with a couple of broken bricks. The builder's steel-toe-capped boots have tracked brick dust across the discoloured old carpet to a pile of junk stacked in front of the fireplace.

'I'll skip the lot if you like, but I thought I'd better check first.' He grins at me. 'You never can tell what some folks will keep.'

'I'll have a quick rummage through in case there's anything that should go back to Mrs Havers. It's all stuff she left behind.' The builder watches me, raising his eyebrows. 'The attic was full of her children's things. Can I let you know?'

'I'll be here a while clearing that lot.' He's nodding towards the office. A smell of damp plaster seeps through the house. Broken bricks, snapped lathes and debris spread across the office floor.

'I'll skip the carpet, shall I? It makes the room smell bad and it's not worth the trouble to clean it. I doubt that stain beside the hearth will shift anyway.' He nudges the grey-pink fibres with the toe of his boot. The sourness is here, hiding beneath the smell of the office. I can't place exactly what it is.

'That would be great, thanks. I suspect my husband nips

in here for a sneaky smoke. He won't be able to get away with it if the room's fresh and aired.'

I rattle the brass doorknob, turn it, the catch retracting in and out, the mechanism works fine. 'Can you do anything with this? The key's downstairs in my bag, but it opens even when I've locked it. The balcony's unsafe and I don't want the children getting in here.'

George Cooper tries the lock, runs a thick calloused forefinger along the door edge. 'I'll give it a go. The lock's probably worn; it might need replacing. I can fix a bolt top and bottom, if you like.' He smiles again, then winks. 'It'll keep Shirley happy. She went on and on about a bird getting in the house – it was this room, wasn't it?'

I laugh.

'She's a funny old thing, Shirley, superstition sucks her right in. Don't you be listening to any such nonsense.' He smiles and I suspect she's told her brother-in-law how I feel about Haverscroft. 'Her heart's in the right place. Coming over, she reckons.'

He walks off towards the office, pulling up the collar of his donkey jacket. 'It's not her day today,' I say to his retreating back.

'Oh, our Shirley loves a drama, don't you know? She said something about it being a good drying day. She intends washing the curtains, on account of the dust.'

He walks into the office closing the door behind him.

I still haven't spoken to Mark. His mobile was on voicemail this morning when the twins and I tried calling from the high street on the way to school. His clerk said he'd arrived at chambers late yesterday afternoon and had my message about the chimney. He would say I'd called again today. Why hadn't he been in contact? Has he tried? I pull my mobile from my pocket. No signal. I'll try calling again when I take Riley out.

This room feels different today. The door wedged open, George Cooper along the landing, fanciful thoughts can't take root. Stained floral wallpaper is scarred with dirty outlines of old pictures. Furniture dents in the carpet, a paler patch where the bed stood. Sunlight scatters through strands of climbing rose and grimy glass. Like the house, the space feels abandoned. I head for the chaise longue and sit with my sketch pad on my knees. Last night had been okay. The twins snuggled in my bed, Riley a fixture on my feet. The dust hasn't worsened Tom's asthma, Sophie didn't bombard me with questions and my weird behaviour wasn't mentioned.

I started a sketch last night to stop my mind racing: the park beside our London home, drawn from memory, a hot summer's day. I begin to fill in the chequered detail on our picnic rug, the intricate criss-cross of coloured woollen fibres. Hammering starts up in the office.

'Only me!'

Shirley sounds miles away. A few minutes here to gather my thoughts, then I'll go and make some tea, have a natter, see if we can't get through a few of the WI cakes with help from George. The pencil is light and lively, my shoulders relax. I'm doing okay. No pills, no strange drawings. Yesterday would have been enough to test anyone's resolve. Everything came at once, even Stephen, after months of no contact. But I'll feel easier when I've spoken to Mark. Where has he been all this time? Doing what and with whom?

I hold the sketch up, turn it towards the light streaming in from the French windows at my back. Not so bad. I drop it to my lap, the golly's one eye stares at me from the junk pile.

How did you get into the office? Did someone, Mark maybe, put you in there? I bought you in the house the day Riley came, didn't I? There's a gap, between Mark kicking you across the drive, to now. How did you get upstairs? It must have been Mark, trying to avert another fight between the twins. Another question to ask my husband.

Light glints on metal, something shiny poking out of the golly's breast pocket. I kneel down, my fingers fumble, too big and clumsy to release it from such a tight space. At last it comes free. I rest back on my heels and look at a tiny key in the palm of my hand.

The document box is on the hall table waiting for me to take it to the locksmith. George Cooper hadn't fancied having a go at it when I'd asked him. Why would this key be anything to do with the metal box? Both the golly and the box were in the attic. I jump to my feet and dash downstairs. The kitchen door is shut, Shirley's radio on. I grab the box and head back to the spare room. It could be a key to anything. I drag the chaise in front of the dressing table, sit down and place the box on the empty table in front of me.

The key fits easily into the lock but doesn't turn. I wiggle it. It's almost certainly not the right key for this lock. I take it out, replace it and try again. Attempts to open the box with various keys from the shoebox, with screwdrivers and bits of wire might have damaged the mechanism, it's probably shot by now. I try again, shake the box. It half turns, a small click. The lid lifts a fraction.

I glance up and see myself in the old triple mirrors. Three of me, my face shining with excitement, blue eyes wide in anticipation. Get a grip, Kate. The box is too light to be the treasure the twins hope for. The lid is stiff to open, the hinge rusting, grinding. The musty mould smell of the attic seeps out. I tease back folded layers of navy velvet, a second box, black cardboard, about two inches deep. I pull it out and lift the lid. Crisp transparent paper crackles as I unwrap a dozen or so watercolours. Botanical studies of wild grasses and flowers, seed heads and rose hips. The wild roses are beautiful, so lifelike I can almost smell their scent. Cramped, neat writing labels the images: a dog rose I recall blooming in the hedges when we first found Haverscroft, a blood-red climber, none are signed. I place the paintings back in their cardboard box. I'll ask Mrs Havers about them when I visit. They're so lovely it's a shame not to frame and display them.

There is also a black hardback book, snug in the box, tricky to prise out. I wedge my fingers between its edge and the metal side, pull the blue ribbon tied around it like a parcel until it comes free. Its spine is broken, the cover and pages loose. I untie the ribbon and leaf through a sketchbook similar to my own, and a journal. Judging by the style of the drawings, this is the same artist who painted the watercolours. Rough studies of plants and grasses, the river, the church and high street. Portraits of long-ago people: a small blond boy, a scruffy white terrier and pages of cramped neat writing about day-to-day events.

I put the journal to one side. Shirley will be thrilled, the twins might be less so. Several bundles of letters remind me of Mrs Havers correspondence, tied with string, twine and ribbon of varying colours. Envelopes are addressed to Mrs H. R. Havers, the letters to Helena. Mrs Havers will know who Helena Havers was. Two brown envelopes are all that's left in the box, neither is addressed or sealed. I look in the smaller of them. A birth certificate for Frederick Henry

Havers, born at Haverscroft to Edward William Havers and Helena Rachel Havers in July 1946. The second document is his parent's marriage certificate for two years earlier. Is this Edward Havers the same man Mrs Havers married? Families used names multiple times back then. What happened to these people? A trip to Fairfields might get some clarification if Shirley doesn't know.

The larger envelope has several black and white photos of varying sizes. Portraits of unnamed people whom presumably Mrs Havers will recognise. A group of four sitting on a blanket, a picnic around them on a summer's day taken, I guess from the style of clothes, in the late 1930s. A man and two women in their twenties and a girl of about Sophie's age. The girl smiles a beautiful wide smile at the camera. She clasps the golly in front of her, his blank eyes staring, his grin complete. The women smile at the lens. One has a short dark bob, her features familiar. My heart quickens. Maybe she was in one of the photographs in the attic? But I'd sketched this woman before I went up there.

I sit back, look up into the mirror and jolt with horror. Everything has changed. The glass is clear and unblemished. The face staring back, not mine. A woman, her eyes empty and unblinking. Her hair, a similar chin-length bob to mine, but so dark as to be practically black. Smooth with a sharp fringe, it frames her pale face. The face in the photos. And my sketch. I'm sure of it. My heart hammers against my ribs, I'm imagining things, seeing things again. I try to breathe, but the stench in here has worsened. I can't take my eyes from the woman's. On the periphery of my vision, I see the dressing table cluttered with all manner of things. A silver-backed hairbrush and comb, a small glass dish with hairpins and rings, bottles and jars of cream. A bottle of perfume. A square green stone and diamond ring. Where have they come from?

Voices scream in my head. I put my hands over my ears, scrunch my eyes tight shut. A man, a woman. Can't hear what they say. Raised angry exchanges. Am I screaming? I can't tell. I can't hear. Their voices get louder and louder, my head might explode with them. I open my eyes, look in the mirror. Foxed and pitted old glass, my own ashen, terrified reflection.

The dressing table vibrates, coming in waves, growing in strength. Bottles and jars rattle, the perfume bottle topples over. The hairbrush and comb, the glass dish, rings, bottles and jars fly across the surface as if a hand swiped them away. They smash with a terrific sound against the fender, glass and mess spill into the hearth and across the carpet. I launch myself away from the dressing table and jump to my feet.

The door to the landing vibrates against the broken bricks, the doorknob rattling. The corridor is gloomy, the green runner filthy. Something is there, not a shadow, a tall column of dark space. The bricks fly, crash against the wall, the door slams shut. Silence. The lock turns, a soft thunking into place. No one was on the landing. No one to turn the key, which is still tucked into the side pocket of my handbag.

I dart towards the door and grab the knob, it's solid, fixed, locked. I can't shake the voices from my head. I'm shaking from cold and terror, the doorknob slipping beneath my sweating fingers.

'Unlock the door, let me out!'

Laughter invades my mind, a cold deep sound full of menace. I cover my ears, I can't keep it out.

I hammer my fists on the door, kick at its base and scream. My voice doesn't sound real, my throat rasping.

The door flies open and I fall forwards. He grabs my wrist. My legs bend like rubber beneath me. He has hold of me, Mark stops me falling. George Cooper is here. My husband's lips are moving, but the silence in my head hisses too loudly to hear him.

They pull me from the room, onto the landing, their arms beneath mine. We reach the top of the stairs as my legs gain some stability. Shirley's in the hall at the bottom of the stairs, staring up at us.

'Who the hell is Edward?' says Mark.

CHAPTER 13

I SIT ON Mum's sofa with my feet curled beneath me, my sketch pad on my knees. Mark piles dinner plates into the dishwasher.

'You're taking your meds, right?'

'Of course.'

The little white lie trips off my tongue with a smile.

'It was just a panic attack then. An isolated thing?'

I nod and smile at Mark's stony face as he stands hands on hips with his back to the stove, Riley at his feet.

'I must have gone through the box, dozed off and had a nightmare.'

We've been through this already. If I stick to the story, hopefully this will blow over. I can't blame Mark. To come home and find your wife screaming another man's name at the top of her voice needs some explaining. Thank goodness I wasn't shouting Stephen. The 'nightmare' was the only logical explanation I could come up with. I overheard Shirley recounting to Mark my blurting out about the Havers' children's deaths. No doubt Mark will have spoken to the twins, probably when he collected them from school this afternoon. What will they have to say about their mother's behaviour?

'The botanical sketches are very good,' I say, changing the subject. I pick up the broken journal beside me on the sofa and turn a loose page. The cramped writing in faded blue ink rendered the notes in the margins difficult to make out. 'It would be interesting to know who the people in the photos and sketches are. Maybe they lived here.'

'Old Lady Havers will probably know, won't she?' says Mark. He pushes himself away from the stove and comes to sit beside me on the sofa.

'You look knackered,' I tell him, shifting my feet and journal out of his way.

'We were at A&E for hours. Mother was her usual demanding self. I've forgotten what sleep is.' He puts his arm round my shoulders. I try to relax and lean against him.

'I was worried when no one could reach you.'

'I guess you would've been. It wasn't a great time for my mobile to die, but it pretty much sums up the whole situation.'

His voice sounds flat, exhausted. It's been one thing then another here, but it's been as bad for Mark too. I believe him about his phone, Jennifer and her demands at A&E. The story has a ring of truth about it. But then, I desperately want his absence to be nothing more.

'And she's, okay?'

'She's back home. Low blood pressure. She doesn't eat properly, plus her age doesn't help. They've sorted it now.'

Jennifer doesn't eat at all. I've lost count of the times she's told me she's the same dress size now as she was in her twenties.

'It would make sense if she came and stayed here for a few days,' says Mark.

I try to keep my face neutral, but the thought of Jennifer staying here, presumably with Mark in London, doesn't appeal one bit. It must be obvious from my expression.

'She helped out loads when you were ill, Kate. She'd be

able to help out now so you wouldn't need Mrs Cooper about all the time.'

I don't want Jennifer here analysing, criticising everything I say and do. I can manage the twins perfectly well on my own.

'She's one morning a week. She was extra today because of the chimney and all the mess.'

'I'm not saying you can't cope. It's just that it's been hard for her on her own, since Dad.'

A knock on the kitchen door. It opens, George Cooper pokes his head around the door jamb.

'I've done all I can for today. The spare room's clear and the carpet's skipped. I've put bolts top and bottom on the door like you asked for, Kate.'

'Thanks for doing it all so quickly, George,' I say. I'll feel better tonight knowing it's sorted.

'I'll be back in the morning, just to pick-up the last of the rubble.' He nods and smiles a farewell. My smile feels tight. The bathroom mirror earlier told me I look washed out and strained.

'Your girl's about on the landing. Just so you know.'

The door closes and I look at my husband as we listen to hobnail boots retreating across the tiles, the front door banging.

'I'll go and sort out Sophie,' says Mark, hauling himself from the sofa.

Mark's shouting at the children, footsteps running along the landing. Tom evidently is out of bed too. Mark had been confident when he'd finished stories earlier that they would stay put in their own beds. If he was here more, he'd know how unsettled the children are at night.

What had I seen in the mirror? I turn the pages of the journal, Helena's journal, her name neatly written on the flyleaf. It's possible I just dozed off. It seemed so real, though. I can't bear to think I'm going backwards. How would I tell the difference between something real or imagined?

The last third of the journal is blank. Never used. I flick through the empty pages and notice notes scribbled towards the end of the book, upside down, going back to front. I turn over the journal. The same hand, the same faded blue ink, but no drawings. Just short notes.

Edward cried out again last night, his words slurred by sleep and whisky. The fear, the horror in his voice chills me. How to help? How to reach him?

There are no dates. No way to know when these notes were written or the length of time between them.

Edward went utterly berserk, smashing the dinner service across the hall, kicking several spindles out of the staircase.

My eyes run down the page, turn to the next. Rages and outbursts of temper.

'Trapped in the bedroom. Hammered his cane against the door, threatening to smash it down. Freddie wet my bed again, the child's terrified.

Panic tickles the pit of my stomach. Had I been dreaming earlier or wide awake? The writing is deteriorating. Scribbles difficult to decipher. Who was this woman, was she writing in secret? In haste?

'Denies I'm his wife, Freddie a bastard.'

'Kate?'

I look up. Mark handing me a mug of steaming liquid. I hadn't heard him come back into the kitchen and pour our coffees.

'Thanks,' I say, taking the mug. My hand shakes, Mark can't fail to notice.

'You, okay? Something interesting in there?' He's looking at the journal open on my knees. 'You were pretty engrossed.'

My mouth is dry, my heart is beating too fast. I try to smile and hope I look calmer than I feel.

'It's just tricky to read. The writing's faded and old-fashioned.'

I blow on the coffee, play for time as I gather my thoughts. I can't explain any of this to Mark just yet. He'll most likely dismiss it all as ancient old nonsense or worse, think I'm unhinged. I'll speak to Mrs Havers. Find out the history of the place then see what I've got. I must have imagined it, dreamt it, surely? Maybe I should check with the GP, ask if it's a side effect of coming off the medication? But then I'll have to explain about dropping the dose, coming off faster than he'd advised.

'Sorry, it's such a flying visit, Kate.' Mark still stands watching me. I close the journal.

'Six hours or so is better than nothing. At least you've been able to see what's gone on with the chimney. I wasn't looking forward to explaining all that over the phone.'

He heads to the kitchen table. His holdall gapes, clothes piled beside it along with a half-dozen battered LPs, which Mark had given to me as Shirley bustled about making tea and chatter. More charity shop booty, he explained. Late 70s disco and punk. Not Mum's style, way after her time. By then she hardly went out and I'd no spare cash for extras like records.

Mark stuffs the clothes into the bag, the holdall straining as he swings it off the kitchen table and onto the floor.

More stuff, casual things too. Is he intending to spend longer periods away?

'You spoke to Blackstone yesterday.'

The statement takes me by surprise. Mark knows I call the clerks when I need to, but not his colleagues. Not Blackstone. Did he get a rollicking when he finally turned up to chambers?

'He spoke to me actually,' I say, hoping to explain the conversation.

'He didn't mention Southampton then?'

'Southampton?'

'The Southampton fraud trial. It came into chambers a couple of weeks back. It's a big case, six defendants, and it's likely to become a high-profile thing.'

A sinking feeling rolls over me. I know what's coming next.

'Blackstone's asked me to junior for him. A case like this could really help my career and the fee's obviously good. You know we could do with the money, what with the chimney and everything.' . Mark strides to the stove and looks back at me across the length of the kitchen. 'I'll have to take it, Kate.'

Weeks in court. Six, eight, ten weeks staying away most nights in Southampton.

'Charles is one of the other juniors, along with Cassandra Lewis-Brown. You remember her? You met at the summer drinks thing.'

Cassie. Do I remember? I remember far more these days than my husband realises.

'When's it listed for?' I ask, my tone flat.

'Pretty much all of March and a few days into April.'

'You're kidding?' I stand up, put my mug on the table and brush dust from my jeans. 'That's five, six months away.'

I take a breath, hold it in, bite back the words sticking

in my throat. I just don't get it. If he isn't planning to work locally, what was the point of moving here? If he's playing around I'd rather know. Know what I'm dealing with. But now's not the time, better to wait till the weekend. Mark picks up dirty glasses from the table and brings them across to where I stand.

'Let's finish tidying here and then we'll go up and say goodnight to the twins. I've ten minutes before I have to leave.'

I pick up a plate and begin stacking the dishwasher.

'I'm back Friday night. We can talk about Southampton then.'

'Is Friday a definite?' I say, looking at him.

'Absolutely. I've got a guy coming over on Saturday morning to look over the Armstrong Siddeley to see what kind of a state she's in and what we need to do to get her moving.'

Has he failed to notice one of the chimneys has taken out half the roof?

'Till then, though, Kate, take your pills. Perhaps speak to the GP, see if you need the dose increased, or maybe your old counsellor, okay?'

I nod. What else can I do, for now? I wish I could tell him I dropped the meds weeks ago and have been doing just fine but I can't. No way will he see today as a blip in an otherwise stable period.

'Is Mummy ill again, Daddy?'

The startled surprise and horror I feel is reflected back at me in Mark's face. I look around his shoulder as he spins to face the hall. Our daughter stands in the doorway, dark hair sleep-ruffled about her shoulders, skinny arms clutching tight the greying blanket she has loved since babyhood. Her eyes, huge in her pale face, glisten brightly.

'Hey,' says Mark, hurrying towards her, 'Mummy's just fine . . .'

'Mummy!'

The shout, high pitched and scared, is from upstairs.

CHAPTER 14

OUR SON SITS bolt upright in bed, duvet heaped about him, pillow on the floor, Blue Duck gripped in his hand. As soon as he sees me, he bounds from the bed and clamps his arms about my waist.

'Did you have a bad dream?' I stroke his hair, damp with perspiration and kiss the top of his head, the warm scent of Tom. Mark, with Sophie trailing behind, pads along the landing.

'Did you hear them too, Tom?' Sophie asks, peeping around Mark.

'Hear what, Sophie?' Mark's tone is short, irritation barely concealed. When our daughter doesn't answer I turn and see she's standing, gazing at her naked toes.

'Well? Come on, Sophie, what are you talking about? If it's more of what we were discussing earlier I'll not be impressed!' says Mark.

'It's okay, Sophie. Just say what's up.' I only have a view of Mark's back as he continues to look at Sophie. Tom clings so hard to me it's difficult to move.

'I told her off, didn't I, Sophie? Telling ridiculous tales to the builder and her brother. Tom's as bad for believing such nonsense.' Mark's voice is getting louder, building to a shout. 'Didn't I say your mother had enough to cope with without you adding to it, Sophie?'

Our daughter gives a tiny nod, all the while keeping her eyes fixed on her feet.

'You both have school tomorrow, so back to bed,' I say. Tom clutches me tighter, Sophie glances up at me in alarm.

'I did hear something, honest. I came straight downstairs, just like you said, Daddy. I never said anything to Tom, did I, Tom?'

Sophie looks at her brother, his face still pushed deep into my waist. He shakes his head.

'So why did you yell for me, Tom?'

I keep my tone calm and patient. Shouting at the twins isn't going to get to the bottom of why they're scared and I need to know what they heard. Was it the same as me?

'Don't know.' Hot breath seeps through my sweatshirt as he speaks. 'I just woke up and was scared.'

'Of nothing?' Mark sounds exasperated. 'And your problem was what, young lady?'

Sophie shrugs, looks at me. She's on the verge of tears, works the blanket between her fingers, clenching and unclenching it as she grapples with what to say.

'It's okay, Sophie. Just tell us what's wrong before you both freeze to death here. Before we all freeze to death here!' I look at Mark. 'And before Daddy has to catch his train.'

Sophie glances back along the corridor, past the stairs and towards the spare room. The door is ajar, a slice of grey moonlight around its edge. It was shut when I went downstairs earlier, leaving Mark to finish the bedtime stories. Had George Cooper left it open after fitting the bolts? Surely not. He knew how much I wanted it locked.

'I did hear them, honest I did.'

Mark strides off along the landing. 'For God's sake, Sophie. It was Mummy and me talking in the kitchen.'

Sophie is looking at me, eyes wide, shaking her head. Mark

clicks the landing light at the top of the stairs, but there's nothing, the bulb useless and dead above his head. He snatches up the torch and strides towards the spare room.

'I *did* hear them, really Mum, I did. I didn't dare come downstairs until Daddy opened the kitchen door cos of the dark.'

Sophie's whispering, but there's no need as Mark is banging and crashing about, the torch light flicking wildly about the spare room. My heart pounds my chest. Is this what I heard? Voices screaming in my head? If so, what the hell was it? Are we safe?

'Nothing in here at all! Completely empty.'

Mark's voice is muffled by his thudding footsteps. Tom presses closer, his hands locked at the small of my back. Dare I mention anything to Mark? He's minutes from leaving. Nothing he can do.

'Where did you get the idea for Riley's name, Sophie?'

My daughter stares at me before she speaks in a whisper so low I hardly hear her. 'Like the other dog that's here sometimes. The lady's dog.'

My heart thuds so hard I think Tom must hear it.

'Who are they? The people you hear in the spare room, Sophie?'

She shrugs and looks back at the spare room. Mark still thumps around. 'I don't know, but the man's scary. He locks the door and bangs it with his stick.'

Tom's head pops up. 'You'll be in so much trouble, Sophie. Dad'll go nuts when he knows you've told Mum.'

'Why will he?' I say, looking at the twins.

They exchange a glance. Tom's eyes are bloodshot, his face tear-stained.

'If we make you more ill you won't be able to look after us,' says Sophie.

'I'm not ill! I'm fine,' I reassure her, looking angrily towards the spare room.

'Nanna Jen will have to come and take care of us again,' Tom says, as he reburies his face in my side.

'Do you hear these things too, Tom?'

Tom shakes his head. Just Sophie. Our daughter's fanciful imagination, Mark will conclude.

'Look, kids, hop into my bed for now while I talk to Daddy.'

Tom's head pops up. 'Can we have Riley with us?'

I look from his face to Sophie's. 'Can we, Mum?'

'I'll bring him up, just as soon as Dad goes for his train. That's my best offer. Off to bed – now!'

Sophie grabs her brother's arm and pulls him off me. They run, bare feet slapping the floor to our room. The beam of Mark's torch catches their backs as they vanish through the door. Our bed creaks as he stops at the top of the stairs.

'That room is empty, which is no surprise to me at least. The kids need to sleep in their own rooms, Kate.'

He switches off the torch, bangs it back down against the bannisters. I hurry towards him. He speaks loudly knowing the twins will hear him.

'Don't leave the door unlocked, Mark!' I say as we meet at the top of the stairs. Moonlight floods the spare room, the door wide open. I catch his expression, surprise turning to fury. I won't sleep unless the door is locked. I run to the end of the landing, grab the brass knob and slam the door. I shoot top and bottom bolts home, turn the key in the lock. I pause, catch my breath, relief floods over me. I retrace my steps and Mark heads off downstairs so fast I can't close the gap between us.

'Mark! Wait, just a minute!'

'You make the kids nervous with your absurd behaviour, Kate. What the fuck do you think is in there?'

He snatches up the holdall and grabs his keys, knocking sheets of paper off the table and onto the floor. He scoops one up as I reach him. The sheet is A5 and covered in handwriting, lots of capital letters and figures. I pick up two more pages from the tiles. *G.W.Cooper and Sons – Builders*. Mark snatches them from my hands, stuffs them in his jacket pocket, but I've seen the number at the bottom of the page. I stare in dismay at Mark. He slings the holdall over his shoulder.

'I asked the builder for an estimate.'

He pushes past me towards the door. All I want is to delay him, not let him leave like this. I've no idea what time we have. How long before he would miss his train?

'We're insured, aren't we, for the work?'

He stops dead on the top step, I collide with his back.

'What the hell's the matter with you, Kate? Of course we're insured. Do you think I'm utterly incompetent?'

He clicks the key-fob and lights blip on the Audi, headlights picking out the skip at the edge of the drive piled high with a mess of broken plaster and rubble.

'It'll be okay then, won't it?' My voice sounds small and whiney, more like our daughter's than my own. I'm better than this. I take a breath. Try again. 'They'll send out loss adjusters for something this big. I can deal with all that. It's what I've done for years, Mark.'

He doesn't move or say anything. Short dark hair curls at the nape of his neck onto his collar. He'll have it cut soon, one night after work, on his way back to Charles' flat. Does he go straight home from chambers like he did when we lived in the city, or is he tempted out, to the wine bars, theatres?

'You're so busy, Mark. Don't worry, I can get the quotes sorted out and call the insurers.' My voice is firm and calm. Not panicky, not angry or needy. I want to say don't treat me like a child or an invalid. Trust me like you used to. Listen to me. But I don't.

'I'll try and get away a bit early on Friday, even if I bring prep back here.' His voice is without any emotion, his anger spent. He stares down the front steps. 'I'm going to take the Southampton brief, Kate. I thought you and the twins could stay by the coast over the Easter holidays as it will be difficult for me to get back here so often. The brief fee is more than I'll get doing anything else.'

'Are we that hard up? Don't feel you have to take it, Mark. We'll manage . . .'

He turns around and faces me. 'I wanted to speak to you about it first. Whether it would bother you, possibly bumping into Blackstone again. If you and the twins stay around the Southhampton area?' He shrugs. We both know how closely they'll work together. I would almost certainly 'bump' into him at some point and would hear about the case constantly from Mark for months as they prepared it. I'm sure it wouldn't bother me to see Stephen around. Not like it would have done a few weeks ago. No time to explain this to Mark right now.

'Take the medication, Kate. I need you well, not spooking the hell out of everyone with insane tales about kids dying here, okay?'

It's like I've been frozen, I just stare silently at my husband, at the angry frowning face. He turns away, walks down the steps and I don't know if I should follow. He opens the boot and throws the holdall in beside bundles of briefs, thick law books and journals. He slams it shut, heads for the driver's door and looks up, his face in shadow, I can't make out his expression.

'Mum, how long will you be?'

I fold my arms across my chest against the damp chill, glance over my shoulder. Sophie, with Tom at her side, peer over the landing bannister.

'Get back into bed. I'll only be a minute.'

The engine starts as I look back to the driveway, lights blaring into the darkness as the car scatters gravel and heads towards the road, brake lights flare at the top of the drive, the car barely slowing before turning into the lane. I stand on the step staring into the darkness until the engine fades to nothing.

CHAPTER 15

WEDNESDAY, 20TH OCTOBER

'JUST THINKING ABOUT it gives me a headache, George.'

We stand in the doorway of the morning room admiring the first three drops of pale cream and green striped wallpaper.

'I can't fathom how to keep the pattern straight on the corners.'

'That'll be a challenge for sure, Kate. Symmetry and old houses don't mix.' George grins and fusses an ecstatic Riley. 'You should've gone for the floral print like the room upstairs.' He raises his eyebrows to the ceiling.

'I'm okay, thanks,' I say with a grimace.

'It's coming on well though, Kate. You're nearly done in here. Amazing the difference a week makes.'

'A walk to the church and back will clear my head, I'll get on again then this afternoon. The paint fumes aren't helping.'

I tug Riley's lead and head into the hall. 'Slam the front door when you're done, George. I have a backdoor key with me.'

I drop my mobile into my pocket and grab the keys from the glass bowl on the hall table. The corner of Mark's work laptop pokes out from beneath the stack of Sunday papers waiting to be recycled. He must have forgotten it last night in his rush to leave for London. I'll call him when my phone picks up a signal.

I follow Riley through the kitchen and lock the back door behind us. The front door sticks so badly it's almost impossible to use. I cross the lawn and head down to the pond. Beneath the willows, overlooking the still black water, is a rusting metal seat, just wide enough for two people. I'm never tempted to linger here let alone sit a while. Mr Whittle saw me shiver that first day we looked around. Something about the water, the deep shade and isolation beneath the draping willows jangled my nerves then and still does now. If I'd found the place sinister then, when the sun burned in a clear blue sky, the lane frothing with cow parsley, a dank day like today isn't going to alter my opinion. I hurry towards the back gate and out into the lane.

Riley already has a scent and I follow the bustling little dog to the fingerpost where the loke splits left to the village and right to the church and river. I stop and call Mark's mobile, leave a voicemail about his laptop, say the morning room's coming on well. Over the last week, since the argument on the landing, things have settled down. Mark's managed to be here an extra night or two. It helps that George is about the house. Even so, the spare room remains locked and the twins, Riley and I share my bed when Mark is away. Mark will be home tomorrow night. Until then I'll continue decorating and do a bit of sleuthing into Haverscroft's history.

The churchyard is empty. I find the children's grave easily with Shirley's directions. A single polished white marble headstone, boys aged seven and nine years with identical dates of death. In loving memory but no details of their parents, just the children's names and ages and an urn of freshly arranged mauve Michaelmas daisies and ruby-red dahlias. I take a photo on my mobile and move to a larger grave behind the children's.

The name in gold letters, carved into black marble, catches my attention. *Helena Rachel Havers, wife of Edward, mother of Frederick*. I take a second photo. I can follow up dates of birth and death when I get internet access, maybe head over to the cafe in the village before I pick up the twins this evening. The more facts I have before I meet Mrs Havers tomorrow the better. Old fashioned crimson roses fill a wide china bowl sunk into the ground at the foot of the head stone. I kneel beside the grave, reach out and touch a petal, soft as velvet, its heady scent threads the damp air.

'Hello, there!'

I practically jump out of my skin and drop the mobile as I stand. A thickset man, black biker leathers and Doc Martins, strides towards me between gravestones. His warm friendly grin has me smile back although I'm sure we've never met.

'Alan Wynn. Kate Keeling, isn't it?'

He holds out a very square hand, as warm as toast as I shake it.

'I'm the reverend here. Sorry we haven't met sooner. I missed you when I dropped by Haverscroft.'

'Shirley Cooper mentioned you called.'

He grins again, perhaps he's aware Shirley doesn't quite approve of him. I pick up my mobile.

'She tells me you've had a real problem at the house. Is there much damage?'

I nod. 'George Cooper's rigged up something temporary so we're water tight, but it's good to get out. I'm looking for the Havers family graves.' I turn back to Helena's headstone. 'She was a very young woman when she died.'

'I understand there's quite a family history. The house is the subject of many fascinating local legends and tall tales, like so many large country piles. I've only been here just over three years so I don't know much myself. It takes a while to fit in.' He smiles again.

The twins spoke of the carrot-topped vicar who makes them laugh in assembly. I wonder what his regular congregation make of him.

'The registers are here: births, marriages and deaths. You're very welcome to take a look.'

'Great, thanks. Do you know Mrs Havers?'

'A little. She attends an occasional Sunday morning service,' he says, turning back towards the gravel path. 'May I show you the church? The tower's Saxon in origin, and parts of the building date from then too. All rather fascinating.'

Alan steps past me into the church, one arm held out to lead me into the building. The interior is gloomy to the point of darkness until my eyes adjust to the light filtering through stained glass windows. It smells of damp stone, polish and dying flowers. At the end of the dozen or so oak pews, posies of cream lilies and pink carnations sag in shiny white ribbons.

'So, what do you think of St Mary's?'

Shafts of light dapple spots of colour across peeling whitewash along the wall to my left. The roof soars away from me, the black rafters like thick ribs above our heads.

'It's exactly as I imagine a small village church,' I say. 'Very tranquil.'

'I'm here most afternoons so you can come and go as you please. No one will disturb you.'

He's quite serious, his pale eyes rather piercing. I look away, glance around the church. What has he heard about the family that moved into Haverscroft? Shirley's unlikely to spare the details.

'You might find the Roll of Honour over here interesting.'

I follow him along the aisle until he stops and looks up at a large wooden plaque. The names, rank and ages of local men fallen in combat over the last century are painted in black and arranged in columns filling the space.

'I asked the WI ladies what they knew about the war dead. Lots of intriguing and poignant tales, as you might imagine. Three Havers brothers fought in the Second World War. Only the youngest, Edward, came home.'

'Mrs Havers' husband?' I ask.

He nods. 'Edward got lucky. He was injured; something to do with his ankle so got sent home.' He glances at his wristwatch. 'All the registers are in the vestry,' he says, moving towards the area behind the altar. 'They must remain in the church, but you can inspect them in your own time.'

He opens a door set flush in the wall revealing a small cluttered room.

'Paperwork's not a strong point as you'll see,' he says, stepping towards a table in one corner. He shuffles papers into a pile. 'These are the registers going back about a century and a half.'

Thick black hardback books remind me of Helena's journal.

'We found some old documents in the attic.' I explain about the metal box, the journal, the entries I'd read.

'Sounds like post-traumatic stress, doesn't it? So many suffered in silence back then. Speaking out wasn't acceptable in polite society: stiff upper lip and all that.'

'I'll show them to Mrs Havers, I'm visiting her tomorrow. Maybe she'll speak about it.'

'Richard Denning might be worth a word.' Alan looks at me and smiles. 'He's an introverted fellow, but once you get him started he's fascinating. Trained as a doctor apparently, but was seriously ill years ago. He had a bit of a breakdown, I think.'

I remember Shirley saying something about Richard Denning being ill, not speaking of it. I had not realised what had been wrong, perhaps I, of all people, should have guessed.

'Never judge a book by its cover, so they say. We all have a past, don't we? I'm sure he's no different from the rest of us. He looks after the churchyard beautifully. Always flowers on the children's grave and roses on Helena's.'

I stare at Alan.

'Is everything, alright?' he says, stepping towards me and lightly touching my elbow. Perhaps he thinks I'll faint or throw a fit. I'm sure he'll have heard something about how I've been lately.

'May I ask you a question?' I say as I gather my thoughts. I probably have such a reputation that I'm sure a bit more nonsense can't do any harm. Alan's nodding. Looking at me. Waiting.

'Is it possible, after someone dies, something of their spirit remains?'

'Ghosts?' he says, frowning slightly.

I nod, grateful he's said it out loud rather than me.

'The Church doesn't really recognise them as such. Why?'

'It sounds insane and it's certainly something I can't explain.'

'At Haverscroft?'

I nod. 'If it was only me, but it isn't.' I tell him about Shirley not going upstairs and get the impression this isn't anything he hasn't heard before. Mr Whittle too, I suspect. About Sophie. Knocking sounds, doors slamming. The odd smells. The voices.

'I must seem quite mad!' I say, laughing.

'Not at all. So much is unexplained or not understood. Is it why you want to look into Haverscroft's history?'

'Partly.'

'Haverscroft has a certain reputation. Many old places do, don't they? Shirley and the WI crowd have much to say, as you can imagine.'

We turn to leave the vestry.

'I keep an open mind on these things. Once you've got used to the place, if you still feel there's a problem we can speak again, if it helps.'

I'm so glad he hasn't instantly poured cold water on the whole idea. Raised angry voices ring through the cold air from outside. Both Alan and I look towards the church door. Two male voices, from what I can make out, shouting.

'Excuse me, Kate,' says Alan. He hurries along the aisle, Riley scampering hot on his heels. The gardener strides in carrying a black bucket stuffed full of lilies. The man's lips are set in a hard, straight line, a deep frown pulls thick grey eyebrows together. He dumps the bucket down with a thunk on the flags. Alan stops as they meet. They exchange a few quick words, their voices low, I can't hear what they say. Winter sunlight streaming through the doorway dims as a figure stops on the threshold of the church.

'Alan, there you are,' says Oliver Lyle. 'Sorry to rush you but I'm due back at the office. Can we make it quick?'

Alan glances back at me, pulls an apologetic smile and hurries out. The church falls silent. Richard Denning stares after them for a moment before turning towards me. The churning sets up in the pit of my stomach. There's no logical reason to be nervous of this man.

'Everything alright at the house?'

'Yes, fine, thanks. I'm looking at the registers.'

I take a breath and steady my nerves. I don't have to explain why I'm here.

'There is one thing, though,' I say. 'We bought some posts and rope at the weekend to fence off the pond. I'd like them in before the twins spend any time in the garden. I can't imagine my husband ever getting round to it. Is it something you might do?'

He stares at me. A long, silent, unsettling gaze. I've no clue what he's thinking.

'You've been speaking to Shirley?' He shakes his head, walks towards the door raising his hand. 'Consider it done,' he says and vanishes into the churchyard.

The builder's van is gone by the time Riley and I get back to Haverscroft, only ladders and scaffolding poles are stacked beside an over-stuffed skip. I'll have some peace and quiet to plot out the Havers' family tree after lunch. I drop my keys into the glass bowl. Mark's laptop is here. I'm not a wife who snoops. I've never gone through pockets, his phone or email as some wives do. I've always trusted my husband.

I take the laptop into the morning room, clear a space on the pasting table and open the lid. The screen flashes, the cursor blinks for a password. I've never used his work-laptop and have no clue what the password might be. I try a couple I know Mark used in the past at home: an old case, his father's middle name. Nothing works. The curser blinks, blinks, blinks. *Sophie-belle*. Mark's pet name for our daughter when she was a baby.

The screen opens to an email, the last thing Mark read. The

solicitor's name is familiar, Mark would go to her, wouldn't he? I've often remarked she's the best divorce lawyer I know. My cheeks flood with heat, a pulsing in my temple makes it hard to concentrate. Her email was sent in May, so two, no, three months after my breakdown, a month before we found Haverscroft. I pull away from the pasting table and stare at the screen unable to drag my eyes from the black text. Does Mark want me to see this? Has he left it open deliberately? I don't think so. I'm sure leaving the laptop here was a genuine oversight. So why is he looking at this right now? I don't want to read it, but I have no choice. I have to try and make sense of what it might mean for me and the children.

The first part is all about the financials: not a good time for Mark to separate while I'm ill and not working. Uncertain if he'd be stuck with high and long-term maintenance payments for me as well as the twins. I'm not interested in the money.

The heading, 'Children's Future Residence', freezes the blood in my veins. My mental capacity, ability to care safely or at all for the twins, is discussed in detail. A good time to move forward with an application for the children to live with their father. The children's welfare is paramount. It ends with advice to think all options through fully, then, if he wanted to move things forward, he should contact her. My mouth is dry, my heart hammering against my chest. Has Mark contacted the solicitor again? And if he has, what has he decided to do? Our family, the twins are my world, I'm nothing without them. I've moved to this horrible place in the hope we'll all be okay, but if Mark is looking at this now, is he making plans to leave and take the children from me?

I scream and lash out, kick the metal bucket full of

wallpaper paste on the floor beside me. It skims across the floor and crashes against the fireplace. Glue sprays out, splashes up the wall and floor. The bucket rolls on its side, the last of the paste leaking across the hearth tiles.

I stand motionless, my heart thumping my ribs, not sure what to do with myself. Riley trots in from the kitchen and stops in the doorway, his eyes on my face. He must wonder what an earth is going on.

The crack slices through the silence, sharp, clear and unmistakably from the empty room upstairs. Riley shoots back into the hall and stops at the foot of the stairs, a low rumbling growl in his throat. His tufty coat stands on end, his ears flattened against his head. I stare up at the ceiling, the knocking comes again, a sharp rapping sound.

I run into the hall and race up the stairs before I have time to consider what I'm doing, before I lose my nerve. I stop at the top of the flight. The landing is gloomy and cold, all the doors to the bedrooms, office and bathroom, closed.

The torch is beside my feet. I snatch it up, click it on and flash the beam along the landing. Riley is barking non-stop at the base of the stairs. The spare room is locked and bolted. The horrible smell that got skipped along with the carpet is back, the chemical scent growing stronger by the second. I realise what the sweet smell reminds me of. My hands shake so violently the torch beam shivers across grey, filthy walls.

To my right, on the periphery of my vision, there's a movement, something coming towards me. George Cooper, a man, striding along the landing, but there's nothing, just the dim corridor. No one here. The torch light flickers, and flickers and dies in my hand. A whispering voice, laughing, an icy breath against my cheek. I'm screaming, the torch hitting the floor.

Riley howls and runs into the kitchen.

Silence.

The strange sensation, the oppressive atmosphere, is gone. Just a dark and empty landing, a fading sense of the stale smell dissipating into cold air. Riley is barking, barking, barking in the kitchen. Not until Alan Wynn spoke of Helena's grave, of the care Richard Denning takes of it, had I been able to place it. That sweet sickly smell, the chemical scent of rotting roses.

CHAPTER 16

THURSDAY, 21ST OCTOBER

I STARE THROUGH the windscreen at Fairfield House, the car growing colder, the solicitor's email spooling in my head. Since yesterday I've thought of nothing but the email and the strange experience on the landing. Even the twins noticed my distraction. I can barely think straight after the worst night's sleep in ages. I'm still undecided what to say to Mark about any of it. A muddy four-wheel-drive moves in my wing mirror, crosses behind me and pulls into a bay a few cars from mine. Mr Whittle's bulky frame rolls out of the vehicle.

I cram my mobile, sketch pad and Helena's journal into my bag and hurry out of the car. The estate agent spots me and waves as I head across the tarmac towards him. He smooths a crumpled green-check jacket over his expansive belly, straightens the glasses perched on his head and beams his broad smile in my direction; happy sells houses.

'Not here to visit Mrs Havers?'

I grin at the astonishment on Mr Whittle's face.

'Well, I never! You don't have to, you know,' he says, lowering his voice and leaning a little towards me. 'She can't sue if you don't.'

I laugh as we turn towards a ramp running from the carpark to Fairfield's central white front door.

'I thought she might have interesting stories about the house, you know, its history.'

Mr Whittle studies my face while I'm speaking. I smile back at him.

'Come in then. I'm here to see my aunt. I'll introduce you to Matron first.'

I follow Mr Whittle up the ramp and into a brightly lit world of beige. Bland prints of local scenes and seascapes blur past along a corridor smelling of bleach and air freshener. We pass a communal lounge, a large television blaring daytime soaps at no one. Doors stand open at regular intervals, nameplates reminding me of school: Mr Henshaw, Mrs Simpson, but no Mrs Havers. The small, not-so-private lives of the residents, defined by patterns on quilts and curtains.

'How does someone live here after Haverscroft?' Mr Whittle sends me a side-on glance as I speak. 'Maybe dementia is a blessing of sorts, if it blurs the edges.' His answering smile is a watery thing.

A large conservatory is at the end of the corridor, the matron, judging by her pressed cotton uniform, stands in the doorway. She has a brief, friendly exchange with Mr Whittle.

'Mrs Havers is in the conservatory,' Matron says to me with a curt nod. 'I'll leave Mr Whittle to introduce you as I'm engaged at present. I'm along here in my office if you need assistance.'

I'd like to ask what assistance might be needed, but Mr Whittle is heading into the conservatory so I follow. Several blinds are pulled, the light bright but diffused. Upright sage-green vinyl armchairs are here and there, some pulled together, others turned to the glass to give a view outside. Several people, sunk deep in their seats, snooze, chins on chests, a group in one corner play cards. The room is stifling, and save for the clack of our shoes on the floor tiles, hushed.

We cross the room to a lady with pure white hair set formally in elegant neat curls. She wears a twinset, pale blue skirt and jacket, a large brooch pinned just below a short lapel. The brooch is some sort of claw, a rabbit's foot possibly, its ankle encased in a silver cuff.

Mr Whittle stops beside her. The old lady's hands, liver-spotted and wrinkled, rest on the curved handle of a dark-wood walking stick, a cream leather handbag on the floor at her feet. I thought she looked out at a rectangle of grass, but as I stop and stand beside the estate agent, I see her eyes are closed. Mr Whittle hesitates and glances at me. He leans a little towards her.

'Mrs Havers?'

He lowers the glasses sitting atop his domed head and perches them on the end of his nose, peers at the old lady and turns to me again, eyebrows raised. I shrug and smile, hoping the estate agent doesn't notice the bubble of mirth rising in my throat.

'Mrs Havers? I've bought Mrs Keeling to see you.'

Rich brown eyes snap open and glare at Mr Whittle. He straightens, steps backwards and smiles, gesturing towards where I stand.

'This is Mrs Keeling, from London, you know. She moved into Haverscroft with her family recently, if you remember?' Mr Whittle's tone is bright and stilted, his wide smile unconvincing.

The old lady ignores me and continues to stare in a hostile manner at Mr Whittle.

'And how is the house? I hope you have kept it secure. I

don't want squatters getting in or thieves stripping out the fireplaces. The kitchen stove needs lighting in this weather, it keeps the damp out. Have you lit the stove?'

Her voice would be at home in an old black and white movie. Clipped, a little shrill, the woman's contempt towards the estate agent is unmistakable. Mr Whittle ignores this line of enquiry and pulls one of the green vinyl armchairs closer to Mrs Havers. The chair legs squeal on the tiles, residents stir and stare in our direction.

'You wanted to meet the people who bought Haverscroft. This is Mrs Keeling. She's come to visit.'

Mr Whittle speaks a fraction too loudly, indicates for me to sit on the chair pulled close to Mrs Havers as he backs towards the door at the far side of the conservatory.

'I'll leave you to chat, ladies!'

He darts off between armchairs as I settle in front of Mrs Havers.

'Can't stand the man!' she says to no one in particular. She seems to be focusing on the array of shrivelled cacti arranged on the windowsill beside her, dust caught between their spines, the plants look abandoned. I'm hoping to find out why she is so keen for me to visit. I'm not sure she really knows who I am.

'You have a beautiful home, Mrs Havers.'

We sit in silence as the old lady doesn't seem to have heard me, perhaps she is deaf. I think it better not to mention the roof and damage to the house as I glance around the room. No staff about to help, Mr Whittle long gone. What do I say? Does she suffer from dementia? Her behaviour suggests she might. I shift in my seat, the vinyl groaning. I smile, she looks away. I follow her gaze and see she's not looking at the cacti, instead at a row of tea roses growing along the outside of the conservatory, yellowing leaves peep above the window sill.

'Can't stand the man. Don't like him, don't trust him.'

She studies my muddy black ankle boots, jeans and finger-nails rimmed with paint. The navy double-breasted cashmere coat Mark bought me for Christmas might pass muster.

'You received my letters.'

'Yes, thank you.'

She lifts the walking stick a little and waves it towards the window.

'No point growing them if they're not looked after. The flies sucked the life out of them. They must be sprayed early in the season. They always are at Haverscroft. Keeps the black spot off too. My man sees to it every year without fail.'

'Richard Denning was pruning some the other day,' I say, hoping this comment sounds vaguely on track.

'He knows what they need. I told the man here, but he doesn't listen to me, doesn't care a jot. Disfiguring you know, the fly.'

She suddenly turns her face from the window towards me and leans forward on her stick as though to impart a secret. I try not to look startled, not to lean back into my chair.

'I never liked them you know, the roses. I preferred the wisteria and the dahlias. They cut wonderfully for the house.'

Her skin is perfectly powdered, her perfume something I don't recognise, perhaps Lily of the Valley, very floral. She's of another age when manners were all-important and time ran more slowly. I see her, tucked up with blankets, tea and muffins, in front of the grate in the morning room.

She lifts her cream bag onto her knees and opens its gold

clasp with a sharp click. The bag is stuffed, springs open, bulges with bundles of papers, letters and documents sectioned into coloured elastic bands. It reminds me of Helena's box. Mrs Havers pulls a bundle out, rests it in her lap and delves deeper into the bag.

'One has to keep one's life in one's bag in a place like this. Nothing is private nor safe from snooping staff, cleaners or, indeed, Matron.'

She pulls a crisp, blue handkerchief free, dabs her upper lip. She doesn't look at me as she speaks and pushes the handkerchief back into the bag.

'You should understand about the attic. You must think it ghastly, ghoulish even.'

I watch her replace the bundle of papers into the bag, click it shut and lower it to rest again at her feet.

'I think you will understand; some would not and may think it quite mad. Perhaps it has turned me mad. Whittle and Lyle say so, I believe. They have so little regard for one's reputation.'

She twists a ring, a dark stone surrounded by diamonds, a wedding band behind it. 'Reputation is everything, is it not? I would urge you to guard it well, Mrs Keeling.'

'Call me Kate, everyone does.'

She studies my face, seems unaware of my discomfort at her long and open stare.

'Events have rather overtaken us, have they not? The damage to the house has rendered the attic quite uninhabitable'

'We managed to save a few things –'

She raises her hand, diamonds flash.

'Had there been a relic, keepsakes to bring me comfort, I would have brought them with me when I left Haverscroft.'

Her eyes are dark, unfathomable. 'As a mother, you will know there can be no such comfort.'

I nod, understand perfectly.

'One blames oneself.'

I know too few details to comment. The last thing I want is to make a glib and meaningless statement. I watch her brown eyes as a tea trolley rattles in from the corridor.

'You are wondering, what happened to my children.'

Her voice is firm, a statement not a question.

'It was a fine June day, a busy time in the garden, but the weather had been inclement the previous week and had quite beaten down the delphiniums. I had much to be getting on with but I could hear them playing in the loke, my boys, Andrew and Michael. Shrieks of laughter, other children from the village had been with them earlier. Then, of course, one hears the car, which was unusual back then. It rather caught my attention, the roar of an engine. The silence that followed never leaves me. Nothing ever fills it.'

She's nodding as she speaks, the rhythm in time with her words, the ring, twisting.

'But of course, you know all this. You have been making your enquiries.'

Accusation in her voice, naked displeasure. Shirley, Richard Denning, the Weldon grapevine will have fed her all the information she might want and more.

'You have my late sister's box and journal.'

Her eyes focus on my bag. The journal pokes out from the top of it, too big to pull the zip across.

'Journals ought to be private things.'

Shirley will have told her I've read the journal and looked at the drawings, the photos. A petite woman in a beige uniform rattles the tea trolley further into the room and stops beside a group of card players.

'There is no adequate excuse to poke about in another's private affairs. It's quite intolerable.' She looks at the journal, then at me. 'Are one's own thoughts not entirely one's own?'

'There are things at Haverscroft that I don't understand.'

I can't meet her gaze. It had never occurred to me I might offend her reading the journal. I turn my head to follow the tea lady's progress to a group nearer where we sit as I gather my thoughts. I try again.

'When I found the journal I didn't know who if belonged to, who Helena Havers was.'

She raises her hand again. 'My sister, Helena, was older than me by several years. She cared for me like a second mother. I like to think she watches over my boys.'

She taps her stick, click, click, click on the tiles. I try to move the conversation on and smile as I speak.

'I saw they're buried near her, not with the Havers.'

'Quite right. Quite right.'

The stick stills.

'Not with their father, her husband.'

'You don't stop, do you, Mrs Keeling. As bad as that nosy fellow, Whittle.'

She leans forward a fraction, both hands a fist around her stick.

'The family plot is ancient, full and overgrown. It floods in bad weather. It's no place for her or my boys. Do not read things into other people's misery that is not there. Shirley Cooper has much to answer for, I have no doubt.'

'There's something at Haverscroft that worries me. You'll know what it is and why I'm here.'

We stare at one another, her gaze unflinching.

'The room above the morning room: my daughter has heard things, and I have. Shirley refuses to go upstairs. She says you lived for many years on the ground floor.'

'As you can see,' she taps her swollen knee with her forefinger, 'I have long suffered with arthritis. The attic became quite impossible for me, as did, later, the main staircase. By the time I came here the front steps were beyond me. One loses one's independence as the years advance.'

She glances towards the rattling tea trolley. 'Will you take tea? I'm afraid I can't recommend it. Tasteless, milky stuff, but it's surprising what one gets used to.'

'No, thank you. My daughter called our dog Riley.'

I watch her face, but she remains impassive.

'Is that the same name as the dog that lived there before?'

'I've never owned a dog of that name,' she says. Her sharp, snappy tone surprises me, it must show on my face as she continues. 'Children can be fanciful, can they not? Is she at school? A boarder?'

'Sorry, what do you mean?'

'Will your children board at school? Some time away rids them of childish nonsense. There's nothing at the house.'

'The room above the morning room has a strange smell and the door sticks for no reason.'

'Really, Mrs Keeling! You should consider a new-build.'

'I've heard voices, in particular, a man's when the room is entirely empty.'

Mrs Havers is silent, watching me, her lips pressed together her coral-pink lipstick a thin line. When she speaks her voice is so low I hardly catch her words above the murmur of conversations.

'You have been unwell, I understand.'

Her simpering tone and humourless smile, infuriate me.

'Who's listening to gossip and jumping to conclusions now, Mrs Havers?'

She bangs her stick on the tiles, the crack ricochets across the room and kills the hum of conversation. The tea lady pauses, cup and saucer held out midway to its recipient.

'There can be *nothing* at the house, Mrs Keeling. Nothing.'

She raises her stick, I hold up my hand, for an instant I think she will strike me. Instead, she waves it at the tea lady, another beige uniform and the matron strides in from the corridor. Mrs Havers rocks in her chair, back and forth, back and forth. The stick cracks on the tiles. She's trying to stand. I get to my feet and put out my hand to help her, she slaps it aside.

'Mrs Keeling does not wish for tea.'

Mrs Havers looks at me as she speaks to the tea lady hovering at my elbow.

'Mrs Keeling is leaving.'

CHAPTER 17

TUESDAY, 26TH OCTOBER

'LET'S TRY AND call Dad before we head home. I'm not sure where he is today, but a voicemail will be better than nothing.'

We walk to the turn in the high street and sit on the bench outside the solicitor's office. Sophie dials Mark's number. I expect her to splutter a message to voicemail so I'm surprised when Mark answers and has time to talk.

The twins tell him about half-term, the rowdy Halloween morning at the church hall, Alan Wynn's plans to trick-or-treat, the new vegetable patch in Haverscroft's rear garden. They couldn't have made it sound more idyllic if they'd tried. I watch Mr Lyle talking at Mr Whittle on the pavement opposite as the twins chatter on. The estate agent pulls a white handkerchief from his pocket and pats his brow. He glances around the busy street, takes a step back from Lyle.

'Sounds like fun,' Mark says, when the mobile eventually gets to me.

'This morning's been great: Halloween stuff in the church hall and kids their own age.'

Last weekend was good, the morning room finished, a fire lit, no weirdness in the house. We've all settled down. I haven't mentioned the solicitor's email. After a string of sleepless nights I decided to let it ride for now. It's months old, why would Mark move to Weldon if he was thinking of divorcing me? If he knows I've seen the email he hasn't mentioned it. All I can do is carry on and hope things work out.

'You, okay?'

Always the same questions: Am I alright? Am I coping? At least no question about taking the medication.

'Just fine. The weather's so warm in the middle of the day we're picnicking in the back garden for lunch, then finishing the twins' veggie patches if we get time. It's getting dark early now.'

Mr Lyle crosses the road, dashing behind an estate car as it crawls up the high street. Tall and thin, his body is all sharp angles, his dark suit ill-fitting. He sees the three of us sitting on the bench as he steps up onto the pavement, no glimmer of recognition in his hollow features. Mr Whittle wipes his brow and stuffs the handkerchief into this pocket. He's staring across the road, I raise my hand, but he turns away and hurries off along the street.

'Two things: the phone company are coming on Tuesday morning to fix the landline and sort out an internet connection. Can you be home?' Mark asks.

'You bet I can!'

He's laughing, his easy low chuckle.

'And the second?'

'My trial's gone short so I'll be back Thursday evening. We can go out somewhere, take the kids to the coast maybe on Friday.'

'Great idea!' He'll be working too, immersed in the Southampton case, but at least he'll be here. He's making an effort. I'm more than willing to reciprocate.

'I'll be back around seven with a bottle of wine and reinforcements.'

We turn off the high street into the lane. Sophie holds my hand, hers tacky from too many sweets. Tom strides ahead whipping the weeds in the verge with a stick, Riley springing around his ankles and knees. Mark was right about the dog, is he right about Haverscroft, all just moving-in jitters? If he is, perhaps he's right when he says Mrs Havers can't be believed, that she's just a demented old lady. Even Shirley seems better. But my unease hasn't completely dissolved. I'm reluctant to even raise the subject with Sophie, but I need to be sure.

'Mummy?'

Sophie's tugging my arm and staring up at me, her eyes searching my face.

'Are you listening, Mummy? They've gone away, haven't they? That's good, isn't it?'

'Who's gone?'

'The shouty man and lady. And the dog, cos I haven't heard them, have you? It will be okay now, won't it?'

I squeeze Sophie's hand as we walk past the church. She's looking up at me, her eyes huge in her face. Funny how we've been thinking about the same thing.

'So you won't be ill again and we won't have Nanna Jen make us eat vegetables.'

I laugh.

'I won't be ill and we'll only eat Mrs Cooper's cakes from now on. Will that be okay?'

Sophie smiles and nods.

'If you get the picnic rugs out you might find the water

guns tucked behind the lawn mower,' I say, squeezing her hand again. 'I'll fill some rolls for lunch.'

Sophie drops my hand and runs to catch her brother.

'Dad's put the water guns in the shed! Come on!'

They hurtle down the drive, Tom shouting to his sister to keep up.

Haverscroft seems a little sorry for itself. Sunken into the hollow at the end of the driveway, it's as if it's hiding from view, a child sulking over a grazed knee. Green tarpaulin ripples across a section of roof. Once it's repaired, peeling paintwork and wonky guttering all sorted, Haverscroft will be beautifully elegant against its backdrop of dark yew and beech. A dream home. Inexplicably though, as I reach the front steps, cold unease creeps into my chest and tightens, fixing itself there, exactly the same as that first day we came.

Sunday's blazing fire has eased the front door, a sharp kick to the bottom corner has it closed at my back. Perhaps I'm finally getting the knack Shirley refers too. I'll clear the ash from the grate, relay and light another fire tonight. It transformed the house at the weekend, chased the shadows away, the house lively and warm.

I head into the morning room, fresh paint and wood smoke. I open the French windows, a creaking crackle of new paint. Sunlight skitters through the trees, mellow rays streaming across the clipped lawn. The twins chase Riley around plastic white goal posts, a game of tag and water guns, Tom's coat, Sophie's gilet and hat litter the grass. I step across the terrace and lean my elbows on top of the wall. Sophie's screams might shatter glass, but no one will hear. No need to hush them or worry about neighbours. So much space. We could be happy here.

'Come and play!' Tom beckons me to join them.

'I'll make lunch first. You go and get the blanket and the plastic liner from the gardener's shed, the grass is wet.'

The twins race off, shouting to one another, Riley at their heels. Richard Denning's made a start with the rope-and-post fence. Mark's right though, the twins don't hang around the pond, I'm being paranoid as usual. I step back into the morning room. The wallpaper dried well, the pattern perfect at the corners. A beautiful bright room. I look at the ceiling. Perhaps decorate the spare room next, chase away the ridiculous notions for good.

I cross the hall towards the kitchen and catch my knee against the heap of oddments from the office stacked one side of the hall hearth. George Cooper left it here for me to sort though, mostly stuff from our London home. The smashed computer monitor, books and dirty old folders are likely to be good for the skip. I pick up a folder, Mark's handwriting on the front – *Bills/Receipts*. I flip back the cover. Not the old paperwork I was expecting but pages printed off the internet. Old newspaper stories about Haverscroft.

I carry the folder into the kitchen and sit down on Mum's sofa. Mark's made notes of dates and events. I shuffle newspaper reports, nothing's in any sort of order: Edward Havers' cricket outing for Weldon, their youngest son, Andrew's christening, and an earlier story, headlining for several weeks. The date at the top of these sheets shows when Mark printed the pages in the weeks before we moved here.

Riley barks and the twins' laughter echoes from the garden. My heart races as I scan the pages. The woman in my sketch, the face in the dressing-table mirror, stares at me from an ancient copy of the *East Anglian Daily Times*. Helena Havers smiles at the camera, a family snap taken only weeks before she died, her arms about a young fair-haired boy and a scruffy white dog, the man accused of her murder beside them. The coroner's comments about head trauma, that she was likely to have been conscious and aware of her injuries for the few minutes before she died, turn my stomach. Why had Mark never mentioned this?

A rattle, vibration, growing louder, coming from the hall. I jump to my feet, sheets of paper, the folder, shoot across the floor. For an instant I'm frozen to the spot as if my brain can't take in what my ears are hearing. A bang, tinkling. I stare into the hall, my heart thudding against my ribcage. Glass shattering. Have the kids put a ball, a stone, through a window?

I run into the hall and cross into the morning room. The French windows stand open, a mess of fallen leaves and rose petals scatter the terrace. Something glitters amongst the petals. The roses finished before we moved in here, the blossoms long gone. The window to my left catches in the breeze and bumps my elbow. I stare at it as if I've never seen it before. But I know its every surface, hours spent prepping, sanding, painting. All of the glass, each and every pane, is smashed, barely a shard remains.

A scream pierces the silence, the barking howl of a dog. Low sun blazes, I raise my hand to shield my eyes and squint into the glare. Shafts of light wink off the wet grass. No sign of the twins.

'Tom! Sophie!'

Sophie's purple gilet lies on the grass beside a goal post, just beyond it something moves. Not quite a shadow, a dense darkness seeps into the bank of willow. The sky is cloudless, the garden glimmering in the early afternoon sunlight. Terror creeps through my flesh, raises the hairs on the back of my neck and arms.

Where are my children?

A second scream, the sound longer, louder and full of terror. Frantic, terrified, it goes on and on, filling the stagnant air. The garden is deserted, the scream, a child's, high-pitched and filled with panic. Despite the distortion in its tone, the voice is unmistakable. I would know it anywhere, know it comes from my daughter.

'Mummy! Mummy! Mummy!'

I'm shaking violently, the fear is paralysing. I have to get to her.

Glass crunches beneath my boots as I run across the terrace to the steps, sprint down them and onto wet springy grass. I race towards the willows. Nothing here but the languid sweep of foliage on a lawn smattered with fallen, rotting leaves and dappled shade from sunlight between bare branches. Michaelmas daisies crowd and bully russet-red dahlias. The football abandoned, caught in the planting at the front of the border. Hot, dry breath catches in my throat. The world slow-motions, every leaf and blade of grass harshly bright, the buzz of insects unnaturally loud.

I snatch willow branches aside and screw my eyes to peer into the gloom. Sophie kneels at the water's edge, her back to me, still screaming, her voice rasping. On the ground beside her lies her acid-pink water gun. She leans forward, one hand stretched out into the weeds at the pond's margin. Her other hand is braced against the ground. She doesn't move.

"Sophie!'

Momentarily the barking stops as Riley sees me, runs to my feet, then back towards Sophie's side, his green lead dragging behind him. The barking resumes, I follow the dog. Tom's lurid-green water gun floats on the pond's surface, drifting towards the mass of black water lilies on the far side. Sophie is hanging onto something. Something small and grimy. The muddy slime-covered thing is a hand. Tom's hand.

My knees buckle and I land heavily beside Sophie.

'I can't hold him. Mummy, I can't hold him!'

Sophie's eyes never leave the water's surface. Her cheeks are tracked where tears run through dirt. I grab Tom's wrist and pull. His head tilts backwards, face turned up towards the sunlight. His eyes are staring balls of terror, his mouth open to the water washing across his features. We both pull, his face just clears the surface. Choking, filthy water spurts over my arms, face and neck. I have him but can't pull him free. Something anchors my son so firmly that my efforts barely move him towards us at all. Tom is as heavy and immovable as a block of concrete. His face slides back beneath the bubbling surface.

'Pull, Sophie, hard as you can.'

We heave with all of our strength, getting nowhere. All the while my son's face, yellowed by the dirty water, stares back at me, his mouth open, lips moving frantically. His arm is slippery with mud and weed, I can't get a good grip. I edge into the pond, my boots find water and sludge, nothing firm or solid. Mr Whittle's words fill my ears: *A natural pond, very deep I understand . . .*

Tom isn't coughing this time as his face breaks the surface for an instant.

'He's drowning, Mummy!'

'Keep pulling, Sophie. If we keep pulling he must come free.'

We're hardly moving Tom. Terror's left his eyes. Vacant and unfocused, he's no longer fighting. No longer with us.

My grip on my son's arm slips. Tom's face slides deeper into the churning filthy pond until all I see is blond hair swishing with the motion of the water.

'No!'

If I jump in there's no way out.

'Hold on to him, Sophie.'

I let go of Tom's wrist, grab the weed at the pond's margin, slide into black silt and mud as close to my son's body as I can manage. My feet find no purchase, nothing to take my weight. I gasp as water covers my face. Sophie screams, holds Tom's hand. Blond hair washes like weed beneath the surface. I grab the bank, slithery mud squelches through my fingers, but I steady myself. Tom's legs tangle mine as I hook under his armpits, haul him towards the surface.

'Grab his coat, Sophie!' Water spits from my mouth as I shout at my daughter. She has hold of his arm, his jacket as I push Tom upwards.

'Pull, Sophie!'

I push my son's back, grab his jeans belt, shove him up onto the bank. Sophie struggles, her heels digging into the soft ground. She drags Tom up and away from cloying black mud and weed.

'Is he, okay?' Sour water fills my mouth, my nose. I don't hear Sophie's words, just her voice, her high-pitched scream. My son's dead. Too late. We are too late.

My boots are like lead weights, my legs stiff, immovable in my tight jeans. I should've taken them off, my jacket too, before I went in. No time, though. I scrabble and claw at the bank, weed comes away in my hands. No way out.

Pain in one wrist, then the other, makes me gasp and choke. I look up into a sun-darkened face, bright green eyes. He pulls, the toes of my boots dig into soft mud, the top half of me clears the water's surface. Sophie has one arm, Richard Denning the back of my coat. I lie gasping for breath on the bank.

We pull Tom a few feet from the pond edge before we let him go. He lies motionless, face half buried in willow debris. Sophie kneels beside her brother. Her skinny body shivers, her hands clenched over her mouth as though the screaming will escape again if she pulls them away. Tears run down her cheeks and through her filthy fingers.

'Tom?' Sophie's voice cracks, is practically a whisper, it sounds unnaturally loud as the three of us bend our heads close to peer at her brother. I hear only our panting breath and Riley's whining as he licks mud from between lifeless fingers. My son's face looks unreal, someone I don't know, just an ashen-coloured mask discarded by its owner.

'Go call Doctor Langdon. He'll be here long before an ambulance.'

Richard Denning's voice is deep and steady, head lowered so I only see the top of his cap, fawn and grey weave. I can't see his face at all. He turns Tom's head sideways resting his cheek in the dead leaves and begins pummelling my son's narrow back. Brown-green pond water spews out of Tom's mouth and nose with each effort.

'He won't die, will he?' Sophie asks as I push myself to my feet.

'Stay with him, Sophie. I'll run and get the doctor.'

CHAPTER 18

WEDNESDAY, 27TH OCTOBER

'IT'S NUMBER EIGHT you're wanting?'

The man, the cab driver, stares at me huddled into my coat in the rear of the taxi. His gaze falls to my hands, the shredded mess of paper towel in my lap grabbed from the ladies' toilet in A&E. I'm better now, the diazepam quietening it all down, the tension, in my shoulders, neck and jaw, melted away. He looks out through the front passenger window. Low cottages huddle close together along a street no more than a car's width. A light has come on behind a front door, it opens, a woman in a dressing gown hurries towards us, the driver looks back at me expectantly.

The taxi door opens.

'There you are, love. I've been that worried.'

I get out of the taxi, rummage through coat pockets, my jeans, find a note, some coins, pass them across to the outstretched palm, look into the man's face. I've no idea how much I owe him, but it must be okay, he's nodding, a farewell wave. Shirley has her arm about my shoulders guiding me. We head towards the brightly lit threshold.

'Come into the kitchen. I've just made a brew. I couldn't sleep a wink for worrying.'

Her voice is hushed, a hurried whisper as she pushes the front door closed, takes my elbow, tugs me along a short hall into a tiny, low-ceilinged kitchen. Her voice is soft and undulating, the words like a warm bath, wash over me. She pulls out a chair. I sit, watch her getting mugs, milk, sugar.

'Where's Sophie?' I ask.

Shirley glances at me, continues to pour tea, one mug, then the next.

'Asleep, upstairs. She's alright.'

She puts a mug on the table in front of me. A pile of Sophie's drawings are anchored beneath an iPad.

'I've tried to keep her busy, poor little thing.'

'Has she said anything, about what happened?'

'Not much, but I didn't like to press her. Something's not right though.' We stare across the table at one another. 'I thought it might be better if she chats to you, when she's ready. Your husband called. They had a chat and she was a bit better after that.'

'You've spoken to Mark?'

'Haven't you, love?'

I shake my head, words gather in my brain, I try to slow them down, put them into order. Shirley's hand is warm on mine. I take a breath.

'I left messages, but I couldn't get hold of him. My phone's flat now.'

'Well, he knows what's happened. He spoke with Sophie and says he'll be here.' Shirley looks at the clock on the wall, a cockerel, its legs swing back and forth. 'He should arrive later this morning.'

It's 1:13am. I've lost track of time, it flowed by as I waited in A&E, a side ward, waited and waited for news.

'George boarded up the French windows temporary for

tonight. He's back in the morning. He'll re-glaze them for you then.'

Shirley looks towards the kitchen door, a stair-tread squeaks, feet pitter patter along the hall.

'I'm not surprised she's awake, poor little soul. She kept asking when you'd be back.'

The kitchen door is ajar, it moves a fraction, doesn't open.

'Sophie?' I say, starting to stand. The door flies back, bangs the wall, my daughter hurls herself at me and onto my lap.

'Where's Tom?'

Her breath is hot on my cheek, her lips brush my ear, arms clamp around my neck.

'He's on the children's ward for tonight so the doctors can keep an eye on him. They need to make sure his asthma's okay.'

I hug Sophie, feel her shivering, a small skinny bag of bones. I bite my lip as my eyes sting.

'I'm worried about him cos he's not got Blue Duck.' Sophie lets go of my neck and holds the sagging rag toy between us.

'Don't worry, he was sleeping when I came away. We'll take him with us to the hospital when we pick Tom up.'

I smudge warm tears off her cheek with my thumb. 'Mrs Cooper says you've been busy,' I say, looking towards the drawings. Sophie grabs the iPad.

'Shirley bought me a new game. Look! I'm on level three already! Tom will think it's so cool.'

The screen lights, bright colours, an electronic tune starts up as Sophie's brow creases in concentration. I look across the table, raise my eyebrows as Shirley smiles.

'We made a bed for Mummy on the sofa, didn't we, Sophie.'

Sophie glances at Shirley, nods and smiles, back to the screen.

'I didn't think you'd want to be heading over to Haverscroft at this time of night.' Shirley looks over the top of Sophie's head. 'It's a bit of a squeeze, but I'm glad of the company.'

'I can't thank you enough, Shirley.' There's a wavering in my voice, I pick up my mug, take a sip.

'It wouldn't have felt right with you and the children at the house on your own.' She drinks her tea, her cheeks flushed, I've underestimated how distressed she is over all that's happened.

'Where's Riley?' I say.

Sophie wriggles off my lap, hands the iPad to Shirley.

'His basket's in here with Mrs Cooper's cat.' Sophie dashes off into the hall as she speaks.

'I didn't know you had a cat.'

Shirley's laughing. 'Come and meet Hercules,' she says, getting to her feet.

Sophie kneels beside the hearth in Shirley's sitting room fussing Riley. An enormous ginger tomcat is curled asleep next to the dog's basket.

'He passed away shortly after I lost Nick. I couldn't bear to part with him so I had him stuffed.'

Shirley shakes out a duvet, plumps a pillow on the sofa. 'There's a throw here if you're chilly, but I think you'll be warm enough. There are some logs in the basket for the fire. Make yourself at home.' She looks towards a low table beside an armchair, 'Phone's there if you need it, bathroom's at the top of the stairs, first left.'

'You need to be back in bed, Sophie,' I say, aware that Shirley looks shattered.

'Can I sleep with you?'

Shirley and I exchange a glance.

'Just this once.'

Sophie jumps on the sofa and I tuck the duvet around her.

'Would you mind if I borrow your iPad, Shirley?'

She looks at me, one of her long stares, smiles and nods. 'I'll nip off to my bed. Sophie knows the password, don't you, love.'

Sophie's asleep already, her arm crocked about Riley's neck when I carry a mug of coffee through to Shirley's sitting room. I throw a couple of logs into the embers of the fire and get settled on the sofa with Sophie's head in my lap. I send Mark an email.

> Sorry I've missed you, mobile's flat. We're at Shirley's tonight, picking Tom up tomorrow lunchtime. He's on the children's ward, he's okay, just keeping him in to be sure. I'm on Shirley's number if you need to contact me. If not, I'll keep you posted tomorrow, see you around 7pm.
> Kate x

Mark will blame me for Tom's dunk in the pond. Maybe, in part, I am at fault. How long had I left them unsupervised, absorbed in Mark's file? Five, ten minutes, certainly no longer. They've played out for an hour or more at weekends when we've been busy working on the house. But what was it I saw? Clouds scudding across a brittle blue sky, light and shade, shadows shifting across the garden? Or something different, something I won't be able to convincingly explain to Mark, or a court, if it comes to that. I can't be sure what Mark intends to do. If he decides to leave and make an application for the twins to be with him, I must be coherent.

I google solicitor's firms, find Amy, a fellow trainee from years back, now a partner in a niche firm specialising in family law. I send an email, ask if she might spare me a few minutes' advice. I trawl through websites, get the basics about the Children Act 1989, court orders, when and why they make them. As a lawyer, I see how the solicitor's email builds Mark's case, trashes my care of the children, my inability to focus on the day to day, my mental health, the children's best interests. I've never spoken about it, not to Mark, the GP, not even the quiet and patient counsellor. It worried me, my inability to speak about her, to seek any help or advice. Now I'm relived it's my secret.

The iPad glows bright in my lap, the curser blink, blinking in the search engine box. The room is dark, silent save for Riley's snuffled snores, the puttering of the fire. My fingers hover, brush the screen. Where to start? I type Haverscroft House into the search box and press the return key.

CHAPTER 19

THURSDAY, 28TH OCTOBER

'I'LL BE FRANK, Kate.'

A tractor roars down the high street spewing claggy mud across the road. I press my mobile to my ear and pull my scarf up to my chin. River fog crept through the village overnight, blurring buildings and smothering the horizon.

'Sorry, Amy. Come again. That was a bit of rural life butting in there.'

'A court is likely to order a medical if Mark presses for one, but that won't be an issue, not if you're okay now. It's not like you'll be ill again, and a GP's letter will clear that up. You've got your hands full so I'll let you go, but come back to me if you need anything more. Don't worry though, you're the twins' primary carer, always have been. Mark's got to prove good reason to remove them from their mum.'

I thank her for contacting me so quickly and end the call. Sophie and Shirley sit on the bench outside Lovett and Lyles, Riley lying at their feet. I hurry to join them.

'Sorry guys, all done. Let's go.'

Sophie sets off towards the river, tugged along by a willful Riley.

'Everything alright, love?'

Shirley claps her hands together, her breath mingling with the mist.

'I think so.'

I don't want to go into all the trouble between Mark and me, but she must have guessed some of it. Shirley's antenna won't fail to pick up the vibes.

'Just over an hour before we need to head off to get Tom,' I say.

'Time for a stomp by the river, get us all warmed up a bit. Riley'll snooze then while you're out. How did you get on last night?'

Shirley doesn't look at me as she speaks, just keeps staring straight ahead along the narrow lane sloping towards the river.

'Someone else got there first,' I say.

Shirley's smile is flat, a short nod. 'I did a quick google search after Sophie went to bed. It brought up old bits of local gossip, stuff my parents spoke about. You know how it is when you're a child, you pick up things, but don't pay full attention.'

'You knew though about Richard Denning, being put on trial for the murder at Haverscroft?'

'Oh, yes, that's no secret. He apparently found Helena Havers badly injured, and was wrongly accused of her murder. He was acquitted but only because they say there wasn't enough evidence. Mrs Havers would never speak about it other than to say he was entirely innocent.'

'She must have been convinced, otherwise he'd be the last person she'd have anything to do with, surely?'

'You'd think so,' Shirley says. 'They go back a long way. They were childhood friends; their families knew one another.'

'And he was ill? Did he have some kind of breakdown?'

'He ended up in the old asylum on the London Road after he was acquitted. It's closed now. Once Mrs Havers lost her boys and her husband, she visited regular. She got

Richard treatment and eventually he came out. He's worked at Haverscroft ever since.'

Shirley walks on, eyes fixed on the muddy path.

'Helena's murder sounded horrible – brutal,' I say.

'No one local thought Richard was guilty; he doesn't have a malicious bone in his body. He's a quiet one for sure, he doesn't pour out chatter and nonsense. Sometimes, when folk have been ill like he was, they're not ever quite the same, are they?'

Am I somehow different since I was ill? Perhaps I am and can't see it. Maybe it's why Mark is so constantly anxious I take medication, or do his motives lie elsewhere? Shirley looks at me and I smile at her.

'After all he did yesterday for Tom, I'm not going to argue with you.'

'No-one else was ever charged over the killing. It's only gossip and rumour, you understand, love, but they say it was Edward Havers.'

'That seems unlikely, doesn't it? Surely Mrs Havers wouldn't have anything to do with someone if she thought they had something to do with her sister's death, let alone marry the man?'

'You'd like to think so, wouldn't you? Maybe she didn't know. Maybe it wasn't Edward Havers. Just because he was disliked doesn't make him a murderer, does it now?'

'What has any of it to do with Haverscroft now? I don't see how it all fits together.'

'There's something, you feel it don't you? Something not right. It gives me a right bad feeling. Some say it's her spirit trapped there on account of how she died, others say it's the pair of them trapped together for all eternity.' She shivers, her smile flat, humourless, 'That's the village talk, anyway.'

'Why didn't you tell me about any of this?'

'For the same reason you don't talk about what's happened to you. Folk who haven't felt it think you're a bit daft, a bit soft in the head, don't they?'

Mark would. Even knowing the facts, the history of the house, there's no way I could convince my husband there's something at Haverscroft. He'd assume I was just like Mum.

'I didn't want to worry you, love. What can you do about it?'

I should tell Shirley about Mum's voices, she'd understand how I worry it might be the same thing, nothing else at this horrible house. Sophie is waiting with Mr Whittle where the lane joins the towpath. The estate agent is trying to make conversation. From Sophie's stiff body language it's not going well. They glance repeatedly towards us. I must speak more with Shirley, pick a good moment when we have more time.

'I swear that man is everywhere!' I say laughing, glancing at Shirley.

She's watching Sophie and Mr Whittle, her hands deep in her coat pockets, a small furrow crinkles between her brows.

'Mrs Havers isn't keen on him, but I rather like him, don't you?' I say.

Shirley looks away across the fields, flooded since the storm, they merge with the fog and sky. 'The man's a menace, always hanging around.'

'Morning, morning ladies! I was just on my way over to yours, Shirley.'

'Oh, whatever for?'

Mr Whittle grabs the glasses perched on the front of his forehead and puts them in his top jacket pocket.

'Just to say,' he looks at me, then back at Shirley, 'well, to see if you're alright, all of you.'

He pats the pocket. Is he going to take his glasses out? He runs his hand over his bald head, all the time looking at Shirley to respond. I guess the incident yesterday is all around the village. Just the ambulance alone would be enough to feed the grapevine.

'We're perfectly fine, as you can see. We're just out walking the dog.'

Shirley's tone is short and snappy.

'You could come too,' pipes up Sophie, 'and show us the water voles, Mr Whittle.'

'Well, yes, I could do that. I was just telling Sophie here about them.'

He looks at Shirley and offers her a smile as my phone buzzes in my pocket.

'Let me get this,' I say and step back into the narrow road. The screen flashes, at last, with Mark's number.

'Where the hell are you? I've been trying to get hold of you; as always, nothing,' he says.

'There have been no missed calls on my phone. I'm with Sophie and Shirley taking Riley for his walk. We've just bumped into Mr Whittle. Did you get my messages?'

I don't want to row about who has tried hardest to contact the other. We both know the phone situation.

'I've picked up Tom.'

I'm astonished. So much so, for a moment, I say nothing.

'Is he alright? What did the hospital say?'

'He's totally fine. He's wondering where his mother is.'

'The hospital said to collect him after 11am, are you sure it was alright to bring him home now?'

'Of course I'm sure! He had a good night, the consultant was happy to let him come with me. Keep him warm, let him rest, he'll be fine.'

Mark's tone is so cold, condescending, and I'm on very thin ice to make an issue after yesterday. Shirley and Mr Whittle stand together watching me, Sophie looks worried. I smile at her but she's not silly, she knows we're arguing.

'Where are you?'

'Standing in the road outside Haverscroft.'

'You're in Weldon? Are you locked out? George Cooper should be there to let you in.'

There's a pause before he replies. Sophie and the rest of the little party are clearly keen to get off to the river.

'I'm not locked out, I just couldn't get a damned signal in the house.'

I'm not sure if it's resignation or faint humour in Mark's tone. Sophie beckons me to hurry.

'We stayed over at Shirley's last night. After all that happened yesterday I didn't want to stay at the house. We're out walking the dog by the river. Why don't you and Tom come too? We can wait while you drive up here.'

I'm dreading going back to the house, even for a short time, even with Mark here.

'Are you listening, Kate? How can you suggest taking Tom for a walk when he's just out of hospital?'

'I'll sit with him in the car.'

'What? Don't be ridiculous. I've not taken a day out of chambers to go dog-walking with the cleaner and an estate agent. We need to get a few things straight. How long will you be?'

I've never heard him sound so like his mother. Has he

skipped the Southampton conference? My grip on the mobile tightens.

'Five minutes.' I cut the connection and walk towards where the little party waits for me. How dare Mark speak to me like that?

'Everything alright, love?'

I nod and try to show a relaxed smile as I push the mobile back in my pocket.

'Daddy's at Haverscroft wondering where we all are. He doesn't fancy a walk, I'm afraid. You all go though.'

'Don't go back, Mummy.' Sophie's voice is a whisper.

'It'll be fine,' I say, putting my arm about her shoulders, pulling her close. 'Dad collected Tom from the hospital on the way over.'

Sophie's shoulders tense, her eyes, widen. 'Tom's at the house now?'

'George Cooper's there as well and we need to pick up our things anyway, don't we?'

My voice is too bright, fools no one, but Sophie nods.

'On no account go near the river unless Shirley and Mr Whittle are with you.' Images of Sophie toppling over the bank in enthusiastic search of voles rush through my mind.

'We'll be fine, Kate,' Shirley says. 'You go and sort things out. We'll be back with you by lunchtime.'

I turn off before the high street, run along the lane towards Haverscroft and pass the church. My husband marches towards me, no sign of Tom. I instinctively smile but let it drop, the annoyance in Mark's long strides is clear. He's smartly dressed in a striped pink and blue casual shirt, dark jeans and the brown brogues I bought him last Christmas. He's good with clothes, with colours, not scared of them like many men. It was one of the things I'd liked about him when we met. I still do. He must have driven this morning from London, picked up Tom and then come straight here.

'Where's Tom?'

'Like I said, at the house. Where's Sophie?'

Mark stops dead in his tracks. I walk towards where he stands, taking in his stony expression, purple-blue patches hang beneath his eyes, lines at the corners of his mouth. He flicks a cigarette butt into the grass verge.

'She's gone for a walk. Shirley's dropping her back for lunch.'

'Since when has the cleaner looked after the kids? You seem to be getting a bit casual about things, Kate.'

I stop just a couple of feet from him. How dare he say that?

'Who's with Tom then?'

The shirt is new, at least not one I remember. His hair is cut shorter at the back, a more modern version of his usual style. It suits him.

'The house is just there!' He points across the hedges towards Haverscroft. 'I came to meet you, it's not the same thing and you know it, Kate.'

He runs a hand through the front of his hair and turns away from me. Panic flutters in my chest. He starts to walk back towards the house, but I don't immediately follow. Just stand and watch him stride away. His accusation hangs between us. I can't let it go.

'What did you mean, a bit casual?' I start to follow my husband. My voice is only slightly less than a shout. I need to keep calm and under control, the last thing I need to appear is irrational. He keeps striding towards the house.

'Nothing. I didn't mean anything by it. I'm tired. I have a lot on in chambers at the moment, as you know, so don't go overreacting.'

I'm following him, breaking into a jog to keep pace. Haverscroft's roof, the tarpaulin, comes into view above the front hedge. Mark swerves into the drive. I slow and let some distance pull out between us. The gravel scrunches with each step he takes as he heads down the incline towards the house. George Cooper's van is parked out front, its tailgate open.

Mark shoulders the front door and vanishes into the gloom of the house without a backwards glance. I let my pace slow further, reluctant to go inside and with a row brewing too. But Tom is in there and I'm desperate to see he's okay.

I climb the steps to the front door and walk to the middle of the hall, sunlight streaming across the tiles. When we moved into our London house, just us two, little furniture or money, we'd sink into Mum's old sofa with the Sunday papers, warm croissants and strong bitter coffee and stay there until lunchtime. When did we last do anything, just the two of us: a film, curry, as we used to on Thursday nights, before Stephen, before the breakdown? The kitchen door is ajar, the kettle beginning to boil, the fridge door sucks open and closes. The morning room door is open, George Cooper on his knees, a stack of glass beside him, putty knife in hand.

'Taking me longer than I thought,' he says, sitting back on his heels. 'Got Tom here for company,' he says, grinning.

'Tom?' I say, rushing into the room. Behind the door, pushed against the wall and opposite the fireplace, is Mum's sofa. Sitting on it is my son and beside him, my mother-in-law.

'Hello, Katherine.'

I must look astonished. I smile, try to cover my surprise.

'I do hope Mark let you know I'll be staying for a few days?'

Tom looks up, pulls a face, beams a smile. 'Dad got me an iPad!'

'So I see,' I say, moving towards the sofa. Jennifer shifts forwards and stands. She brushes down coffee-coloured trousers she calls slacks as if they are infected with something. A cream scarf, Hermes or similar, is tied at the neck of a brown polo neck. She adjusts the scarf and pulls the hem of a fitted fawn jacket over narrow hips. I sit next to Tom and put my arm around his shoulders. He leans into me, warm and so alive. My eyes well and I blink furiously, how differently things could have turned out.

'Are you okay?'

He nods, eyes glued to the screen. 'It's got games on already. Dad says we'll have the internet on Tuesday.'

'Have you had breakfast?'

'Mark treated us in Costa,' says Jennifer with a smile. If I did that, fed the kids fast-food, she'd have something to say about it.

I watch Tom's face, the slight curl of his lips, the crinkle of concentration, the same snub nose as Sophie. My throat tightens.

'Where's Sophie?'

'She'll be back shortly with Riley,' I say.

'Is she okay?'

Tom snuggles closer, tucks himself under my arm, rests his head against my chest. I smooth my hand across his hair.

'She's fine. She might actually be pleased to have you back,' I say, my voice jolly and bright.

'Are you staying now?'

'What do you mean, Tom?'

He glances towards his grandmother. Jennifer is standing beside the hearth facing the room, watching Tom and me.

'Of course I'm staying, we all are. You need to rest a bit and if you're okay we'll go to the cinema tomorrow, like we planned.'

'I like what you've done with the room, although I didn't see what was here before.' Jennifer looks about the walls and ceiling. George Cooper grins, winks at me through French windows smeared by putty fingers.

'It hadn't been decorated in decades, so we couldn't do too much damage,' I say.

'I prefer white paintwork. Don't you find the grey a little dark?' She directs her question towards Mark. He crosses over to the sofa, hands a tablet-charger to Tom. I try to catch my husband's eye as he turns away and heads back towards the hall.

'Mark chose the dove grey,' I say. 'I rather like it. It's softer than a white gloss.'

Mark stops in the doorway and looks at me.

'A word in the kitchen,' he says as he turns and walks out of the room.

CHAPTER 20

MARK DOESN'T LOOK up as I enter the kitchen, he just carries on opening cupboards, finds coffee, sugar, and starts putting milk into mugs. How little time he's spent at Haverscroft. How unfamiliar with our life here he is.

'Who moved Mum's sofa?' I say, leaning with my back to the kitchen door. The space where it stood has a muddle of bags and suitcases, Mark's and his mother's things.

'The builder helped me with it.'

I wait to see if he'll explain more, lessen the tension with a bit of chit-chat. I've lost count of the times Jennifer suggested the sofa be moved to the sitting room, or preferably, a skip, when we were in London.

'So what happened yesterday?' Mark says. 'How did Tom end up in the pond?'

He's pouring boiling water into mugs, stirring coffee, spoon clinking. Where do I start? How much do I tell him, what to leave out. I take a breath.

'I don't really know. I haven't raised the subject with Sophie, she's been too upset to talk about it. I thought it best to leave her and let her to settle down for a while. It was so awful, you can't imagine, Mark.' My voice trembles as I finish speaking.

He puts one mug on the surface near where I stand and starts putting away the milk, the sugar, anything rather than look at me. I watch him and wait, but he says nothing.

'Has Tom said anything?' I say.

The kitchen table has yesterday's shopping, picnic things, my sketch pad, pens, Mark's file. Beside them is a stack of legal papers, Post-it notes, a screwed-up pack of Lambert and Butler's. When he doesn't respond, I continue: 'If we give them a bit of time, no doubt they'll explain what happened. We're all still so shocked.'

'He nearly drowned, Kate. It's not a bumped knee or a scraped elbow.'

'Don't you think I know that? Don't you think I feel as guilty as hell? I was the one worried about the pond, who wanted it fenced off. They were playing in the garden, good as gold until I heard the glass in the French windows smash.'

'How the hell did they do that? The builder says he's never seen anything like it.' He stops moving about the kitchen to stand in front of the window, his hands shoved in his jeans pockets, his back to me. 'I took a look at the doors while trying to figure out where you'd gone. How did all the glass smash in every pane? Tom's football wouldn't do that. They need entirely reglazing.'

I don't know the answer. It doesn't make sense. How can I say what I saw? Shirley's right, he'll think I'm soft in the head, the very last thing I need.

'Why weren't you out there keeping an eye on them?'

'They're nine, nearly ten years old! They've played out in the garden at weekends without us standing over them. If you must know, I was looking through your house file.'

The file and papers are still scattered where I left them. He has to have seen it.

'All the things you've kept secret from me. Is it any wonder

I was distracted? Don't you think I should have known all that stuff?'

'It was decades ago.'

'You researched the house after you got Mrs Havers' letter, didn't you? Why keep it all from me?'

Mark leans both hands on the work surface and stares outside. Silver patches of spider webs dot the lawn. With his back to me I can't gauge what he's thinking, if he'll say anything more.

'Did you plan on telling me about the house? About Richard Denning?'

I snatch up the file, pull out the copied pages from the *East Anglian Daily Times*, and wave them at Mark's back. The papers crackle and flutter in my hand.

'Some one was murdered at this house, the prime suspect is our gardener!'

'He was acquitted.'

'Only through lack of evidence! Don't you mind someone like that around your wife and children?'

Mark doesn't move a muscle, he just keeps staring out at the garden, which enrages me more. I take a breath and try to speak calmly.

'And what about Edward Havers, found dead in the pond? I can use google too you know, Mark!' My voice is raised as I finish speaking. I can't help thinking Jennifer will be listening, maybe George Cooper as well. I'm all over the place today.

'Clever old you. Then you'll know there was nothing suspicious about his death, Kate. People die, sometimes in their homes. You knew Mrs Havers was a widow, so naturally her husband had died. Would you usually raise questions about that? No, you wouldn't.'

Mark turns around, folds his arms across his chest and looks me straight in the face. 'This was all decades ago. Ancient history, all old houses have their stories.'

'I had the right to know though before we decided to come here. Maybe I wouldn't have wanted to buy Haverscroft if I had. Doesn't my opinion count for anything? Aren't we both supposed to want this house together?'

'You were ill, Kate, just starting to get better when all that came to light, but no stress, the GP said. If you took things slowly and quietly, most likely you'd be okay. What would you have done if I'd told you about the children, about any of it? You'd have gone nuts, got stressed, become hysterical.'

We're fighting as soon as he's here and he's right about me back then. The medication either made me as dopey as hell or had me screeching like a banshee. Whatever I say, whatever he says about the house, won't change the fact we've moved here. I want to get back to Tom.

'Can't we leave it for now and let the kids tell us in their own time? How long are you here for?'

'I'm going back Sunday afternoon.'

'Is Jennifer staying here until then?' I make my tone light, inquisitive.

'She's here for a few days, there are no fixed plans. I've asked George Cooper to put our old double bed back together now the spare room's cleared of junk.'

'She's sleeping in there?' The surprise, alarm is clear in my voice, Mark frowns. 'I mean . . .' Words jumble in my brain.

'The room's fine now the carpet's skipped,' says Mark. 'She's been a bit wobbly lately. She has some new tablets for her blood pressure that her GP says should settle her down. I'd like her here, just until I'm sure she's okay.'

I have to say something, try to change this plan. It's the only empty bedroom, it makes sense for guests to use it.

'Maybe she's safer downstairs if her blood pressure's erratic?'

'She'll be fine. The builder has plastic sheeting to cover the French windows – that should help keep the draught out. Maybe you'd light the fire in there for her? If we get the house good and warm, everyone will be more comfortable, won't they?'

He knows. I can tell from his tone, his patronising smile. He knows I want to say the kids and I hate that room.

'I can't explain it. There's something here,' I say.

Mark studies my face. I hold his gaze.

'Something's not right about the house, and that room in particular.'

Mark shrugs, waits for me to carry on.

'Isn't it what Mrs Havers' letter was about?'

'What are you suggesting, for Christ's sake, Kate? Ghosts and ghouls, things that go bump in the night?' His laugh is a sneer, cold and menacing in a way I've never heard before.

A tap tap on the kitchen door makes me jump. I spin around, wrench it open and stare into my mother-in-law's face. Knowing Jennifer, she's been there ages and heard all we've said.

'Sorry to bother you.' She looks past me into the kitchen, at Mark, back to me. 'Your builder's upstairs in the spare room. He says he's unwell. He's asking for you, Kate.'

CHAPTER 21

GEORGE COOPER SITS on the bottom stair, his head bowed so I only see the top of it. I stop just in front of him and touch his shoulder. He looks up at me, his face ashen, his brow beaded with perspiration.

'Are you okay, George?'

Mark hovers beside me not sure what to do with himself.

'I had a bit of a turn in that bedroom I'm working in. I feel such a fool now. Bloody door slammed and I couldn't open it. I came over all panicky.' His eyes are full of fear and confusion.

'Can I get you something, George? Water? A cup of tea? You look dreadfully pale,' I say.

He shakes his head. 'I'll be alright in a minute. I don't know what I'll say to Shirley about it.'

I crouch beside him and put my hand on his arm. 'I think she might understand perfectly well, don't you?' I say, my voice low, aware of Mark and Jennifer behind me.

He glances up, then back to staring at the floor tiles.

'Where's Tom?' I say, a cold wave of panic washing over me as I get to my feet. No plink plink of the iPad. I stare at Mark, at Jennifer, they stare back. I rush across the hall to the morning room.

Tom hasn't moved, still in the middle of Mum's sofa, his pale face stares up at me, the tablet in his lap.

'Are you okay?'

He flings the iPad aside, jumps from the sofa and rushes at me. 'I heard some noises upstairs, but they've stopped now.'

'It's okay.' I take his hand and turn back to the hall. Mark stands in the doorway. 'It was only George Cooper putting the bed together for Nanna Jen, okay?'

Tom nods, Mark goes back into the hall. I exchange a glance with my son and we follow my husband to where George still sits, head in hands.

I look up to the empty landing. Nothing but shadows and dust.

'I was trying to get the door open.' He looks at Mark, then at me. 'From the landing side, it was. A banging – not a random thing. It sounded angry like . . . like someone trying to get in.'

I hold George's stare, words fail to come. I know exactly what he means, a shiver gooses my skin.

'No one else is here, unless you think it's Tom playing tricks,' says Mark.

Tom gasps, I squeeze his hand to stay silent. George has no chance of explaining this to Mark in a way my husband will find credible.

'It weren't your boy, I'm sure.'

'Well, what, then?' says Mark, frustration clear in his voice.

George Cooper looks at me and I know he's struggling to explain what's happened. I can't help him. I've no words to express it either. I don't know whether to feel relieved it's not just me, or sorry for George.

'I'll make some tea,' says Jennifer, taking Mark by the elbow and heading towards the kitchen. 'Something hot and sweet, isn't it, for shock.'

'Have you had a shock?' says Tom, sitting next to George.

'I'm not right sure what I've had, Tom. I'm feeling a bit more myself now. That door's open up there though, Kate. Can't say I fancy going back right now to bolt it.'

'Don't worry, George. Can I call anyone for you? Your wife?'

'I'll be alright, just give me a minute and some of that tea.' George smiles, his face has some of its colour back. 'You and me, hey Tom. Been in a bit of bother, I'd say.'

Tom nods, smiles at George.

'Sophie!' says Tom, leaping to his feet at the sound of crunching gravel. He runs outside, down the front steps. Sophie tugs Riley along, Shirley a few metres behind. No sign of Mr Whittle.

'Here comes the cavalry,' says George, relief clear in his voice.

'I'll be intrigued to hear you explain all this to Shirley,' I say with a flat smile.

George Cooper's van turns out of the drive towards the village, Shirley's promised to call later to confirm he's okay.

'Well, it's been quite a day, hasn't it?' Jennifer walks down the front steps buttoning a camel coat to her neck. She has a black beret over her short grey hair, black bag and leather gloves. 'There's no food in, so Mark's taking the twins and me shopping.'

'I hadn't expected you both to be here. I thought it was just going to be me and the children.'

Mark's at the front door yelling for the twins. The lights on the Audi bleep as he jogs down the front steps.

'Are you taking Tom?' I say as Mark approaches me.

'He wants to come and says he feels fine.'

'He's only just home . . .'

'Mother can sit with him in the car or the kids can have something in the supermarket cafe with her if he feels wobbly. We won't be long.'

I want to argue for Tom to stay home, but then I want the kids out of the house . . . Mark waves a scrap of paper towards me.

'Is there anything else we need?'

I take the list, cast my eye down a long, scribbled column all in Jennifer's slanting handwriting. Broccoli is underlined. I look up at Mark.

'It's not great to find the fridge empty. What the hell do you do with your time, Kate?'

I'm aware of Jennifer hovering beside the car, tucking her gloves into her bag. I smile at Mark.

'You should have let me know you and Jennifer were coming, Mark. Had I known, I would have had food in and asked Mrs Cooper to bake us some of her wonderful cakes.' I hold Mark's gaze. 'While I'm not working, I don't spend money when we don't need to, as you know.'

The twins stand shoulder to shoulder looking entirely fed up. Tom has his feet jammed into his trainers, the backs flattened from not unlacing them, Sophie's hair is wild, wind-blown strands lose from their clips from her walk with Shirley.

'We'd planned a trip into town today, the cinema and the supermarket. But our son nearly drowning rather disrupted things.' I smile so pleasantly I know it will piss Mark off.

He says nothing, snatches the list from my hand and heads towards the car.

'Have some time to yourself, Kate. It would be nice if the

fire's going by the time we're back. We'll probably be a couple of hours.'

Sophie has Tom's coat tucked under one arm.

'Have you got your inhaler, Tom?' I ask, taking his coat from his sister and holding it out for him. He pushes one arm then the other into the sleeves.

'It's in Dad's pocket.'

'You're sure you want to go? We can find something to do if you're not feeling up to it.'

'Stop fussing, Kate, I tell you he's fine.' Mark is herding the twins towards the car. 'Would you lock the spare room before you go, Mark?'

As the words leave my mouth I watch his expression alter from irritated annoyance to disbelief.

'For God's sake, Kate, get a grip. Do you honestly think I'd let mother sleep in there if I had any concerns?'

He gets in the car, Jennifer in the front passenger seat. The Audi heads down the drive, the twins' faces peering anxiously from the rear window.

I can't be here alone, even with Riley for company, not with that door unlocked. I can't bother poor Shirley, not again today, she's seen far too much of us lately as it is. But I can find Richard Denning and thank him for all his help yesterday. And it would be useful to speak to Alan Wynn.

The boathouse is in darkness, the cabin doors closed with brass cabin hooks. Fog is seeping back, clinging to the river-bank, creeping through the reeds.

'Come on Riley, let's try the church on our way back.'

I'd never thought I'd talk to a dog the way I've started to chatter to Riley. I like to think he understands and agrees with me most of the time. At least he doesn't argue back. It's barely three in the afternoon and already the light is fading, the brightness, what little there is of it, dull and flat. It'll be dusk by four, dark by five. We reach the lych gate and I'm relieved to see the tall leaded church windows illuminated from within, the heavy front door open.

'Kate, how are you? How's Tom?'

Alan Wynn sits at the crowded desk in the vestry.

'He's doing okay, thanks. We're all bit shocked, but thankfully there's no permanent damage. But I imagine,' I say, smiling, 'you've heard that already?'

'I confess all,' he says, throwing up his hands in feigned horror.

'I was looking for Richard Denning. I didn't get a chance to thank him before we were whisked off in the ambulance yesterday.'

'He's on the annual Horticultural Society trip to a local nursery. He stocks up on all sorts for next season. I'll see him tomorrow and can let him know you wanted a word.'

'Thanks, that would be great.'

I stand in the vestry doorway not knowing how to broach the subject, the idea that was building in my head on the walk over here.

'Was there something else? Something I can help out with?'

Alan's eyes never leave my face.

'Last time we spoke, about the house, Haverscroft, you mentioned you might be able to do something.'

'I've had a bit of a look into it all since then,' he says, turning back to the desk and rummaging through piles of papers. He pulls out a single sheet. He looks down the page and then back at me. 'Two things came up. The first, a simple blessing can be done quite easily; anything more would need permission from the bishop. I see no reason why I can't ask about it if you wanted to pursue that avenue.'

'We could try a blessing first, see how it goes?'

He pauses, still watches me. 'I understand Mrs Havers may have tried something similar some years ago. My predecessor carried out the service for her.'

I'm amazed. I must look surprised as Alan raises his eyebrows and smiles.

'She must believe, or at least she did then, there's something at Haverscroft,' I say.

"Presumably she did.'

'Then why did she flatly deny it when I asked her?'

Haverscroft is in darkness as we dash up the front steps, it was silly to have rushed out without leaving some lights on. For once I get the front door open and closed again without too much of a battle. I switch on the hall lights as Riley happily scampers off to the kitchen. It'll be dark within twenty minutes or so, Mark can't be long coming back. Time enough to ramp up the stove and light the fire in the morning room. There's no way I can light the fire in that upstairs room, not until Mark is back. I can't shake off my unease about it being unlocked, I won't feel happy until it is. I head for the stairs.

Halfway up the flight I glance back down the stairwell. Riley sits quietly waiting, his tail wags as I look at him. I'm gripping the banister, can smell only a hint of stale cigarettes. Mark, most likely. There's no rancid, sweet smell. And no sign of our torch, Mark presumably has moved it. The landing is dark, but the room isn't. Light filters through from the south-facing French windows, the last room to lose the daylight, what little we've had today.

I let go of the banister, my knuckles ache from the force I've been gripping it with. I run towards the door, my focus on the doorknob. I reach out my right hand as something brushes my cheek, cold, icy, a stench of stale nicotine. I don't move, I'm shivering, my breath frozen in my throat and still a metre or so from the door.

A punch, a terrific bang between my shoulder blades shoves me forward, my hand misses the door entirely, my feet tripping over themselves as I try to keep my balance, my shoulder cracks against the door, an outline of the bed-frame, the mattress half-on, half-off the bed. My boot catches on something, I throw out my hands into darkness.

A sound, a yowling, distant and far away.

'Mummy? Hello?'

Pain in my head, worse as I move, try to open my eyes.

'Kate, where the hell are you?'

The yowling is Riley, I've not heard him sound that way, not since the storm.

I'm cold, my shoulder aching, something touches my arm, I jolt upright and stare at the room. Harsh light, a bare bulb overhead, the dark dressing table, a half-made bed.

'Whatever happened, Katherine?'

I raise my hand to my forehead, feel it swollen and tender where my hairline starts. Coffee-coloured trousers.

'Wait right there, don't try and get up, you've a great lump on your head.'

Quick footsteps, heels click, click, click on the floorboards. Soft thuds along the landing.

'Mark! Mark, darling! She's up here.'

There's urgency in her tone, an old woman not sure what to do. My fingers gently explore the lump, hard, extremely tender, but I guess I'll live. My left leg feels heavy and dead, blood rushing in, pins and needles. I rub my thigh, keep my eyes from the dressing table. Mark's heavy tread on the stairs.

'Mummy!'

Tom, Sophie? I can't tell, the shriek so high pitched. Riley's barking, claws scratching, scampering up the stairs.

'Go into the kitchen, Kids. Stay right there.' Mark, more worried than annoyed.

Riley's here, pushing his wet nose into my hand. I scruff his soft head, pull his warm fluffy body to mine. Jennifer here too, she's speaking, her voice concerned, softer than usual.

'Kate, can you move? What the hell happened?' Mark's kneeling beside me, his hand pushing back my hair, his fingertips brush the sore patch. I wince. 'That's quite a lump you've got there, Kate.'

'It was dark in here.' Jennifer's speaking, has hold of my hand, is rubbing the back of it with hot thin fingers. 'This room's such a state. I nearly caught my foot on some old junk when I came in. I know he was taken ill, but your builder shouldn't be leaving the room this way.'

'You probably tripped and banged your head on the fender as you fell,' says Mark. I almost certainly did. I'm right by the fireplace, somehow. 'What the hell were you doing up here in the dark? Come on, let's see if we can get you into the kitchen. You're freezing.'

CHAPTER 22

THE CHILDREN'S VOICES murmur against the pop and crackle of the morning-room fire. Their words undulate, ripple and rise before Sophie hushes Tom. A furtive glance towards Mum's sofa, they see me peeping at them from beneath the thick throw Mark tucked around me earlier. Tom's head jerks up, a hurried look at the hall door, it's pushed to, not closed.

'We didn't wake you, did we Mummy.'

A statement, a worried small voice. My daughter's face is blotched and red, her eyes glitter.

'Hey,' I say, propping myself onto my elbow. Sharp pain cuts cross my temple. I raise my hand to my forehead, the lump is there, harder, smaller now. A wave of nausea grips my stomach. I sink back into the pile of cushions pushed under my head. Mild concussion, the Weldon GP said, I'll be fine in a day or two.

'You didn't wake me. What are you two up to, whispering away over there?' I force a bright tone into my voice, push my hand out from the throw towards the twins. They scamper across the space between us, Tom grabs my hand, they sit with their faces close to mine.

'What's up?' I say. Even frowning hurts. Gingerly, I push myself back, pull the cushions into place and sit with my feet tucked beneath me.

'Come on,' I say, patting the sofa, 'jump up.'

A mad scramble of skinny limbs, shoving and jostling at my feet.

'What's going on?' I ask, looking at Sophie. She drops her gaze, worries a corner of the throw between her fingers.

'Tom?'

My son shrugs, looks at the door, back at me.

'Are you two in trouble?' I ask with a feigned scowl. Tom's shaking his head, Sophie watches me from beneath dark wet lashes.

'Where's the iPad? Dad's not taken it away already, has he?'

I pull a face, smile at the twins. If there's been trouble, the first thing Mark would do is confiscate whatever's presently in vogue.

'It's flat. Dad's charging it in the kitchen. I don't want to go in there and get it though.' Tom looks at Sophie, their eyes hold one another's, that silent communication they used so much when they were tiny.

'Nanna Jen's cooking dinner,' Sophie says, nodding at Tom. Tom nods back at her.

'Vegetables? *Broccoli?*' I say.

'Carrots and parsnips too. I hate parsnips! And roast pork. I said we don't like it when we were in Tesco's, but Dad didn't listen, did he, Tom?'

'Shush, Soph.' Tom looks at me. 'We mustn't bother you, Dad said.'

I laugh. 'You're not bothering me, don't be daft. Please be polite to Nanna Jen and eat some dinner. I'll see what we can do a bit later – there's a pizza in the fridge. Where's Riley?'

Another exchange of looks between the twins.

'Dad put him in his kennel,' Tom replies. 'He got under Nanna Jen's feet. He's been making a horrible sad sound for ages now, you can hear him in the kitchen. Nanna put the radio on. She turned it up really loud.' Tom's eyes widen as he speaks, great ovals of concern.

'Well, maybe we can have him in here. Dad's probably worried that he'll trip Nanna up. She's been a bit wobbly lately, hasn't she.'

'She seems fine to me!' says Sophie, eyes blazing.

Mark and Jennifer's voices in the hall, getting louder, coming closer. The twins both watch the door. Mark's thudding footsteps on the stairs, Jennifer's shrill voice growing fainter.

'They're going upstairs,' says Sophie as we all look at the ceiling. Floorboards creak overhead.

'Is Nanna really sleeping in there? On her own?' asks Tom.

'I've told Daddy I don't think it's a good idea and that she could sleep in here, but he thinks it'll be okay,' I say.

'But he doesn't know, does he?'

'Shuuuush, Sophie! You know what Dad said.'

'But he doesn't, does he, Mum.'

Tom puts his hands over his ears, scrunches his eyes shut. I can hear Mark raking the grate in the room above, the low hum of conversation.

'Nip out and get Riley you two, while the coast is clear.' The twins stare at me. I smile. 'Go on! I'll say I insisted. He'll be freezing outside, he's not used to it.'

The children rush for the door, feet pitter patter across the hall. Quite what's been going on while I've been out of it isn't clear. I grope on the floor, find my sketch pad and pencils. I'd tried drawing for a few minutes after the GP left, but it had been exhausting.

The sketch isn't quite right, Sophie's profile is flat, none of her is here. Tom walked onto the page. I erase a section and try again, from memory this time. I've drawn the children so often, watched them sleep, eat, play, so it's not hard to do. I attempt to catch the tilt of her head, the dip of her chin as she watched her brother firing Lego bullets at aliens while they sat before the fire earlier. I can't get Sophie, just Tom, the little boy he once was, still is so often in my mind. I drop the sketch pad to my lap. Perhaps it's the bang to my head, my eyes throb, a dull headache making me tired.

Raised voices, Sophie and Mark. A door slams. Fast, light feet running this way, the morning-room door flies open, Sophie crying, jumps onto the sofa.

'Sophie? Whatever's the matter?'

I sit up, put my hand on my daughter's back, her face buried in the throw at my feet. I've been dozing, how long have I been out of it this time? Mark's swift steps crossing the hall, he stops in the doorway, his face red, contorted in anger. He sees I'm awake and comes into the room.

'What's going on?' I say.

'I told the twins to keep out of here and to let you sleep.'

Sophie's back shivers beneath my hand.

'Where's Tom?'

'Still eating dinner. Mother's spent half the afternoon preparing it. Sophie was badly behaved. I won't have her spit food onto her plate.'

Sophie's head pops up, her face wet and red. 'It isn't that. You all keep saying I pushed Tom and I didn't. I wasn't anywhere near him.'

'I won't have you tell lies, Sophie. Get back in the kitchen and finish your meal!'

'Hang on a minute, Mark. All this shouting is only making things worse.' I nod towards the door to the hall. 'Let me speak to Sophie, you have your food while it's hot.'

Mark stands like he's in no-man's land. I can almost hear his brain whirring, calculating what to do. He says nothing, stares back at me, his eyes full of anger, turns on his heel and heads into the hall. The kitchen door slams.

I rub Sophie's back and wait for her to calm down.

'What's this all about then, Sophie?'

'I didn't mean to spit out the carrots, but they made me upset and they got stuck and just came out.' Her breath is hot through the throw, her words jerking between sobs.

'How did they upset you?'

I stroke her hair when she doesn't respond. Mum did just the same thing when I was ill, angry or upset.

'I'm listening and there's no one else here to argue with what you say, so before Tom or anyone else comes in, *you* tell me what happened.'

Sophie peeps up at me.

'Come on, sit up, you're squishing my ankles,' I say, pulling the throw straight.

Sophie gathers herself, sits in a tight little ball at my feet, her arms wrapped about her knees. She sniffs, wipes her nose across her tights.

'They say it's all my fault Tom nearly drowned cos I pushed him in, but I didn't. Honestly, Mum, I really, really didn't.'

'How did he fall in, do you know?'

Sophie shakes her head.

'I heard him yelling when I was filling my water gun at the tap.'

'Beside the gardener's shed?'

She nods. 'Tom did his first, then he ran off to hide. Now he's blaming it all on me and it wasn't me.'

'Tom says you pushed him?'

She nods and nods, her eyes never leaving mine.

'I think Tom's scared. Dad and Nanna Jen asked him loads of questions on the way home from the hospital.'

'Tom told you that?'

She nods again.

'What happened at the pond, Sophie?'

She sits completely still, her eyes unblinking, staring at me.

'Do you know?'

Sophie's silent, so I wait, knowing that she's holding something in, something that will burst out if I wait.

'There was no one there, only Tom and his gun in the water. And Riley who was barking all the time. I tried to pull him out, but he was really heavy, wasn't he?'

I nod and wait for her to continue.

'So I yelled and yelled for you cos I couldn't leave him there, could I? I mean, he might . . .'

Her eyes are glassy, her chin shivering.

'Hey, come here,' I say, pulling her close. 'He's fine now and no one's going near the pond again, that's for sure. It'll be okay, Sophie. You did really well out there, I'm proud of you'

Sophie tucks in closer, her arm about my waist.

'It was the shouty man, wasn't it, Mummy?'

CHAPTER 23

SATURDAY, 30TH OCTOBER

MARK OPENS THE front door as the twins and I reach the end of the drive.

'A visitor's waiting for you in the morning room,' he says, turning back into the house.

'Who?' I ask, running up the steps.

Mark strides across the hall and jogs up the stairs.

'I need to get on, see if Mother'll make tea,' he says as he vanishes along the landing.

The Southampton-case prep. Papers swamp our bedroom, with both the office and spare room out of bounds. Yet he's managed to spend almost two hours this morning looking over the Armstrong Siddeley with the mechanic. I unzip the neck of my windcheater and shoo the children down the front steps.

'Take Riley the back way. Don't let him off the lead till you've got the mud off his paws.'

The twins race off around the side of the house, Riley yip yipping at their heels. I win the battle to close the front door and head across the hall, drop my keys, gloves and scarf on the table. The morning-room door is wide open: two brown leather chesterfields, coffee table, the bookcase Mark and I moved in there this morning, the record player and a stack of paperbacks waiting to be sorted onto shelves. The room looks like our space now.

I walk in. She's standing in front of Mum's sofa, immaculate in a navy coat, shoes and wide-brimmed hat, clutching a pair of cream gloves and her stick in one hand, my sketch pad in the other.

'Mrs Havers!'

'Good afternoon, Mrs Keeling.'

She lowers the sketch pad and smiles at me. 'I do apologise for the intrusion. One would usually make arrangements, but the matter is quite pressing.'

We stare at one another, my brain scrambling for something to say. I suspect I look like a rabbit in headlights. After our last meeting I never expected to see her again. She raises the sketch pad.

'You draw very well.'

The half-sketch of the children stares up at us.

'Thank you, though that one didn't come off for some reason.'

She studies the drawing for several seconds, the pad trembling as she continues to regard what is only a very rough thing.

'The boy is very good . . .'

'Our daughter, Sophie, is the easier of the two to capture usually. Tom looks much younger there.'

I can't make out her expression, her brow crinkles into a frown and the paper shakes. I think she might say something, instead she turns abruptly and drops the pad onto the sofa.

'I hear you have been unwell. Are you quite recovered?'

Jennifer's shoes, clickety-clack, across the hall.

'I'm much better, thank you. I had an accident, in the bedroom above here. I can't quite explain how it happened.' I watch for a reaction from our visitor, but there's nothing. The hall is suddenly silent. I step towards the door and stare into my mother-in-law's face. She covers her surprise with a swift smile and comes into the room to stand beside me. Her make up looks fresh, a whiff of sandalwood.

'We were so concerned,' she says to Mrs Havers. 'My son had to go out into the lane to call the doctor. I really don't know how you manage without any sort of telephone.' She smiles at me, looks at Mrs Havers. 'Shall I make tea? Only breakfast blend, I'm afraid, Lady Havers.'

Mrs Havers smiles. I raise my eyebrows, turn away as laughter bubbles up.

'I'm sure that will be delightful, thank you so much.'

Jennifer hurries back across the hall. I suspect tea won't be long arriving, my mother-in-law won't want to miss her share of the conversation. We listen to the clickety-clack of her heels receding across the hall. Mrs Havers' smile is entirely mischievous.

'How long are you going to let that go on?' I say.

'I rather think it suits me, don't you?'

She taps her stick on the armrest of Mum's sofa.

'They don't make them like this any longer: good, solid framework and wonderfully turned legs. Will you have it reupholstered?'

'Possibly. My mother bought it years ago from a flea-market in London near where we lived.'

Mrs Havers studies my face. I smile. What does she think of the new family at Haverscroft?

'Would you like to sit down? I can bring a chair in from the kitchen if you'd prefer?'

I glance past her, look at Mum's sofa. How hadn't I noticed it before, surely it wasn't just sitting there? My breath is a stone in my throat. Where has it come from, this horrible thing?

'Mrs Keeling?'

The indentation in the sofa where the twins and I sat earlier is still there, it's so ancient, the stuffing so compressed, there's no spring in the saggy old seat. Its balding, curly head tilts slightly to one side, one black button eye stares at Mrs Havers' back. Sitting bolt upright in the indentation, the throw on its lap, is the golly.

Mrs Havers follows my stare. I can't see her face, only her hat. She hooks the throw on the end of her stick and flips the fabric aside. I take a step backwards, a shiver runs through me.

'Where did he come from?' she says. I shake my head, there's a quaver in her voice.

'I found him in the attic, on one of the children's beds.'

Mrs Havers' stare is fixed on the ragged old toy. 'I've not seen him in more than sixty years.' Her voice is a whisper.

'Your children's?' I ask.

'My sister, Helena, gave him to me one birthday. I was terribly keen on him for years. You know how children become attached to such things.' She pulls her eyes away from the golly and stares at me.

'I thought we'd thrown him out with all the other things from the attic. I expect one of my twins rescued him.' I doubt the twins would have done any such thing, but I can't immediately think of another explanation.

'When the chimney came down, we were clearing up and found the key to the metal box in the golly's pocket.'

Mrs Havers stares at me, her eyes hold mine. I'm reminded of the woman in the mirror, that empty, blank stare. It's impossible to guess what's in her head. She turns away from me and walks towards the French windows.

'I suggest you dispose of it.' Her tone is clipped and sharp. 'I've been admiring your room,' she continues. 'It's beautifully decorated. I thoroughly approve of the decor, it's so much fresher and brighter than before. I'm glad to see you light a fire.'

The grate is full of yesterday's ash waiting to be cleared and relayed. I glance back at the sofa, half expect the golly to be gone, but he's still there.

'Would you like to walk around the garden?' I ask, keen to escape the golly's fixed stare and Jennifer's inquisitive ears.

'I thought you would never ask,' she says, tapping her stick against the windows.

Pockets of frost linger on the terrace, the sun low and yellow. She walks slowly, each step carefully taken, all the time pointing out this plant and that. I can't get the thing with the golly out of my head.

'My sister put in that climber, only a bare root at the time, no more than a foot tall. It smothers the wall in June with deep red blooms and has such a lovely heavy scent. It was her favourite rose. You won't have seen it yet?'

Mrs Havers watches me, expects a response. I shake my head. 'We first looked around at the end of May, just as the wisteria was going over at the front of the house.'

'Yes, yes. Now I remember.'

She heads for the terrace steps, puts her elbow out for me to take her arm as we descend to the path. We make our way along the gravel to the long border.

'You need a map,' she says, pointing her stick at the turned black soil. 'A plan of what's here. Richard will be unlikely to tell you. I'll put something together, if it will help?'

She's friendly again and, I suspect, making an effort to be so.

'Yes, certainly, thank you.'

'You don't want to dig up something precious!'

What does she think of plastic, white goal posts, a football caught in a shrub at the front of the border? Here and there the lawn is scuffed from skidding, kicking feet, Riley's scrabbling paws.

'Richard told me that he'd put the posts in.'

'I thought it might keep the children away from the pond.'

'He said as much. He's been giddy recently, a bit of tummy upset. It troubles him greatly to think that if he'd finished the job sooner your boy may not have taken a tumble.'

'I'm sure it made no difference. If they'd been determined to go near the pond they only needed to duck beneath the rope. I can't understand though why they would. I'd been so clear, perhaps too clear, about not to play near the water.'

We reach the end of the border, I put out my hand and catch a strand of willow. I've no wish to go any further and realise Mrs Havers also hangs back.

'There's a little metal seat,' she jabs her stick towards the willow. 'Helena's favourite spot, we often sat there together. Like you, she was a talented artist. I keep a number of her sketches still. There are many of the pond, with the church tower rising in the distance. You're like her in many ways.'

She's silent, her eyes unfocused on the swaying willow branches.

'I came here today to discuss a private matter with you. It requires a little explanation, if you can bear with me?'

'Of course.' I wait for her to continue, wondering what could be so urgent.

'Some think it odd Richard and I are such firm friends. It is, of course, absolutely none of their business.'

She purses her lips into a coral-pink line.

'We both felt Helena's loss keenly; a shared grief is a little easier to bear. Richard says he feels her here still, particularly on a warm summer's evening, in the scent of the roses.'

She looks me full in the face for an instant before turning towards the house.

'Richard is a dear man and would never have harmed Helena in any way. Gossip in the village says it was my husband.' She glances at me as I catch up. 'I'm sure you'll have done your research or Shirley will have told you.' She stabs her stick into the grass with each alternate step and puts her elbow out again, I take her arm, the grass uneven, she leans against me, then the stick.

'I do not make excuses for Edward, I merely seek to explain. He was convinced Helena was unfaithful although I have her word she was not.'

We reach the gravel path, she points her stick back the way we have come. 'Just after the start of the new year, you will see a great swath of snowdrops all across here. Quite stunning on a sunny winter's morning. It would be better to keep the children off the grass then, if you can.'

She stops at the bottom of the steps that lead to the terrace, turns to face me and lowers her voice so I barely catch her words.

'I have only ever spoken to Richard about the matter I now refer to. You know me a little, you know I value my privacy. I must have your discretion: not a word must pass to anyone.'

I'm astonished. 'Of course.'

'I only tell you at Richard's insistence. He is quite right – you need to know. The inquest found that my boys died by misadventure caused by my husband Edward driving in the loke here.'

I recall the news reports of the inquest, its outcome and fail to imagine how this woman must have felt.

'Some weeks later Edward claimed that it was no accident. Like my sister before, he accused me of being unfaithful and said that the boys weren't his. Absurd, but once a thought fixed in his head, there was no shifting it. Logic and reason played no part. Fear was his friend, he used it to control both his wives.'

She stares at the end of her stick, silence pulling out. I wait as she gathers her thoughts.

'I tried to put it all out of my mind. I did not wish to believe Edward, who would do such a thing? But his paranoia was such . . .' She breaks off, her thoughts left unfinished. She presses her lips together. 'As a mother, you might try to imagine how impossible it was to erase that accusation from my memory. Should I have done more to protect my children? Andrew was just nine and Micheal only seven years old when they died.'

She looks up at the terrace steps, but makes no move.

'Before I mustered the courage to challenge him he suffered a fatal heart attack.' She points her stick back towards the willow. 'I found him there, quite dead, floating in the pond. He died before he had time to drown.'

'I'm so sorry. I can't imagine how you coped being here alone.'

'Richard is a dear friend, a great comfort, and I had my garden.'

'What happened to your nephew, Freddie, Helena's son?'

Her dark eyes look at me. I'm pushing too hard, too fast, but I need to know.

'Edward moved to London after my sister died.' It's impossible to gauge her, what she's thinking. I tilt my head to one side, make it clear what she's said isn't enough. 'He continued to maintain the boy wasn't his, then the child died within a few months of his mother. Scarlet fever – it was quite common back then.'

She looks away, out across the garden. Does Mark know about all this? How far has his research into Haverscroft and the family gone? Another thing to put me off moving here.

'I'm so sorry.' It sounds so trite, inadequate but words fail me. 'And here, what is at the house?'

'What do you mean, Mrs Keeling?' She takes a step towards the terrace.

'You know what I mean.'

She lowers her head, her hat shields her face.

'What does one know, exactly?' She rakes the gravel with her stick, short, deep strokes scarring the path, a line of dark earth. 'There was nothing which concerned me before my husband passed away. Since then . . .' She looks at me. 'You have experienced the room above here.' She nods towards the spare room. 'It was my sister's room when she was married. They argued there, I heard them myself. And she claimed Edward locked her and her son in there. Her journal, I assume, referred to some of this?'

I nod, recalling entry upon troubling entry.

Mrs Havers shakes her head. 'Get Wynn, the new man, in. Reverend Haddingley did something for me, quietened it all down for some time, but of course by then only I was here and kept myself to the ground floor rooms.'

'Why didn't you warn me? I thought I was imagining things!'

'I wrote to you, I warned your husband before you bought the house. He chose not to listen. Most do, Mrs Keeling, most do.'

'Mark came to see you? When?'

For an instant, she looks at me, then taps her stick again into the gravel.

'I don't recall exactly. I can be forgiven the occasional lapse of memory at my age.'

She twists the ring on her finger, glances up at the terrace and takes a step forwards.

'You might at least try,' I say, my voice terse.

'It was shortly after I first wrote to you, I'd say. The roses were in full bloom.'

Tom, Sophie, then Riley hurtle around the corner of the house and race across the lawn. Tom picks up the football and flings it across the grass sending Riley sprinting after it. The children's laughter, the dog's excited yap, yap yapping ring through the cold air.

'He's like his father, although very fair, of course.' She watches the children chasing after each other and the ball. Riley scampers up to Mrs Havers, tail wagging nineteen to the dozen, then turns, sprints back to the twins. 'He's a friendly little fellow.'

Jennifer comes onto the terrace and stops at the top of the steps, her jacket pulled tight across her chest. She smiles down at us. 'Tea's getting cold.'

Mrs Havers waves her stick. 'We're on our way!'

She puts her elbow out, I take it, hold her back for a moment. She looks up into my face.

'Are my children safe here, Mrs Havers? At least tell me that.'

CHAPTER 24

SUNDAY 31ST OCTOBER

I CLOSE THE back gate onto the lane, let Riley off his lead and head along the narrow winding path towards the house. Haverscroft was quiet, the twins, Mark and Jennifer having a Sunday morning lie-in when we left over an hour ago. The damp chill from our march through empty lanes, deserted village and towpath has seeped into my bones, all I want is the warm stove and a piping hot mug of tea before the household stirs into action.

The walk gave me a chance to mull over my conversation with Mrs Havers. Once the children are in school on Monday morning, if I manage to dodge Jennifer for an hour or so, I'll see if I can pick up Wi-Fi in the café on the high street. I can't shake off the feeling Mrs Havers holds back more than she reveals. And if Mark intends his mother to be here for the week, I'll be cheerful and on top of things. A cooked breakfast of pancakes, coffee and newspapers will set things up nicely before Mark heads back to London this afternoon.

The path widens to a clearing, the dark expanse of the pond spreading away towards the thicket of yew, the round church tower beyond. Fog hugs the banks and curls across still black water. Near-naked trees drip against my windcheater as I duck a low branch. No sign of Riley. The ground at the pond's edge is scuffed, ridges and dents in the soft leaf matter where knees and heels and hands struggled to get a grip. My throat tightens, I look away toward the rusting metal seat. Richard Denning stares back at me.

'Sorry to startle you, miss. I sometimes sit here. I hope you don't mind.'

'Not at all,' I say, trying to cover my shock with a smile. 'I've wanted to speak to you, to thank you properly for your help with my son the other day.'

'Alan Wynn mentioned that.'

I'm breathing hard, he sees it, I rush on. 'I didn't expect to see anyone at this time of the morning.'

'The river's always moving; the water's more restful here.'

I can't think of a reply. I've always felt on edge beside the pond and still do, worse since Tom's accident. And this silent man is so hard to gauge. I glance at the curtain of willow separating us from the house and garden. Riley's distant yap, yap, yapping, no one about yet to let him in.

'Alice called then?'

Alice Havers. I've seen her Christian name on the old deeds, the contract we signed when buying Haverscroft and her letters. I'd never given it a second thought until now, but it suits her.

'She says she told you about me being a bit off colour. Still, I should've had that rope and post fence done for you.'

'Please don't blame yourself. I'm sure they won't make the same mistake again.'

'I swept the terrace after you and your boy went off in the ambulance. Whole lot of glass and mess there was.'

I stare back at his calm features, his green eyes, milky in his sun-darkened face.

'You saw the glass, on the terrace?'

He watches the water for a moment, glances my way as if to check I'm still here. He smiles and pushes his cap a little further back on his head. He's far friendlier looking when he smiles. I've only ever seen him with a glower.

'I get the feeling Mrs Havers holds out on me,' I say to him. 'I just want to know my children are safe.'

'She'll tell you what she wants you to know and ignores anything she doesn't. I told her it won't do, not any longer.'

He leans forward, resting his elbows on his knees. The seat's small and shallow, it can't be comfortable for a tall man. Riley's barking. 'Mummy?' Tom, yelling from the terrace, by the sounds of it. Wondering where I am.

'She reckoned if there was any trouble here it was her family's. It wouldn't be a bother to anyone else.' He looks at me before staring back across the water. 'Things don't always turn out like you think they will, do they?' He stops speaking and looks at me again.

'Mummy, where are you?' Sophie, concern in her voice.

'The night Helena died, I found her badly hurt and knew right away nothing could be done. I stayed with her. It's a bad thing to leave this world alone.'

A shiver crosses my shoulders, a tight knot in my chest. He's paying me little attention, talking to himself, his eyes all the time watch the water.

'Mummy! Mum?'

The twins sound frantic, I should go.

'You know what happened to her?'

He doesn't respond, continues to stare at the water. I glance towards the house, its invisible from here behind the cloak of willow branches. He nods, a small rocking motion of his head. His eyes turn towards me, he looks me full in the face.

'I've always known what happened to her.'

He takes a deep breath. It's taking a great deal for this quiet, private man to speak of these things. He looks tired and drained. Just how old is he? He stands up and brushes down his baggy old cords as he looks beyond where I stand, back towards the house.

'Kate? Where the hell are you?'

Mark now. Can't I have five minutes!

'You'd better be looking after those children.'

He turns rather stiffly, heads towards me, passes where I stand. He stops at the path and looks back at me.

'Come and join us for a cup of coffee. I'm about to cook pancakes, bacon and eggs.'

I want to know what he has to say, it might be better if Mark hears it too, although he's likely to dismiss it, but at least it won't be coming from me.

'It's waited half a century, it'll wait another twenty-four hours.'

He glances at me, tired eyes. Now we're close I see his skin's grey, his cheeks hollow.

'Weather's due to be bad for the next few days. I'll be about my boat tomorrow afternoon. You're welcome to come over anytime.'

He sets off along the path towards the rear gate. I can't think of any reason to delay him.

'Kate?' Mark holds back the draping willow branches. He's come out in a hurry, tee-shirt and jeans, deck shoes, no socks. 'There you are. We were worried with Riley back.'

'For goodness sake, Mark. Did you think I'd got lost walking the dog?'

I look towards the path, Richard Denning holds up his hand and calls over his shoulder, 'See you tomorrow. I'll fill in the gaps for you.'

CHAPTER 25

'WHAT HAVE YOU said to Mother?'

Mark pulls open the garage doors. I follow him inside and wait for him to turn around and look at me. He leans with his back against the Armstrong Siddeley's bonnet. I shake my head, no clue what he's on about.

'What do you mean?'

'She wants to catch the next train back to London.'

'I haven't said anything.'

'Something's upset her. Last night she was talking about being here for the next few days.' Mark glares at me.

'I haven't had a conversation with Jennifer about any of that. I've no idea.'

'You've hardly been welcoming though, have you? It's no wonder she's decided she can't stay.'

'That isn't fair! I told you I didn't appreciate being dumped with your mother. You say how difficult she is. I've tried to be friendly. You know what's she's like.'

He looks away, out towards the house. The car looms behind him, a great dark hulk of decay.

'Has she said why she's going back?'

He shakes his head. 'It's too soon to be sure her new pills suit her, I'd rather she was here until we know she's alright. Blackstone's threatening to find another junior for the Southampton trial if I have any more time away from chambers.'

Maybe I have been a bit standoffish, Jennifer has a talent for putting my back up. Nothing particularly bad springs to mind though, I have been making an effort.

'You need to start trusting me, Mark.'

'It's only you says I don't.'

'Rubbish! You should've asked me about Tom's accident. How dare you cross-examine the children! I won't have you or your mother reduce them to gibbering wrecks. They're nine years old, not criminals in one of your witness boxes!'

'I need to know what the hell's going on here. It's one thing after another.'

'If you trust me like you say, you'd speak to me, listen to what I say instead of ignoring me or dismissing what I tell you as being my imagination on overdrive.'

Silence.

I cross my arms and wish I'd grabbed my windcheater. It's damp in here.

'Mrs Havers says that you visited her during the summer.' My voice is level, no accusing undercurrent.

'You've met her. The woman's unhinged, and that's being polite.'

'But you said nothing about it.'

'We've been here already, Kate. You were ill. I kept stuff away from you on doctor's orders. I thought I was doing the right thing. Doctor Langdon says you're fine.'

'You've spoken to the GP about me?'

'Only after we found you knocked out. I just asked if you'd be okay to look after the children. You know he can't tell me more than that. Don't go getting paranoid.'

His phone buzzes in his pocket. I haven't realised there's

a signal out here. It buzzes again, loud in the silence between us. Chambers? Who calls him on a Sunday morning?

'How have you got on with the insurers? I was thinking we might need another estimate if George Cooper isn't coming back. They'll want three, won't they, before they authorise any work?'

'Why wouldn't he come back, Kate?'

Mark's eyes bore into mine, challenging me to explain George's absence. His phone buzzes again.

'Shouldn't you get that?'

He shakes his head, waiting for me to answer his question. 'It's nothing that can't wait.'

'It's such a big job, maybe we need more than just George?'

'Leave it for now.'

'Why? We need to get on here – at least repair the roof.'

I don't want to argue but guilt's kept me silent, on the back foot for too long.

'Are you seeing Cassie? Is it her on the phone now?'

He shakes his head, drops his chin to his chest. My question hasn't surprised him. Why then, deny it?

'You never explain why you're not here, where you are, what you're doing. I've had enough of being lied to. If it isn't Cassie, then who? Just tell me, it's cruel to leave me hanging.'

'Don't judge me by your own standards, Kate.'

'That's no answer.'

He turns to face me, his eyes cold and hard, always this when we get near Stephen. His phone buzzes again.

'You should get that, you've no idea who it might be.' The sarcasm is plain in my tone. 'It might be urgent.'

I take a breath, my heart's a knot in my chest, getting tighter, my palms sweating. I have to know what's going on, what I'm dealing with, but I won't lose it and give him an excuse to shout me down.

'I've still no answer about Tom. Just you deflecting the blame, Kate. How can I be sure the kids are safe around you? I'm not even confident you take your medication.'

This, yet again. Why does he want me on pills that make me as dopey as hell, all these months?

'I read the email from your solicitor.' My voice is flat and quiet. I watch his face, see surprise blend to anger.

'Considering the circumstances, I don't think anyone's going to blame me for taking advice. Checking out my options. You'd do the same, Kate.'

'Don't you think you shoulder some responsibility? A marriage doesn't hit trouble because of one person, it takes two for it to fail.'

'I didn't fuck Blackstone and half of Lincoln's Inn.'

The slap makes the silence that follows seem unreal. My palm tingles, rough stubble and jaw bone. Mark's face jerks from the force of it. He turns back towards me, his eyes full of shock, eclipsed instantly by fury.

'What the fuck? That was utterly unforgivable, Kate.'

I'm as appalled as Mark looks. I haven't hit anyone since primary school. He steps away from the car towards the open garage door. I'm so shocked for a moment I can't think of anything to say. I can't screw up now. I try to take a breath, to speak calmly, not to make this any worse than it already is. 'And it's not unforgivable to say that sort of thing to me? I was with Stephen once, no one else.'

'Was he any good?'

'Stephen? You want to know? You really want to know that?'

Mark stares at me, less than a metre between us. Stephen's older than us, early 50s. Does that bother him? Why would he care?

'I honestly don't remember.' I shake my head, it does no good to go here again. We've been over and over that night. 'I was so drunk.'

'Blackstone says you used him, can you believe that?'

'Used him, how?'

'To get at me.'

'Get at you?'

'You were pissed off with me that night for not turning up to the party. I was working remember, for us?'

'That's utterly ridiculous! It's not always all about Stephen, he's absolutely unbelievable!'

Mark is shaking his head, his laugh a low humourless sound.

'Everything was fine with us until your thing with him.'

So finally we get to the point. The place Mark refuses to go.

'But it wasn't fine with us before, was it?'

I wait, he won't answer. He never does.

'Once we did everything together. We came first. I'm not a foolish romantic, I know passion cools over time and becomes something more steady, but you went missing. It seems anything and everything is more interesting for you than being with me and your family, Mark. You worship at the altar of your career. Nothing gets in the way of it. You and the twins are everything to me, you always have been. I came here hoping to keep all that safe, but if you can't or won't let Stephen drop, we've no chance, have we?'

Mark doesn't answer.

'I've apologised countless times, I've moved to a house I hate away from all I know, but you're never here. That's why it's not working – because you're not here and won't take any responsibility for your part in any of this.'

Mark turns away, stares out across the drive. Silence pulls out into a monstrous thing between us. I'm too scared to ask if he still loves me. What would I do if I get the wrong answer?

'You said we could sell up if it didn't work out. There's something here, I can't explain it. I don't feel safe and neither do the twins. I'm going to move out and take them with me. I'll rent somewhere local for now. Even if you can't understand, I hope you'll still come with us.'

Mark turns around, watches my face as if there might be more. More nutty nonsense to fling at him.

'If you're going to leave us, Mark, don't keep stringing this whole thing out. It's too painful for words, but don't consider taking the twins. I am a good mother.'

'Are you? How can I be sure?'

I stare back at him. I don't flinch, don't pull my eyes from his.

'How do I know you're not just like your mother, Kate?'

My heart thrums my ribs, pulses in my throat. Words fail to come, my brain paralysed. I stare at my husband and wonder who he is and how we ever got here.

'I'm just fine. Absolutely fine. If you suggest otherwise, even hint I'm not fit to care for our children, you'll have to prove it. I'll never let you take the twins from me, Mark.'

Footsteps crunching on gravel, we both turn to the open garage door. Jennifer in her camel coat, beret and gloves.

'Not interrupting, I hope?'

She looks between us, her smile falsely bright. My cheeks

burn, my eyes, hot. I can't find a platitude to smooth things over. She knows damned well we've been arguing. Mark's probably already told her his plans.

'I suggested a trip to the cinema this morning, Katherine, before I travel home, but the twins say they have too much homework.'

'That's a first,' says Mark, stepping out of the garage to stand beside his mother. 'Surely they can go out for a couple of hours, Kate?'

Mark's looking out across the lawn towards the lane, a taxi is coming down the drive. Jennifer's, I assume.

'They promised me they had no homework over half-term, but Sophie suddenly remembered a history project that's due tomorrow. I've said they're going nowhere until it's done.'

Mark's phone buzzes. Jennifer looks at her son, towards the sound. Whoever it is is as persistent as hell.

'Shouldn't you know what homework's been set, Kate? You don't have anything else to do.'

Mark's glaring at me, but I'm not backing down. I won't have this conversation in front of his mother. His mobile stops buzzing.

'Anyway,' says Jennifer, the insipid smile again, 'that builder chap might say he's secured the balcony doors, but I can assure you he hasn't. You'll need to speak to him darling. Don't use that room for now.'

Mark's phone buzz, buzz, buzzes.

'For goodness sakes, answer the phone!' Jennifer frowns at Mark. 'How do you know it isn't important?'

'That's just what I've been telling you, Mark. Take the call why don't you?'

❧

'What have you been saying to Nana Jen?'

'Nothing,' the twins say in unison.

I pull a face, and glance at their books, not much done so far. To say I'd flown off the handle earlier is putting it mildly. The twins had looked so shocked, but I hate being lied to. Perhaps I should have let them go with Jennifer for a couple of hours, given Mark and me space to talk. We clearly need to. Riley snoozes beside the stove. I put on the kettle, do I dare take Mark a coffee? Better to leave him to work for a while, time for us both to calm down. I stand at the sink and stare out of the window. My car is blurred by fog, parked beside a jumble of scaffolding poles and George's overflowing skip. One of the golly's legs pokes up from the heap of debris. After Mrs Havers' taxi left for Fairfield, I'd pushed the doll amongst the broken lathes, plaster and tiles. If it was the twins messing about, it's out of reach now, well and truly rammed in amongst the rubble and rubbish.

The twins whisper behind me.

'You two need to get on,' I say, turning to face them. Their heads lean together, eyes looking up at me. 'You can sit there until those projects are done. Dad's furious and blaming me. I'm not having it, so I suggest you get on.'

'We need the internet,' says Tom, curling the corner of his textbook.

'Tough,' I say. 'If you'd told me earlier instead of lying about it, we could've used Shirley's or gone to the library.'

'We're not lying, we forgot,' says Sophie. I wait for her to look at me, stop her detailed study of the table top.

'What else have you been up to?'

'Nothing.'

I tip my head to one side, press my lips into a flat smile. I know when the twins are hiding something.

'Nanna Jen hasn't packed all her stuff.' Sophie sticks her pencil between her teeth, gnaws the end of it.

'What do you mean? She's forgotten something?'

Jennifer's organised, even at her age. I find it hard to believe anything would be overlooked.

'Dad can take it with him when he goes tonight, if she has,' I say, trying to keep my tone even. The row with Mark has made me anxious, angrier than I should be with the kids.

Tom nudges Sophie with his elbow and jolts the pencil from her mouth.

'We saw things in the spare room, her things. Nail stuff and shoes.'

'You've been in there?'

Sophie shakes her head, alarm in her face at my raised voice. I rarely shout at the twins, twice in less than an hour is practically unprecedented.

'Nanna Jen's upped and left and Dad says it's because of me. I'll be furious if you two have done something.'

Sophie looks at Tom, her eyes bright.

'I'm fed up with you being naughty. Is it you two putting that bloody golly everywhere? I've thrown it out once already. It's not funny.'

'It isn't me, I hate it!' Sophie looks at Tom.

'I haven't done anything,' says Tom, shoving his sister's exercise book.

'You took it from the attic and chased me with it!'

'Who put it in the morning room? Someone took it out of the skip. Was it you, Tom?'

Neither speaks. Both look down at their homework, Tom scribbles small circles round and round on the corner of his page.

'The spare room door was open. We saw Nanna Jen's stuff from the landing when we got up, didn't we, Tom?'

Tom's nodding, stares up at me, blue eyes, wide. 'It's still open.'

'I'll close it.' I say.

If I sort it before Mark goes it'll be okay, we can stay downstairs. The twins' heads huddle close, more whispering, their eyes turning to me.

'And another thing, I still don't have any proper answer about Tom's accident. Now what's going on with you two?'

'Nanna Jen was in the morning room when we got up, wasn't she Tom?'

Tom's nodding.

'So, why shouldn't she be?'

The twins exchange a glance and look back at me.

'She slept there all night.'

CHAPTER 26

MONDAY AFTERNOON, 1ST NOVEMBER

'THIS'D BE A lot easier if George helped out,' says Shirley as she flops down on Mum's sofa.

I sit beside her, Riley at my feet.

'We're most of the way there now,' I say, looking over my shoulder across the hall to the kitchen door. 'Well, halfway.'

Shirley laughs and shakes her head.

'I've missed it. There's nowhere comfy in the kitchen without it,' I say.

'You're right about that, love.'

'George isn't coming back, is he?'

'Shook him up good and proper, it did. Said he heard something.'

I shiver, not just the door sticking then. Shirley pats my knee.

'For goodness sake, tell me, nothing about this hideous house will shock me now.'

'He wouldn't say much,' Shirley says.

'What *did* he say?'

'He asked me if I'd heard anyone laughing.' Shirley tugs her pale blue scarf, pulls it tighter. 'He thinks he's losing his marbles. He said it all seemed a bit daft once he got home, had a hot shower and something to eat. I thought you might have something else to say about it, love.'

I don't know what to say. The twins tried to explain this morning on the way to school what happened at the pond. Tom's 'scary thing' and Sophie's 'shouty man' leave me no clearer about any of it, just more determined not to stay here a moment longer.

'George isn't one to let you down and there's nothing needs doing in that spare room now, is there?'

No point mentioning Jennifer's concerns about the balcony. If the spare room stays locked, the French windows aren't an issue.

'The roof's the most urgent thing. It's impossible to heat the place.'

'If you're staying with me, it won't bother you, not for now. You're all right, are you, love?'

'Me?'

'I didn't like to call round, what with your husband and his mother staying. It got Mrs Havers over here right sharp though, didn't it, that funny turn of yours in the spare room.'

I had wondered, as Riley and I walked home from school earlier, what to tell Shirley, where to start. In the four days since I'd last seen her, so much had happened. The Weldon grapevine had done it all for me though. I swear it's impossible to ever tell her a fresh piece of news.

We look at the landing, Riley runs to the bottom stair and barks. Was there a movement, a sound that caught our attention? Shirley's body tenses beside me and my heart quickens. Fog presses at the windows, no scudding clouds throwing light and shade across the room. Other than Riley's incessant barking, there's nothing, the hall, silent and still.

'Come on,' I say. 'Let's get this sofa shifted.'

We start huffing the heavy piece of furniture across the hall.

'Riley, that's enough!' I shout as we reach the kitchen door. The dog stops barking, scampers beneath the sofa and into the kitchen.

'I'll pack the rest of our stuff while you finish up, Shirley. It won't take much longer. Then I'll head over to Richard Denning's.'

We edge the sofa through the door frame, Shirley backing into the kitchen.

'Don't forget to take his fruit cake, will you?'

A door slams upstairs. Riley shoots between our feet, claws clattering across the hall. He stops at the foot of the stairs barking non-stop. Shirley's expression is frozen, her eyes wide with concern.

'The sooner we're out of here, Shirley, the better.'

I stop in the lane where it meets the path running past the church to the river. The fog is thick, our familiar walk strangely silent and disorientating. Riley doesn't seem the least bit bothered so I let him off his lead and pull my mobile from my pocket.

> Let me know you got back okay? A real pea-souper here. Hope London's clearer. Kx.

The phone screen is bright in my hand. Mark would usually have let me know he got back safely, but there's been nothing, not even a short text. I read, re-read the message and press send. He left without a word this morning. Yesterday afternoon and evening had been spent avoiding each other. He ate dinner whilst working in our bedroom, claiming to be too busy to join us. This morning the kitchen was empty, no scribbled message, not a single Post-it note.

I shove the mobile in my jeans pocket, shift the cake tin under my arm and follow Riley down the narrow path. If Mark replies the phone will vibrate in my pocket, but at 14:42 he'll be in court, a client conference, or working with Stephen and the team on the Southampton trial. From Mark's perspective, this whole thing must seem crazy. But if the tables were turned, wouldn't I listen, at least try to understand him? It's not as though it's only me. He saw how shocked George Cooper was, how skittish and nervous Shirley and the children are in the house.

'Riley?'

The fog is thickening as the path slopes to the river. If I lose the dog I've no chance of finding him in this. A short yap, scuffling somewhere up ahead. He's been good over half-term, coming when the twins and I call him. The lych gate is a dark mass, growing sharper as I pick my way across puddles and potholes. Heavy, rhythmic footsteps pound the ground behind me. I glance over my shoulder and pull off the path into the shelter of the gate. A jogger, hoody pulled up, a scarf across his mouth, splashes past. I'm gripping the cake tin so tightly it's digging into my hip bone. Familiar things are strange today. Even the dull drip, drip, drip from branches sounds eerie. I step back onto the path and pick up my pace. The towpath is another hundred metres or so, the boathouse only a few minutes from here.

Mark rarely mentions Mum's illness, we don't discuss it. Google will have told him about symptoms, treatments, the hereditary stuff, anything he wants to know. If he didn't check it out after we met he will have before the children were born. Anyone would. So why throw it in my face now? If he's planning to leave me and take the twins, he'll know how difficult it will be for me if he brings all that up. It could be an explanation why he's so keen I take my medication, clear proof I'm not fully recovered. However hard I try, whatever I or the doctors say, doubt will linger. Is she okay, will she relapse, are the children really safe with her? Once doubt is established, any judge will err on the side of caution, order the children to live with the parent who poses no risk at all. I should speak to Amy again, fill her in about Mum. See if that alters her advice.

I reach the end of the path, fog wraps around me, the air still, heavy and cold. Everything is wet. The towpath is busy, dark shapes randomly loom at me, joggers and fellow dog walkers keen to get home before it gets dark.

'Riley?'

We need to take a left here towards the village. I can't make out the boathouse yet, but it's only a few metres further along the towpath. I hear Riley before I see him. I clip on his lead and we set off together towards the village. It feels better with the dog pulling me forwards.

The boathouse is tucked tight into the riverbank, its squat tin chimney spiralling wood smoke into the fog. Across the small deck, a cabin door is hooked open, the interior of the boat in darkness.

'Hello?'

There's no bell to ring. I rap my fist against the side of the boat, unsure how else to make myself known.

'Mr Denning? It's Kate, Kate Keeling.'

My voice sounds disembodied in the silence. Riley tugs the lead, eager to be on his way. I stand beside the boat, not knowing what to do. There's no sign of Richard Denning. Do we wait here a while? We hadn't agreed a time to meet, just Monday afternoon. He's almost certainly nipped out on an errand and will be back shortly. I head for the bench a little further along the river.

I rest Shirley's cake tin on the bench and my bag on my knees. I can watch the boathouse from here, see him easily if he returns. He can't have gone far with the cabin open in this weather. I let Riley off the lead again. The dog stays close, snuffling beneath the hedge behind where I sit. The bench, like everything else, is wet, damp seeps into my jeans. I rummage in my bag and pull out my sketch pad, rummage some more and find a pencil. I quickly fill the page with an outline but it's cold, the light too poor to draw, what am I think of? I stuff the paper and pencil back into the bag, take my phone from my pocket. 14:49. Nothing from Mark. I drop the mobile back into my windcheater. I'll wait a few more minutes.

If there's any chance of saving our marriage, the last thing to do right now is move out of our home. But we just can't stay. It's a massive relief to be out of the place, to be able to stay with Shirley. Too much has gone on at Haverscroft. I can't ignore it or put it down to nerves, mine or the children's. We're not safe there, I'm sure of it. Mrs Havers can't or won't help, that much is clear. Richard Denning knows something. Shirley thinks he has information beyond common gossip and rumour. She's usually right about these things. If he can explain what is there, what it is we are faced with, perhaps Alan Wynn will know what to do. How, or if, this thing can be sorted.

A few days at Shirley's will let me relax. Stress caused the breakdown. It still stops me thinking clearly now. It scares me, all this stuff about the house, with Mark, all whizzing round in my head getting nowhere. I can't be ill, not again, not now. Maybe when I know more I can understand it. Maybe then I can explain it to Mark, if he's prepared to listen.

I stare across the path to the still and silent boathouse. Somehow it's changed. Mist still presses at the low, dark windows. Nothing moves. It bothers me, the cabin door left open in such damp weather. I check my phone, nothing from Mark. I've been here far longer than I intended. My feet are numb with cold, my jeans cling to my skin. Riley pushes a damp nose into my hand. He's cold and wet too, I should get him to Shirley's. I look back at the boat. The thin spire of wood smoke no longer churns from the tin chimney. Perhaps I misunderstood our arrangement, maybe Richard Denning has gone to Haverscroft?

My legs are stiff as I stand and I realise just how cold I am. I drop my phone into my jeans pocket, pull my coat closer and my scarf tighter. I'll leave the cake tin on deck with a note and my mobile number. The surface of the towpath is like soup, puddles interspersed with islands of squelching mud. Tom said wellingtons were a 'no-brainer' this morning, I'm grateful for them now. Riley follows at my heel, his coat hanging in wet ribbons under his belly and legs. I glance along the riverbank. Visibility for fifteen, maybe twenty metres at most. No one to be seen.

I reach the side of the boathouse.

'Hello?'

My voice rings with uncertainty in the stillness. No one responds. I hammer my fist against the side of the boat and wait. Nothing. I step closer, grab the wooden handrail and lean over it trying to get a better view across the deck and into the cabin. The varnished rail is wet, my hand skids beneath my weight. I stumble, put out both hands to break my fall.

'Shit!'

The cake tin clatters and skids across the deck and thunks into the far corner. Riley shoots past my legs, claws scrabbling against the boards. He vanishes through the open cabin door.

'Riley! Here, boy!'

Muddy paw prints smear the deck. For a second, maybe two, I hear nothing.

'Riley!'

The dog growls, a low sound growing in volume, breaking into non-stop barking. I glance along the towpath, no one in sight. What the hell is he barking about? Has he hurt himself, fallen down the cabin steps?

'Riley! Get out here, now!'

The barking continues, a relentless rhythmic sound. I'll have to climb aboard and see what the problem is. What can be in there to make him bark like this?

'Riley!'

I swing my bag over the handrail onto the deck. I can leave the cake in the cabin with a note to say we're staying at Shirley's. My wellingtons are filthy, slippery with mud, perhaps I should take them off? I crouch in front of the cabin door and peer inside the dark interior. A brown tweed jacket hangs on top of a pile of coats near the door, a chequered cap on top. My eyes slowly adjust.

'Riley! Come here!'

The dog's barking is like nothing I've heard from him before. The constant noise is making me anxious, my heart racing, my breath coming in short sharp puffs. A long narrow space emerges from the gloom. Nearest the door is a kitchenette, a dumpy silver kettle, a whistle on its spout. A Pyrex jug has pale yellow mixture in it, scrambled eggs maybe, the fork resting against the glass side.

The second cabin door is closed. I pull it toward me, it opens easily, the catch rattling loose against the varnished wood. More light spills down the narrow slatted-steps into the galley. No-one would leave a boat open, even for a short time, with it being so damp today.

The interior of the boat comes into focus, my eyes scan the space. At the far end is a closed door, a bedroom or washroom. Immediately in front of it is a sitting area, bench-style seating attached to the wall piled with mismatched and beaten-up cushions. A large old-fashioned chrome angle lamp must have stood on the table but now lies across the narrow walkway, broken. Splinters of glass from the bulb glint, catching the light that streams in from where I crouch at the top of the steps. I hope Riley hasn't smashed it bounding around in such a confined space.

Something about the smell in here is familiar, constricts my chest, a cold sweat beading my forehead and prickling my underarms. Riley is the only thing that moves as he barks and yowls, his eyes trained on my face. I feel the scream rising in my throat as my hand flies to cover my mouth. I don't look directly at the bulky shape the dog stands next to, I don't need to, I know what it is.

The bloodless grey pallor of the skin on a hand, nut brown when it hauled me from the pond. Where does that colour go? I don't look at the unseeing green eyes or the black shape crawling from beneath the back of his skull. Even though I don't look, not directly, I know beyond any doubt, as my screaming and screaming and screaming cuts through the fog, he is dead.

CHAPTER 27

MONDAY EVENING, 1ST NOVEMBER

'YOU'RE SURE YOU want a solicitor?'

I follow the DCI down the length of a grey corridor, black windows glare strip-lighting back at me.

'I just want to get home to my children, it's getting late.'

'A man is dead, Mrs Keeling. We must have some answers from you.'

I follow him into a waiting room, no windows, a row of battered plastic chairs bolted to the wall. He puts a white polystyrene cup of coffee and a pre-packed sandwich of grated cheese on white sliced on a low table piled with tatty magazines. He straightens and looks me full in the face. 'Some proper answers.'

He knows I lied, so stupid to do that. He's staring at me, I've missed something, zoned out.

'Your children are perfectly safe as we've already told you, Mrs Keeling. Can I get you anything else?' I shake my head. 'We've called the duty solicitor for you. There'll be a bit of a wait, I'm afraid.'

'Actually, I'll be fine without a solicitor, really, there's no need for one. Let's just get on with it.'

I thought the little white lie would get me out of here quickly, before the school pick-up, it must be way past that now. No watch, phone, bag and no clocks about this bloody station either. The DCI is still staring at me. A WPC stands in the doorway.

'I'd rather speak to you when you have a solicitor, all things considered.'

The shock of seeing him there, what was I thinking? I blurted out the first stupid thing that sprang into my head. The lie's made it all so much worse.

'Take a seat, Mrs Keeling.'

He glances at the woman then back to me.

'Have a bite to eat and something to drink, hopefully the solicitor won't be too long.'

I can't explain why the children shouldn't be left with Mark at Haverscroft, it sounds too crazy. Shirley will have the twins, Mark delayed as usual getting out of London. They'll be asleep in bed at Shirley's cottage, not at the house. The two police officers are watching, concentrate. They think I'm deranged, who can blame them the way I've been behaving over the last couple of hours. The good thing about being mentally deficient is no one expects anything of you, so I say nothing. I've said too much already. I sit down with a thunk on an orange plastic chair and pull a calm expression onto my face. I smile at them both.

'Anything you need, just ask the WPC.'

'Can I have my sketch pad and pencils? They were in my bag.'

The expression in his eyes frightens me, like Mark's and the twins. A clue that what I've said isn't quite expected, not right in some way. I need to get my act together if I'm getting out of here anytime soon.

The WPC comes with my sketch pad and pencils, takes away the cold coffee, sandwich and comes back with a mug of tea. White with two sugars, she says, you'll feel better for it. She's right about that.

The sketch I started this morning by the river isn't so bad. If I draw for a while I'll calm down, think clearly. The pencil is light, easy, more of you spills quickly onto the page. The pills must still be in my bag. It's so long since I've taken any I can't be sure. I can't unravel after all these weeks, not now. And I am unravelling. I know I am, but how do I stop it?

Think, Katie. Take a breath. Concentrate.

I watch the pencil, the lines spreading, moving across the white space. Exactly what happened today?

I don't know if I've taken a tablet. Did the police let me take one before they took away all my things? I think they did. The nurse gave me one while I waited for Tom in A&E. It helped, calmed me down, let me think straight. The police suggested I take one as we drove away from the river. I'm sure they did.

The police know if someone is lying and mine's so easy to check out, so why, when the DCI asked if I knew the dead man, did I say no? Panic and desperation to get back to the twins, to make sure they're not at Haverscroft. I'm sure they won't be there.

When the DCI asked if I needed to see a doctor, that was a bit of a clue I wasn't quite right. I lift the pencil from the paper, hold the sketch pad a little up and away from me, your smile is just as I remember. When you lied to me, I so wanted to believe you. The first time they took you away seems like a lifetime ago. I sat on your sofa and waited, you wouldn't be gone long, they said. We'd never been apart before, no one else, no auntie or uncle, no grandparents to stand in your place, just you and me.

I glance up, the WPC stands at the door, her eyes on the sketch pad. She looks at me and smiles. 'It's so life-like.'

I return her smile. Normal, calm behaviour will see me out of here sooner than anything else.

'Thanks. I don't usually draw people. Do you know what time it is?'

'Just after midnight. Easy to lose track in here, isn't it?'

I nod. The pills don't help either, time becomes so elastic. The twins will be in bed, Mark will leave them at Shirley's for tonight. It should be okay if I'm back home first thing. I look back at the page, start to draw.

After that first time, you often went away. A few days, sometimes months at a time. Easier when I was older, A-levels, university and law school. I looked after you, and you were better, didn't go away as you once had. Go live your life, Katie, you'd said, everything's fine. So I did.

My eyes are tired, eyelids gritty with each blink. I put down the pencil and lay the sketch pad in my lap.

'How much longer do you think the solicitor will be?'

The WPC's looking at me, weighing up how I am. I rub my eyes with the heels of my hands. I look at her and smile.

'I'll find out for you.'

Her shoes squeak along the corridor like the matron's at Fairfield. I look back at the page. I found an old man this morning, he reminded me of you. That day at the flat, the air was cold, the place strangely quiet. You always had the radio on, silence was so scary, you said. I stepped into the sitting room and knew something wasn't right, the sofa, empty. You sat in a chair by the window, I'd never seen you sit there before. Visitors, newspapers or books sometimes occupied the space, never you.

'Mrs Keeling?'

The WPC is beside me, nudging my arm, I haven't heard her come back into the room.

'The solicitor's on his way and won't be more than a few minutes now.'

'Thanks. What is the time anyway?'

'Nearly 1am.' She's looking at the page as she speaks. 'Is it you?'

I smile, shake my head. 'No, not me.'

'Well, whoever she is, she has a beautiful smile.'

She goes back to her place beside the door. I look at the sketch, she's right, the curve of your lips plumps your cheeks, crinkles the skin at the corner of your eyes. I don't know how long you'd sat there, why I didn't pick up the signs. You cancelled one or two trips to the cinema and for coffee. Let your hair grow out of its usual neat style. I should've called sooner. By the time I got there, your wrists had long since drained out, the light gone from your eyes. I was angry with you for so long, for leaving me, for letting me find you like that.

The WPC stands very still by the door. I wonder if she too has children asleep in their beds waiting for her at home. I take a breath. Smile at her and hope the solicitor's here soon.

The sketch is done, nothing more my memory can churn out. We're not the same, you and I. I know that now. Deep down, I've always known. You were the best parent you could have been. I must be the same. I must move on, for all our sakes, especially for the twins'. You would expect that much of me, Mum, I know. Footsteps ring along the corridor, getting louder, coming this way.

'That's the DCI for you now,' she says, tugging down her

jacket. I gather my pencils and get to my feet. He stops in the doorway and nods at the WPC.

'Everything alright, Mrs Keeling?'

'Just fine. Is the solicitor here yet?'

'Just arrived.'

'Let's get started then,' I say, moving towards him. 'I need to go home.'

CHAPTER 28

TUESDAY, 2ND NOVEMBER

'YOU TOLD THE police you were just passing by, walking your dog.'

Oliver Lyle looks down as he speaks at a ruled notebook, a counsel's notebook, exactly the same as I've used a thousand times in the past when talking to clients. I feel displaced sitting here on the receiving end of it all. Being the one needing help. And he's taking so long. If I'd known the duty solicitor tonight was this man I would never have agreed to wait.

'Yes,' I say to the top of his balding head. The dome of his skull has a bony ridge, the sides of his angular head falling to a long, thin face. Skin over bone, no flesh beneath to soften his features. I can't see his face as he concentrates on the writing he scrawls on the page.

'But you were seen by a number of people, sitting, watching the houseboat. You were there for some time.' He looks up at me and smiles. 'Why would they say that if you were just walking along the towpath?'

'I sat for a while. It's good to be out of the house.'

'In the fog?'

We look at each other. His smile is fixed, his eyes, cold.

'I need to know the truth if I'm going to be any help to you, Mrs Keeling. I'm sure you understand?'

I do understand, I just can't respond. I watch his closed

expression, find no clues. I just want him to hurry up so we can get out of here.

'Now, tell me. Have you visited the houseboat before?'

I shake my head.

'Why were you going there? You were going there?'

'I was taking him a cake. He hadn't been well lately. But he was dead when I arrived, like I told the DCI.'

'Why not just leave it there? Why go into the boat?'

'I wanted to speak to him.'

'About what?'

'It's not important.'

'When you're in court you'll be asked these things. Others will decide what's relevant. I need to know everything, as will anyone else who represents you. *You* know this very well, Mrs Keeling. Everyone will know you're aware of these things. A qualified lawyer. They'll wonder what you're hiding.'

'I'm not hiding anything! And I'm not going to be in court. He was dead when I arrived!'

My voice has risen in volume and pitch. The fear is twisting, tightening in the pit of my stomach. I suck in a breath, speak more slowly, as calmly as I can manage.

'I need to call my husband. I can do that, can't I?'

He continues to smile and stare, his eyes blank.

'I'm not under arrest,' I say, trying to grasp hold of this situation. Does this man know what he's doing?

'Tell me why you were visiting Mr Denning. Why not speak to him when he was working at Haverscroft? What was so important?'

A knock on the door. It opens a fraction, the WPC peers in. 'You ready? DCI's keen to resume the interview now you're here, Mr Lyle.'

'Five minutes.'

Lyle sounds irritated. The woman nods and closes the door. We listen to her soles squeak a retreat along the corridor.

'Well, Mrs Keeling?'

The truth isn't going to help me, suggesting Haverscroft has weird stuff happening.

'I went to thank him for his help when our son fell into the pond. I was taking him a cake. Shirley Cooper can confirm that. I've no motive to harm him, quite the opposite.'

I hold Lyle's gaze, relieved mine is fixed, that I don't pull away before he seems satisfied and continues. 'The police are aware that you didn't like the man. He was odd, difficult and argumentative. That's common knowledge . . .'

'Who says I didn't like him?'

Lyle holds up his pen, continues ignoring what I've said. There's something unsettling about him, his sneering contempt makes me feel he knows something I don't. It was there that first day we met in his office.

'. . . as is the fact that you have been unwell yourself, Mrs Keeling.'

Do the police really know all this, has Mark or somebody else told them? Or is Lyle making more of it than he should be?

'The police will have spoken to passers-by, people close to you. The towpath was busy today, despite the fog. You were in the vicinity of the houseboat for in excess of an hour. Your bag was found there and your phone. Why were they in the boathouse of someone you barely knew and didn't like? They'll ask you all these things. You must have answers, your silence will be held against you.'

The police know I was there, I used my mobile to call

them. At least they've found it. And my bag, the cake tin, all left there in the chaos that followed my discovery. Why is this man acting as though I'm under some sort of suspicion?

'Do the police know, Mr Lyle, of your argument with Richard Denning? Do they know you didn't get along, and why you argued with him and Mrs Havers?'

A flicker of surprise crosses his features. Why did Mrs Havers despise this man so much? He's a cold fish for sure, but even so, her loathing seems more than just dislike.

'If the police are interested in people Richard Denning had trouble getting along with, I'd suggest they should speak with you, Mr Lyle.' He watches my face intently for several seconds. I won't let him unsettle me. 'You purchased all the Haverscroft land and you want the house too, don't you?'

'None of this is a secret, Mrs Keeling, and it's all above board. You've checked out the Land Registry?'

I nod, remembering all the information I'd read on Shirley's iPad, the land being sold off, lot by lot over the last twenty years. I'd found nothing irregular, but Lyle makes my skin crawl, the sooner we are done the happier I'll be.

'Mrs Havers, like many old families, was asset-rich but cash poor. Her claim she was made to sell is a ludicrous one. All the land was professionally valued, full market-price paid. Richard Denning was very likely mislead, as many have been, by that woman's scandalous and unfounded allegations.'

He holds my gaze as my brain scrambles for words. What he says makes sense. Was Mrs Havers simply distressed about selling her home? Am I letting my own dislike of Oliver Lyle get in the way a rational judgement?

'Her financial situation became critical. Fairfield is an

expensive place to live in; the fees keep coming. Mrs Havers had no option but to sell the house.'

'Her home.'

'She refused to sell to me simply out of spite. I was, by rights, due the house after buying the land. I'm sure you'll agree, now you have all the facts.'

We watch each other silently for a long moment.

'But we digress, do we not? I'm not the one the police are questioning, Mrs Keeling. I'm not the one there today for a period of time I can't sensibly account for.' The smile again. I hold his stare. 'Remember, I'm here to assist you. To represent your best interests.'

'*You* remember, I am here on a voluntary basis. When I saw him, he was lying on his back at the bottom of the stairs. There was nothing I could do to help him. The police know that. They know why my bag and things would be there.'

He's right. I must have answers, sound firm and unhesitating, and at present I don't. The police have to take a statement from me. I found a dead person, they have to check it out, that's all. I know this. I'm gripping the sketch pad so hard I'm scrunching the edge of the page. I look down at the drawing and take a deep breath.

'Where are my children, Mr Lyle? Does Shirley Cooper have them?'

He taps his pen on his notebook.

'They're with their father, naturally. I assumed you knew that. He smiles, a tight insincere movement of his lips.

'Are they at Haverscroft?'

The pit of my stomach turns over just at the thought of my children being anywhere near that place.

'How would I know, Mrs Keeling? It has no relevance to the matters we are discussing.'

I stare at him, my mind racing. Would Mark have taken the children to Jennifer's, or are they at Haverscroft? Mark said he couldn't have any more time away from chambers. The children will be with Shirley or his mother. Not at Haverscroft.

I stand although there is nowhere to move to. The room is only a few feet wide, the door close enough to reach out and touch. I can't bear to be in this room with this repulsive man for one more second. If the twins are at the house, they aren't safe, I'm sure of it. Mark doesn't get it, he won't look for danger.

I stare at Oliver Lyle as he stands. He isn't going to help me, all he does is confuse and delay me and I don't know why. I press the buzzer beside the door and hear the WPC's quick footsteps along the corridor. A sharp rap, knuckles on wood, the door swings open.

'Ready now?' The WPC looks hopeful, it's late, perhaps nearing the end of her shift.

I nod in reply.

'Mr Lyle has given me helpful advice.' I look at the solicitor. 'I'll take it from here now, on my own.'

CHAPTER 29

TUESDAY, 2ND NOVEMBER, 3:13AM

'MY BATTERY'S NEARLY dead.'

The WPC looks up from the form she's completing on the reception desk.

'I can call a taxi for you. Weldon, is it?'

'As soon as possible, thanks.'

She picks up the phone and dials as Oliver Lyle approaches the desk.

'Still here, Mr Lyle?' Her tone is full of surprise.

'I never run out on a client.'

His insincere smile plays again on his lips. 'I'll drop you off at Haverscroft, Mrs Keeling. I'm going straight back to Weldon myself.'

Lyle isn't looking at me as he speaks, his eyes scrutinise an envelope on the reception desk. The WPC holds the phone receiver and raises her eyebrows.

'I'd rather get a cab, thanks.'

'Really, it's no trouble at all.' Lyle looks into my face and smiles again.

'Sign here for me, please.' The WPC holds the phone to her ear with one hand, points a biro at the bottom of the form with the other. A list of my things. I sign, pick up my bag, house keys and purse from the desk as she speaks to the taxi company.

'Here in 10 minutes,' she says, ending the call. 'Just wait out front.'

'What happened to the cake, it's just . . . the tin wasn't mine.'

She smiles. I'm tired, anxious about the twins and just want to be away from here, away from Oliver Lyle. Why am I worried about a cake tin?

'I'll find out and let you know.' She looks at the sketch pad as I flip the cover closed and pack it into my bag.

'A lady hand-delivered this for you.' She holds out the envelope, the paper smooth and stiff between my fingers. 'She insisted that it's given to you immediately. A bit difficult about it, she was. You were giving your statement when she called in. That's right, isn't it, Mr Lyle?'

The solicitor nods, his eyes again on the envelope as I stuff it into my coat pocket. I step away from the desk and head for the exit.

Three percent battery. I call Mark's mobile, straight to voicemail. I could switch off the phone and save what little charge is left. I dial Jennifer's number, it rings and rings and rings. *Answer the bloody phone.* I cut the call and try Shirley's number.

'Anything I can help you with?'

Lyle joins me as I stare out of the glazed front doors. Streetlights bathe the empty, wet road in a sodium glow. I shake my head, take a step away from the solicitor and listen to the ringing of Shirley's phone. Her cottage is tiny, perhaps she's a heavy sleeper. Surely she must be home at this time in the morning? No answer, I end the call. I can feel Lyle watching me, I wish he'd get the hint and leave me alone. I stare out at the street, the taxi must be here soon.

The DCI, along with his sergeant, approaches the reception desk. A hurried conversation with the WPC. She nods towards the door. My stomach drops. Aren't they done with me? There's nothing more I can add to the statement I signed twenty minutes ago. They stride towards me, as tired as I am I muster a smile. Maybe they have the post-mortem results, new information of some kind? They pass me and stop just beyond where I stand.

'We'd like to ask you a few questions before you go, Mr Lyle, about Mr Richard Denning.'

The taxi's headlights pick out fragments of a frost-covered landscape, bare fields, a gateway, twisted branches overhead. My temple bumps the window and jolts me awake. I've dozed on and off all the way back from the police station. The driver's eyes stare back at me from the rear-view mirror. Each time I've woken, he's been watching.

Her letter lies in my lap. I'd torn the envelope open as soon as the taxi pulled away from the police station and read it swiftly from beginning to end. Words and letters ran before my eyes, failed to filter through to my brain. I pick it up and try reading it again.

Fairfields
Weldon

November 1st

Dear Mrs Keeling,

Can you forgive me? I should have written this letter sooner. I wrote to you in the summer and now I fear you may not have received that correspondence.

Richard urged me to act weeks ago. I procrastinated, it will not do. It is vital you understand about the house, Richard was insistent about that, and he was quite right, of course. Whatever you decide, I shall never forgive myself. My punishment is to live on without the companionship of my dearest friend. I shall miss him most dreadfully.

I deluded myself in thinking that any problems at Haverscroft related to my family alone. Not for one moment did I consider your children to be in harm's way. I will explain about the house, but do bear with me, it will take a little time.

My late husband, Edward Havers, was a charming, witty companion, at least in public. Clever and rather handsome, he was well able to get his own way. He was my sister's husband and for some time that was all. When I was seventeen, I stayed at Haverscroft for a few weeks during the summer. I was company for Helena, who, by then, was desperate to leave her marriage. But one thing led to another.

I can hardly believe what I'm reading. Mrs Havers, so careful and concerned about her reputation, is the last person I would have thought capable of such behaviour. The scandal would have been enormous back then.

My husband experienced things during the war that no human being should see. An injury to his ankle caused constant pain and affected his mood. He sometimes walked with a stick. Noise was a problem for him. Loud or high-pitched sound like a child crying or children shrieking with laughter tore his nerves to shreds. You have read Helena's journal. You know some of her terror. I am sorry to say I did not believe her.

I drop the letter into my lap and rub my eyes with the heels of my hands. That day in the garden, before Tom fell in the pond, the children had been shouting and screaming, Riley barking in the garden. Had that noise triggered something at Haverscroft?

The taxi judders as the driver changes down a gear, the indicator, click, click, click. The moon is high and bright in a star-pricked sky. The old asylum looms above the road, its massive arched entrance shackled shut with rusting chains and padlock. How many years had Richard Denning spent in that place? I shudder at the thought of what his life must have been like. The driver slows down, searching for the Weldon turn. I sit forward and grasp the headrest in front of me.

'Just up here, on the left.'

The driver nods.

'The house is all the way through the village, left immediately after the church.'

The driver nods again, I sit back in my seat. Haverscroft will be empty, Mark will have taken the twins to his mother's, I'm sure of it, but I have to check. I have to be sure the children aren't at the house.

I dial Mark's mobile and leave a voicemail to say I'll be staying at Shirley's. The line goes dead before I finish speaking, the battery flat. I can call from Shirley's once I've checked out Haverscroft. I continue reading the letter.

He used me, of course, to torture Helena. She was

horrified when she discovered our liaison. Edward would allow Helena to leave and have a divorce, but if she left, she did so without her son, Freddie, and without me. Helena refused to go.

Unfaithful himself, Edward was convinced his wives were too. He thought Freddie was Richard Denning's child. I am ashamed to say, he convinced me too, for a time. You see, it seemed on the face of it to be quite plausible. Helena and Richard were childhood sweethearts – it wasn't improbable that they allowed things to go too far after Helena married.

We were newly engaged the first time he accused me of infidelity. I denied it. He said he loved me and forgave me. By then I knew what he was like, but it was too late. I dared not leave him and we were married the following summer. Our union was an outrageous scandal, gossiped about for years and brought us nothing but sorrow and misfortune.

When I could stand it no longer, I made plans to take Andrew and Michael to Canada. We had family there to stay with. Edward discovered my intentions before I managed to leave. He told me to go but leave the children behind. Like my sister before me, I would not consider it.

Why he was set on keeping the children I do not know. If they were not his, as he claimed, why not let them go? There were no witnesses to the events in the loke that sunny afternoon. If I raised a finger of suspicion, who would believe me? No father kills his own children.

I gaze through the taxi window, headlights pick out a deserted high street, a front doorstep, a shopfront shuttered against the night. My body sways with the motion of the taxi, the air, hot, stuffy and stale. It's difficult to take in all this woman has endured. Just a few minutes before we reach Haverscroft, I pick up the letter again.

I was devastated by my sister's death. I have never truly come to terms with her loss. The horror of her passing, of poor dear Richard finding her beside the pond. We both sensed her in so many ways in the years that followed. A hint of her perfume, a feeling of her near me as I dug the borders or as Richard sat watching the pond. I believe you thought my golly rather a fearful thing. When Helena gave him to me one birthday he came with a short note in his breast pocket. We continued to exchange messages and secrets that way, as sisters do, until her death. I can not tell you of my alarm when that old toy reappeared. And the shock of your drawing too, of your son, the very image of my nephew, Freddie. Helena was riddled with guilt before her death. She was quite certain it was her fault that Edward had taken an interest in me. She swore she would always keep me safe and I believe she keeps that promise, even after all this time.

Edward suffered a massive heart attack, brought on by sheer terror, so Richard believed. Did Helena haunt him? Of course, we can never know. After he died, a malevolence entered the house I had never detected previously. If Edward's presence remains at Haverscroft, and I somehow believe it does, your children should not be there. You should not stay. Take them to Shirley's, anywhere away from Haverscroft.

My heart is racing, my throat tight. Buildings crowd more thickly now as we head along the narrow street, Haverscroft is only minutes from here. Her letter is almost done.

There is something more I must explain, but I have been writing to you for more than two hours. Exhaustion addles my brain, but I will not sleep. I never sleep. And now, I have no Richard for solace. I have no choice but to finish here. The rest I must tell you in person if you can bear to hear it. Try as I might, I have found it impossible to write it down.

So there is something at Haverscroft, something that may threaten the twins. I look back at the letter, it isn't even signed. She must have been utterly exhausted by this point. What else can she possibly have to say? Isn't this enough for one family? Shirley suggests it was Edward, not Richard Denning, who attacked Helena. Does Mrs Havers know what happened the night her sister died? Richard said he did.

I look at the rear-view mirror, the driver watches the road as it curves and bends along the empty street. The moon slides out from behind thin cloud, huge and bright, washing ghostly silver light across the village. The cafe window is full of Christmas, Halloween swept away. Who will the twins spend the festive season with this year? I can't tolerate Mark's behaviour any longer, I've done all I can to save our marriage, perhaps I have tried longer than I should have. For now though, the most important thing is to make sure the twins are safe.

My body jerks forward, the seat belt snapping like a steel band across my chest. Tyres scream against wet tarmac, a horn blaring. The taxi lurches left, judders, front wheels smack the kerb. I grab the front headrest and hold tight.

Nothing. No crash or bang of a collision. Only silence draws out.

'Stupid fucking cow! Are you blind?'

The driver shouts out of his open window. Damp night air rushes into the car. I sit up and peer out at the street. The cab is on the pavement at an acute angle to the road, the front bumper inches from the black railings outside Lyle's office. The driver has his head out of his window raising a middle finger. A figure stands stock still in the road, deep in the shadow of the bus stop.

The driver thuds back into his seat as the window whines closed. He puts the car into gear, glancing at me as he does so.

'You alright? Stupid woman. Came from nowhere. I could've killed her.'

I'm still staring at the figure, dressed in a dark coat, collar pulled up high and muffled deep into a thick scarf. My fingers fumble to find the catch for the seatbelt. I release it and grab the door handle.

'Wait! I'll get out here,' I say.

CHAPTER 30

TUESDAY 2ND NOVEMBER, 4:12AM

I SLAM THE taxi door, frozen air folding around me. A few lights come on behind upper floor windows, the striped curtain fabric of the flat above the cafe drops back into place. The road is empty, the receding taxi taillights bleeding into the darkness. No sign of the woman, but rapid footsteps ring along the cobbled side street.

I shove the letter into my pocket and hurry after her, pulling my coat tight about me, frost biting at my cheeks. Dawn is several hours away and with no streetlights I'm glad of the moonlight. The clear sky is perfectly black, stars as bright as I've ever seen them. I turn into the narrow alley, shadows from the crowded cottages cut across the cobbles. I slow down, less sure of my footing.

'Shirley! Wait, it's me, Kate.'

The slope towards the river is steep in daylight, but now it's as if the road falls from under my feet. Slippery, wet cobblestones, I have to slow down. I can't hear anything. No hurrying footsteps. I pick my way further from the high street, my confidence ebbing away with each step. Maybe I should go straight to Haverscroft? If the children are there, I shouldn't delay. The prospect of the lane, the dark and silent churchyard, the empty house, does not appeal. Shirley will know where my children are, no need to go to Haverscroft if she has them.

There's no sign of the woman. Maybe I was mistaken, not Shirley, someone else. She's not likely to be running around at this time of the morning nearly getting herself run over.

I stop and stare along the narrow street. The cottage I think is Shirley's is about twenty metres further on from here. It's in total darkness. No lights show in any of the cottages. I only caught a glimpse of the figure under her layers of coat and scarf, it could have been anyone.

A shadow stirs in the doorway to my left. I step backwards, breath catching in my throat. It grows deeper, more solid. My feet slither on the cobbles, the shadow moving closer. No one will hear me if I scream. Can I make it if I run back to the high street?

'Kate! Goodness me. I'm so glad to see you!'

Shirley clamps her arms around me and hugs me so fiercely for a moment I can't move.

'We've been terribly worried. I can't tell you what I've been imagining. Are you alright? Fancy the police keeping you all that time.' She laughs, a small nervous sound in the darkness. 'I wondered who was running after me. Scared me half to death you did!'

I can't make out her face, but her voice is incredibly good to hear. She's so solid, safe and normal. I hug her back, hold her tight. I'm shivering badly, she must notice it.

'Quickly, now, let's get inside.' She grabs my wrist and tugs me behind her.

'Hang on, Shirley, I'll skid over at this rate!'

My feet slither and slip, Shirley drops my wrist and dashes ahead. She stops on her doorstep and gropes in her bag. She's breathing heavily, ramming her key into the lock as I reach her.

'Come in, Kate. Quickly, love.'

She presses her hand into the small of my back, ushering me inside. She puts on the hall light and slams the door, locks it and draws the security chain into place. She stands still staring at the closed door with her back to me.

'Is everything alright, Shirley?'

She glances over her shoulder, smiles and heads past me to the kitchen. I follow.

'Of course. I just gave myself the jitters. Silly at my age, really it is!'

She snatches a tea towel off a kitchen chair.

'Take a seat, love, you must be exhausted.'

I sit and watch her pull clothes off the backs of chairs, off the oven rail and throw everything into a laundry basket. She fills the kettle, puts it on and starts unwinding her scarf.

'Are you sure you're okay, Shirley?'

The kitchen is a mess, the table full of dirty mugs and plates, a casserole, saucepan and bowls scatter the tiny workspace. There's a slew of papers on the table at my elbow, crayons and a half-eaten bag of Sherbet Dip-Dab. The twins have been here. Shirley's stopped dashing about, no stream of warm chatter. She's probably tired.

'I can't believe what happened, really I can't. Shocking, it is. Shocking. Poor man. Mrs Havers is beside herself, so she is.' Her voice is a touch hoarse, has Shirley been crying?

She looks at me properly for the first time, her eyes are bright.

'She was so worried for you, she was. She said she was going to the station to give the police a piece of her mind.'

'She left a letter with them to give to me. I'm sorry about

Richard, really I am, but are the twins, okay? Did you collect them from school? The police had my mobile.'

Her silence, her expression . . . My stomach drops, my mouth suddenly dry. Where are they, where are my children? The kettle starts to rumble.

'I hope they haven't been naughty,' I say, trying to force a lightness into my voice.

Shirley shakes her head, her hand at her throat, pulling at her scarf.

'They're with your husband, love. He picked them up, just after eleven this evening it was. Bless them, they wanted to sleep over here, they didn't want to go back to that house.' She pauses and stares into my face, her cheeks, scarlet. 'I tried explaining why they should stay but, well, it all sounded . . .' she shrugs. 'You know what I mean, and he was in no mood to listen. He just got angry and said something about his mother being as bad; she won't come back to the house . . . He wasn't pleased about that, I can tell you.'

'The twins are at Haverscroft?'

'As far as I understand there's no plan to go to his mother's. He wanted to know if I'd be free to have the children over the next day or two. They've got school, haven't they?'

I stand, grab my bag from the table, panic washing over me in waves.

'You can't go out there, love, not right now.' I stare at her, she's deadly serious. 'Wait, till it's light, at least. The children will be alright, won't they, once they're asleep in their beds? There's no point disturbing them at this time.'

'I don't want them at that house, Shirley. Mark doesn't get it, you know he doesn't!'

My voice sounds angry, sharp. None of this is Shirley's fault, but there's no way I can have my children in that house. I put my bag on my shoulder and reach for the door. I must get to the twins as fast as possible.

'No, love!' Her abrupt tone stops me in my tracks. 'There's so much gone on. It's not safe to be out in the village at this time of night.'

'What do you mean? For goodness sakes, it's Weldon!'

'Let me make some tea and I'll explain what's been happening over a cuppa.'

She's beside me, has hold of my arm before I can move.

'You can't go walking about out there, love, really you can't. I think you should stay here, but if you really want to go, I'll call you a taxi, one won't be long coming at this time. I'll tell you what's been going on while we wait.'

I push the chair back and try to find the space to pass her. I don't want to manhandle her out of my way, but I will if I have to. I don't need a taxi.

'I have to get the children, Shirley!'

Sharp hammering on the front door makes us both jump. Shirley looks terrified.

'Who in the Lord's name would that be at this time?'

Her grip on my arm is fierce, I feel each of her fingers pressing into my flash through the fabric of my coat. The hammering again, heavy, slower this time.

'Wait here, Kate. I'll see who it is.'

'Shall I come with you?'

Shirley stares into my face, shakes her head.

'Wait here, love.'

CHAPTER 31

TUESDAY 2ND NOVEMBER, 4:25AM

THE DOOR IS pulled to, I can't see into the hall, just hear the chain rattle. The village is one of those places where doors are left unlocked, the chain redundant until tonight, as far as I was aware. A rush of cold air floods under the door into the kitchen. A hurried, whispered conversation. A man, judging by the tone, words too low to make out. The front door closes with a rattle of keys and chain. The visitor stays in the hall with Shirley, conversation continues. I can't resist tipping back my chair, pulling the door open a crack.

A slice of the hall is visible, part of Shirley's back and a portion of Mr Whittle in a jacket, slippers and what look like pyjama bottoms. Old fashioned brushed cotton, paisley print. The estate agent is hugely agitated, flapping his arms about in an attempt to explain some issue to Shirley as quietly as possible. They stand very close to one another, noses almost touching. Whittle glances towards the kitchen and catches me watching. I rock forward, my cheeks hot. Their voices get louder, footsteps coming closer.

'It's only Jerry Whittle.'

Shirley looks flustered. Mr Whittle tries to put his hands in his pockets, finds his pyjamas have none. We look at his feet. Wet, rather muddy slippers.

'I came out in a bit of a rush,' he says, turning to Shirley. I can't make out his expression.

'Sit down, Jerry. I'm brewing some tea. You tell her as it's your doing. It'll be all around the village before lunchtime anyway.'

'I really want to be off, Shirley.' I push back my chair and start to stand.

'You sit down and hear what he has to say. I'll call that taxi company for you. I'll not have you wandering around on your own out there tonight.'

I look at Whittle who shrugs. Shirley's never spoken to me in such a way before. I don't feel I can argue. I can't imagine what's made her speak so angrily and so sharply. Has he got news about the twins? How can he have?

The estate agent is too big for the cramped space, heaving his stomach in as he sits down, pulling his chair towards the table. He gives me a sideways glance and begins patting the pockets of his jacket. Shirley's busy at the sink with mugs, teapot, and milk, her back to us.

'Get on with it, Jerry, the girl's in a hurry. Don't leave anything out.'

Mr Whittle takes his glasses from the top pocket, then replaces them. He stares at the table top, clears his throat, his ears a deep crimson.

'You two . . . ?' I ask.

Whittle beams and nods at Shirley. 'Lovely woman.'

'That's not what I was meaning at all!' Shirley chides him, looking more flustered than ever.

She places a mug of tea in front of the estate agent with such force a little slops onto the table. Whittle looks up at her.

'Really! The less said about that the better. Just get on

with it, Jerry. Kate can't wait around all night for you.' Shirley storms into the hall, the quaver in her voice unmistakable. 'I'll call the taxi for you, Kate.'

I look at Mr Whittle. Beads of perspiration glisten across his bald head, his Adam's apple popping up and down.

'Lyle phoned me earlier, just after Shirley had left to come back here. A nasty call, it was. He said he wanted a word and was coming straight over. He quite upset me. He said the police had spoken to him about his buying up Mrs Havers' land. I didn't fancy speaking to him, not with the mood he was in, so I came straight over here.'

'In your pyjamas?'

He nods and shrugs, an apologetic smile.

'The police were speaking to him about Richard Denning when I left.'

'Shirley says I've to let the police know what sort of man Lyle is. Mrs Havers was worried with him representing you.'

'What do you mean?' Anxiety makes me shiver. Lyle hung around like glue this evening, waited while I gave my statement. Why didn't he just go home?

'Lyle wants me to keep quiet, but I already told the police the gist of it last night. I'm going into the station later this morning to make a formal statement. Shirley's arranged it all.'

Shirley comes back into the kitchen.

'The taxi's on its way. I feel so bad, Kate, about you being dragged off to the station like that. I told Jerry you were meeting Richard on Monday afternoon. I should keep my mouth shut, so I should.' She glares at Whittle. 'Jerry went running off to Lyle and told him you were meeting Richard Denning.'

'The police can't have told Lyle I've spoken to them already.

He says we'll both go inside if I let the cat out of the bag.'

'Let the cat out of the bag about what?' I try not to snap, just wish Whittle would get to the point.

'My firm dealt with the valuations of Mrs Havers' land. I undervalued the plots. Lyle paid me a backhander the first time. Back then, Shirley and me were getting married and were short of money. I shouldn't have done it, and I tried to give it back, but he wouldn't take it. I never took any more money, I refused to, but I should've spoken up.'

Mr Whittle pulls out his glasses again and turns them over and over in his hands as if he's never seen them before. I look at Shirley and shake my head in disbelief.

'When Shirley found out what had gone on, she dumped me and ended up married to Nick Cooper instead.'

He half-smiles at Shirley.

'Go on Jerry, out with it all now.'

He continues speaking, looking at me. 'Once you moved in, I thought it was all over with. I breathed a huge sigh of relief, I can tell you, the end of the whole nasty mess.'

Shirley tuts and starts to pick up plates, piling them in the sink.

'Then Richard Denning spoke to me a few weeks back. He said the old lady was short of money and she shouldn't have been. He wanted to know where it'd all gone.'

'Did he know then, about the fraud?'

Whittle is shaking, his face pale and sweating.

'I don't know, but he was suspicious, asking too many questions. Lyle says if I tell anyone about the land going to him on the cheap I'll go down with him. I should've said something years back, when I first knew what Lyle was up to. He wants the house, you see, always has.'

'If you'd spoken up right away Richard might still be here.' Shirley glares at Whittle, her eyes bright. She picks up the last dirty plate and turns to the sink. 'He'll be greatly missed. He was a better man than most, so he was.'

Whittle gives me a sideways glance. He looks utterly miserable.

'Old Lyle couldn't believe it when Mrs Havers moved into Fairfields and still didn't sell the house. He got impatient, he wanted it straight away and said he's entitled to it, you see.'

'How?' I say, looking between Mr Whittle and Shirley. 'Because he bought the land?'

'He says that he's Edward Havers' son. Illegitimate, but all the same, he's got a right to the place.' Whittle raises his eyebrows, turns the glasses between his fingers. 'It annoyed the old girl, making claims like that.'

'Mrs Havers has a reputation to maintain,' I say, sending Shirley a flat smile.

'Lyle wanted me to say the place was about to fall down and to get shot of it quick. I, well, I just wasn't any good at that sort of thing. The old girl knew I was lying. I'd no stomach for it, to tell you the truth.'

Mr Whittle looks at me properly for the first time since he arrived. 'She even thought there was some trickery in you and your husband buying it from her. She thought you were buying on Lyle's behalf.'

'He's obsessive about the place. He has to have it at all costs.' Shirley reaches across the table and takes my hand. 'I was so worried when we heard he was with you at the station.'

I squeeze her fingers. 'Shirley, I'm just fine, really I am.'

She looks at Whittle and again I can't interpret their expressions.

'Lyle was going to speak to Denning, tell him to mind his own business, right worked up about it he was. He went over to Denning's boat first thing yesterday morning.'

We sit in silence, the only sound is Mr Whittle's wheezy breathing. Not used to running, his lungs must have had an extraordinary shock this evening.

'You know Richard Denning's been unwell, don't you?' I glance between Shirley and Whittle. 'I'd wait to see what the post-mortem says before drawing too many conclusions.'

'Do you think I'll go to jail, Kate? I don't think I'd cope with that.'

Shirley stands and turns to the sink, her back to us, shoulders hunched. Whittle looks at her and fiddles with his glasses, his fingers shaking.

'I don't really know. Mark will tell you, it's what he does. Lyle will certainly go inside, he'll lose everything. The land will get taken as proceeds of crime and he'll get struck off as a solicitor.'

Shirley sits back at the table, her face pale and strained. Despite her anger at Jerry Whittle, she's clearly concerned for him.

'No wonder he's desperate.' Shirley's looking at Whittle.

'Go over to Haverscroft first thing before Mark heads off for London. He'll be able to tell you what to expect at the police station and what the likely outcome will be.' I stand and pick up my bag. 'By then the police will probably have the post-mortem results as well.'

'You're not going yet, love. The taxi won't be many more minutes.'

'I can't wait, Shirley. I've waited too long as it is.'

'Jerry, you walk back with her, speak to her husband about

it all if he's awake.' Shirley's on her feet tugging the sleeve of Whittle's jacket.

The estate agent's head is bowed, shaking from side to side. I don't think Whittle will be much use if we do bump into Oliver Lyle, or anyone else for that matter. I head for the door, Shirley's quick footsteps at my back along the narrow hall. She pulls back the chain, top bolt and unlocks the door.

'Fetch the children back here, Kate.' I step past her onto the doorstep. 'Be careful love, won't you?'

The street is empty, dark and alive with shifting shadows. I glance back at Shirley, her brightly-lit hall, Jerry Whittle sitting at the kitchen table, watching. I should wait for the taxi and take Whittle with me, but I dare not lose another second. I pull Shirley into a hug.

'Thank you for everything, Shirley. Go back inside, don't get cold. I'll be just fine.'

CHAPTER 32

TUESDAY 2ND NOVEMBER, 5:32AM

A DARK, DESERTED high street. The only thread of light spilling across the frozen pavement comes from an upper-casement window of Lovett and Lyle Solicitors. A silver estate car is parked close to the railings.

I turn left, run away from the solicitor's office and head towards the church at the end of the street. My footsteps ring in the still air, murmuring in doorways, whispering behind me. My eyes search each shop entrance as I tear past. I glance over my shoulder. I'm being stupid, there's no one hiding, jumping into my path. No sign of Oliver Lyle. Frosty air burns my lungs, rasps cold in my throat. I jog into the lane, drop my pace and tuck my chin deeper into my scarf. I've let Shirley and Mr Whittle, the empty isolation of this place, unnerve me. It's only ten, maybe eleven minutes' brisk walk from Shirley's to Haverscroft. I've covered it in half that time, even Tom will be impressed.

High hedges kill the moonlight as I pick my way past the church. Icy puddles skid and crack beneath my boots, my breath puffs hot and damp against the woollen scarf. The graveyard is black. I fix my eyes straight ahead and don't allow them to find a shadow, a yew tree moving in the wind, a night creature prowling. If the twins were here, I'd reassure them that nothing hides behind the headstones, nothing to fear other than their own imagination.

Haverscroft is lost to the darkness, the twins in there somewhere. I picture them in my mind and keep moving forward, one step after another. They'll be sleeping, night lights on. I hope they're with Mark, or together in Sophie's bed, Blue Duck keeping them safe. The moon slips into cloud. I stop, try to make out any shape to guide me towards the house. I'm at the top of the driveway staring up into a cold sky patched with pockets of stars and streaked with cloud. The moon's not coming back anytime soon. It was stupid not to have stayed on at Shirley's and wait for the taxi. I can't turn back, not now. Mrs Havers' instruction to leave without delay rings in my head. I have to get the twins.

A shriek, sharp and primeval, makes my heart thud harder. A fox most likely, from the direction of the graveyard. We laughed the first night here, spooked by similar screams. Now I don't feel so brave. All Whittle's talk about land sales and Lyle's dodgy dealings unsettles me. I've no idea how we afforded Haverscroft, what we paid for it, what our London home sold for. I don't know why Mark refuses to get the roof repaired. My husband always played straight, that's one of the things I loved most about him when we first met. It made life simple, or so I thought. Usually I'd be certain Mark wasn't involved with Lyle. But lately, I wonder if I really know my own husband. What he's been up to, what he might be capable of.

I have to keep moving. I try to follow the tyre tracks churned into the driveway as it slopes and spirals away from the lane towards Haverscroft. A red glow rises in front of the house, deepening the closer I get, window frames, the front door and steps picked out. Apprehension tightens in my chest. I turn the bend in the drive, feet stumbling on uneven, frozen ground. A taxi waits, tail-lights blaring a warning into the night. The engine hums, a miasma of exhaust fumes behind it. What is it doing here, is someone leaving? Is Mark taking the twins to his mother's after all?

Light chinks through gaps in the kitchen blinds, the rest of the house in darkness. No sign of the Audi. Shirley thought Mark was staying here, for now at least, with the children. Even so, my chest tightens another notch. He knows I'm friendly with Shirley, would he lie to her if he intended taking the children away?

I run the final few yards, at last able to see enough to move without fear of tripping. The overstuffed skip has been replaced by a smaller, empty one, the Armstrong Siddeley parked where the gravel slopes up to meet the lawn. The car's larger than I imagined, the sweep of the coachwork from wing to slim running board accentuates its length. A tall grill, rusted and bent, must once have been elegant. The car that killed Mrs Havers' children. Despite all that's gone on, Mark's still found time to have it towed from the garage. I can hardly believe it.

The taxi driver hunches low in the cab, his eyes watching my approach in the wing mirror. His window winds down a fraction as I come alongside.

'Are you going in the house?'

His voice is full of irritation. I nod and stop beside the vehicle, my breath clouding in front of me. I'm relieved he's not the cabbie from earlier.

'Who are you waiting for?'

'No idea. A guy called to pick up a fare from Haverscroft House. This the right place?'

I nod again, glance up the steps, the front door, closed. No sign of activity.

'I've been here ten minutes or more already. Blasted the horn twice. I can't wait all night.'

5:41am on the taxi's dashboard.

'Hang on,' I say, 'I'll find out what's happening for you.'

Whatever is going on here? I jog up the front steps, my hands shake as I root through my bag and find my keys. I need a clear head, to be calm and rational. I take a breath, put my key into the lock. It won't turn. I try several times, rattle the key and put my shoulder to the door. Has Mark changed the locks?

I stop, how stupid. I must calm down, the door isn't locked. Mark's leaving so he hasn't locked the place up as I do before bed. I try the handle, it turns easily but the door won't budge, stuck yet again. Shirley would have this open in a second. I lift the handle and put my shoulder to the woodwork. The door stays shut. I reach for the knocker. The door rattles and shakes, stops me dead in my tracks. Someone inside trying to open the door. Mark must have heard me. Swollen and sticking, it shakes again, the brass knocker clatters. The door jerks open.

CHAPTER 33

TUESDAY 2ND NOVEMBER, 5:46AM

I STARE IN astonishment. The very last person I would expect to see here stares back at me. It would be usual to speak, to say something, but words fail me. I'd assumed only Mark would be home.

'Good gracious! We were just talking about you. Come in, come in before we all freeze to death!'

I step over the threshold and stand on the door mat gaping at three people staring back at me. The surprise on their faces is nothing compared to the astonishment I'm feeling.

She raises her stick and waves it towards the taxi. 'Wait right there, young man, I won't keep you a moment.'

I can't move from the doormat, she's blocking my way into the house.

'Are you all right, Kathrine? What a dreadful business this has been. Utterly ridiculous the police keeping you like that. Quite absurd. I told them so myself.'

I stare at her, at my husband standing behind her. Why would he be entertaining any visitors at this time of the morning, let alone Alan Wynn and Mrs Havers?

'Are the police finished with you?'

I look into her face. 'I didn't kill Richard Denning, if that's what you're asking.'

'No, no, of course not!' She glances over her shoulder at

the two men behind her and taps her stick on the tiles, her eyes bright beneath the rim of her hat.

On the landing, a soft green light glows faintly from one end. No Sophie spying between the spindles. No Tom shivering at the top of the stairs. But the nightlight is on.

I look beyond her, at Mark. 'Are the twins okay?'

'They're just fine, Kate. Asleep in bed.'

Mark's voice is flat with exhaustion, his face grey. He looks so much more like his father, a worn version of the man I married. I can't begin to imagine how I must look.

'I'm very sorry about Richard Denning, Mrs Havers, but why are you here?'

'I should have come sooner, spoken more frankly when I was here with you and your mother-in-law. I'm here on Richard's mission.'

Her voice is higher than usual, she stops speaking abruptly and looks back at Mark and Alan Wynn standing shoulder to shoulder. The kitchen door is open, light spilling through into the hall.

'There's rather a lot to explain. It all takes so much longer than one thinks. Have you read my letter?'

'I read it on my way here.' My tone is short and snappy. I no longer care if this woman finds me rude.

'Then you know I must trouble you for a short while longer.' She turns away from me and walks past Mark and Alan Wynn. 'The morning-room fire may need a little something, it was getting quite low a few moments ago.'

Mark is looking agitated, clearly expecting me to do something but I have no idea what. 'Mrs Havers has been waiting in the morning room for you Kate, for some time.'

I hurry across the hall and catch up with Mrs Havers. 'I've

had an extremely long and trying day, Mrs Havers. I'm here to collect my children and then head straight to Shirley's and to bed. Perhaps I can call at Fairfield this afternoon or sometime later this week?'

I lay my hand on her arm, she pauses and looks at me, then moves forwards again.

'I must speak with you now, Katherine, it's quite imperative, there must be no further delay.'

Her progress is slow but steady. She grabs the doorjamb as she steps across the threshold into the morning room. Short of manhandling her, how do I make her leave?

'Well, I must shoot off.' I glance back towards the front door, Alan Wynn smiles at me and I realise I have no idea why he is here. 'I have a christening in the middle of the day and must get my head down before then. We've agreed I'll call by late afternoon, Kate, if that's okay with you?'

Mrs Havers stands on the threshold of the morning room waiting for my reply. Her navy blue coat has shiny gold-coloured buttons down its front, her brooch pinned to its lapel. A silk scarf in cream, red and navy is tied at its neck.

'We have a plan in place,' she says. 'One that will work this time, I think, if you are prepared to try it. Reverend Wynn here,' she waves her stick towards Alan, 'has offered, very kindly, to have you all stay while he sorts out . . . what is here. So much more room than at Shirley Cooper's. I will let the gentlemen explain. Do please excuse me but my knees have been dreadful in this damp weather, I really must sit down.'

She heads into the morning room and I look back helplessly at Mark. He looks furious.

'Let's sit in the kitchen for a second,' he says, heading off without waiting for a reply.

I watch Mrs Havers for a moment. One of the kitchen chairs is in front of the hearth, our low coffee table cluttered with cups, glasses and a teapot. My husband has been quite the host in my absence. I glance at the landing, all is quiet, the glow from the children's night-lights still there. I look back at Alan. He smiles and extends his hand towards the kitchen door.

Mark stands with his back to the stove looking as irritated as hell, Alan sits himself at the table.

'We thought it better to fill you in sooner rather than later,' says Alan. 'You know what gossip is like in the village, and it's easy to get the wrong end of things.'

'I've certainly got that lately,' I say, trying to smile and ease the tension. 'Why is Mrs Havers here?'

'She didn't like Lyle representing you.' Mark at last looks me fully in the face, he crosses the kitchen and closes the kitchen door. 'I told her I'd been to the station, but you'd already instructed Lyle, so I couldn't interfere.'

'He was the duty solicitor tonight, but he's the last person I wanted. I didn't know you were at the station, Mark.'

I sink into Mum's sofa, drop my bag at my feet and realise just how exhausted I am.

'I went straight there from London, what else would I do? I came back here after I'd spoken to one of the DCIs. They said they were just after a statement from you and that there was nothing to worry about. You'd taken some medication and were doing okay.' Mark looks at me. 'I thought you'd be fine so I picked the kids up from Shirley Cooper.'

'And Riley?'

'I put him outside when Mrs Havers got here. He barks incessantly at the woman.'

Mark walks to the sink and runs hot water on to a multitude of mugs, plates and pans. I should point out we have a dishwasher.

'Mrs Havers wasn't entirely making sense when she descended on me at the Rectory, but the real reason she's here is something altogether different.' Alan looks at my angry husband, then back to me. 'She said you'd be interested to hear about her nephew, Kate.'

Alan smiles again. I'm glad he's here, it's difficult to fight with a Reverend in the room. Alan's looking at Mark piling dirty crockery into the sink.

'You remember after Dad died, Mother and I did a bit of research into the family tree?' Mark says.

I recollect Jennifer's excitement as they pored over websites and old papers together.

'It was kind of therapeutic when we'd just lost Dad. I knew he'd been adopted and assumed it wouldn't be easy to find much out. It turns out he'd gone looking for his birth family before. He already had legal papers and letters and knew he was born here as Frederick Havers.

Mark stops speaking and looks up at me from a sink full of soapsuds. Knowing my husband, he's probably wondering if I'm keeping up with his tale.

'Mrs Havers is your great aunt?' The astonishment rings in my voice. The family-tree project had been Mark and Jennifer's. They had chattered about it, exclaimed over discoveries and emailed details and updates to one another. Little, if anything, was shared with me. I laugh out loud and notice a smile on Alan's lips too.

'Now I come to think of it, you are a little alike!'

Mark clatters the mugs in the sink and ignores what I say.

'Mrs Havers said you threw her that day when you asked about Freddie, not knowing who it was. She guessed something was off between us and didn't want to put her foot in it.'

'So Freddie didn't die of scarlet fever?' I try to keep the laughter from my voice, knowing it will irritate the hell out of Mark. I daren't catch Alan's eye.

'That was just the first thing she could think of. It turns out Dad met Mrs Havers about fifteen years ago. I don't think they kept in touch, who can blame him, the woman's a menace. When I looked up Haverscroft I saw it was for sale. I hadn't seriously thought to buy it, I was just interested to see where Dad was born and wanted to take a few photos to show to Mother.'

'So we weren't just out for a drive that day?'

Mark shakes his head. More lies, more deception. Sure, I was ill, but I could have coped with a bit of family history. It pisses me off that Mark can't admit he wanted this house and was going to buy it regardless of my opinion. I recall the journey home to London, the twins and Mark making all sorts of wild plans for when we lived at Haverscroft House. All so long ago now.

'When did Mrs Havers know it was her great nephew's family who had moved in here?' I say.

'Mother told her when she came to stay just after Tom's accident at the pond. Mother was rather pleased to tell her there was a family connection, but Mrs Havers didn't take the news at all well. I'd intended to speak to Mrs Havers about it when I met her in the summer, I but never got the chance. She was rude and belligerent, so I was only with her a few minutes.'

I can imagine them both at Fairfield talking, shouting, at each other, but not listening.

'She must have been horrified,' I say. 'You know she's convinced herself the weird stuff here only threatens her family?'

Mark nods as he washes the last dirty mug. 'She's nuts, like I keep saying.'

Alan pushes back his chair and stands. 'To put it simply, Kate, Mrs Havers insists I come over to Haverscroft and offer some prayers for protection and peace.' He stops speaking and smiles.

'That's the plan?' I say smiling back.

'I thought you'd approve of it, Kate. Meanwhile, you're more than welcome to camp out at the Rectory for as long as you like.'

He stands and fishes in the back pocket of his jeans. 'I'm off to my bed, let yourselves in as soon you like.'

I take the key from his hand. 'Thank you. You can't imagine what a relief this is.'

All of me relaxes a little. I can get the children away from here just as soon as I've spoken to Mrs Havers.

Mark wipes his hands on a tea towel. 'It can't do any harm, can it? An exorcism, or whatever you want to call it, to humour her?'

I stare at Mark, I'm aware Alan does too. The silence pulls out for several seconds.

'Do you believe there's something here then, at Haverscroft?' I make no attempt to hide the astonishment in my voice. Mark looks towards where I sit on Mum's sofa.

'I'm the only one who doesn't get it. The kids are petrified of being on the landing, and Mother says I'm insane for wanting to stay here.' He shrugs his shoulders and turns to Alan. 'So you can have a go, at sorting it, can't you?'

I'm irritated Mark wouldn't have any of this from me. I bite my lip, it won't help to challenge him right now, what's the point, we're leaving anyway.

'Absolutely. Whether it has any effect, of course, is entirely speculative. Opinions vary enormously on these things.' Alan looks at me before continuing. 'Mrs Havers has been on at me about it for weeks, and so had Richard Denning.' He zips up his black leather jacket. 'Then you raised it with me too, Kate, that's when I spoke with the Bishop.'

I push myself from the sofa and stand, my heart racing. The whole thing sounds like a scary nightmare.

'We don't carry out exorcisms very often, far from it. The Church doesn't even call them that these days.'

I'm nodding, my mouth so dry I don't speak. I can't imagine any of it making the slightest difference, and even if it does, I don't want to be here. This house will never be a home.

'Did you get it?' Mark says. 'Permission?'

'Eventually. Mrs Havers was persuasive, as you might imagine.'

Alan and I exchange a smile as he heads for the door, Mark right behind him. 'I'll drop by this afternoon if that's convenient. There's no time to waste as far as Mrs Havers is concerned.'

Mark and Alan head for the front door.

'I'll give the taxi guy some cash, Kate, make sure he's okay to hang on while you speak to Mrs Havers.'

I nod at Mark and watch the two men head outside. There's no sound from the morning room. Mrs Havers can wait a few more minutes. I tiptoe across the tiles and head for the stairs.

I stop on the top step, the spare room door is closed and bolted. A small set of stepladders I've not seen before leans against the wall, the fluted glass shade and three blackened bulbs on the floor beside it. A plain white shade, a modern cone-shaped thing, hangs from the ceiling on a much shorter cable. I try the old Bakelite switch.

Click, click. Click. Dead.

There's no odd sensation, no peculiar smell. I hurry away from the spare room along the landing, past my room to Sophie's, which glimmers in soft light from her lava-lamp, bubbles rise, collide and fall, bouncing deep pink shadows across the ceiling and walls. Her bed is crumpled, the duvet sagging down one side, a pillow thrown to the floor. No Sophie. Bloody hell, where is she?

The office and attic doors are closed, the bathroom in darkness. I run towards the green glow coming from my son's room. The door is ajar, I push it wider. Trainers tumble amongst discarded jeans and a tee-shirt, Lego and books spread across the floor. The lamp is on the bedside table, silver glitter rises and falls in the current of green liquid spinning sparkles of light around the walls. From here it's difficult to see my children properly. I pick my way across the cluttered carpet to stand beside the bed. Sophie is here, lying on her back, her mouth open slightly, she looks as if she might say something any second. Her arm is flung out towards the lamp, a tangle of dark hair spread across the pillow. Tom's face presses into Sophie's neck, blond hair sticking up at the front Tin-Tin style, Blue Duck clamped into the crook of his arm.

I watch the slow rise and fall of the duvet, listen to the soft whistle of Tom's breathing. They're safe. My children are okay. The knot of tension in my chest eases, the relief is so overwhelming my knees feel wobbly, my eyes growing hot. I breathe, let my shoulders relax. I watched the twins sleeping for hours and hours when they were babies, terrified one might stop breathing, turn themselves over and suffocate. I watch them now, not daring to move away from the bedside. My face is wet, salty rivulets dribble off my chin and drip onto my coat. One day I'll tell you about her, your grandmother, my mum. How she would have made you laugh, and how she would have loved you both so much. My strong and clever, warm and fragile Mum. But right now, we need to leave. I look up, my breath catching in my throat, a still dark figure fills the doorway.

I didn't hear his footfall, the creek of the landing floorboards. I've no idea how long he's been there, how long I've been watching the twins sleeping. I hadn't noticed earlier how his jeans look looser at the hips, his belt a notch tighter. I wipe the back of my hand across my face.

'What the hell are you doing, Kate. She's still fucking well downstairs. Get rid of her, for God's sake so we can all go to bed!'

Mark's voice is a low hiss, his head jerking towards the stairs.

I look at the sleeping children. I can't imagine what she has to say and why only I must hear it. I need to sort things out with her and with Mark. Especially with Mark.

CHAPTER 34

TUESDAY 2ND NOVEMBER, 5:58AM

THE MORNING ROOM is silent, the single standard lamp in the alcove beside the hearth casts a low yellow light across the polished floorboards. The fire has all but burned out, more ash now than coals in the grate. I only see the top of Mrs Havers' hat, her head dropped forward. I assume she's asleep. She clasps her stick in both hands, her cream bag resting on her lap. For a moment, I wonder if I should leave her here, gather the children and slip out the backdoor and head over to Alan's. One way and another, it has been an extraordinarily long day for everyone.

'Katherine, there you are!' Not so asleep then. 'Come in, sit down.'

'Mark tells me your nephew, Freddie, didn't die of scarlet fever. It must have been a shock to find out your great nephew and his family had moved in here.'

Her hand grasps the handle of her stick as she taps it gently against the fender at her feet. I won't let it pass that I know she lied to me. I want her to know. I'm fed-up to the back teeth with everyone's lies.

'It was indeed, a most unwelcome shock. I have explained all that to Alan Wynn and your husband, but it is something rather more difficult I wish to discuss with you, Katherine.'

'Surely it can wait until later this afternoon, or tomorrow? I really am very tired.'

'I must speak now, it is what Richard would have wanted. No more secrets, he was very clear there. This is something I've told no one other than my late husband, not even Richard.'

She stops speaking, the fire murmurs as it sinks lower in the grate.

'It is about my sister Helena. I hope she is with Richard now, God rest their souls.'

She looks at me standing in the doorway.

'Will you not sit with me? It will only take a moment to explain, this thing that has haunted me my whole life.'

I don't want her here and I guess she knows it. If she weren't so determined to tell me her tale and I so curious to know it, I'd tell her to go and not come back.

I step into the room, and stop of a moment. We watch each other in silence. My ears strain for movement upstairs. I can't help but glance at the ceiling.

She smiles and extends her hand towards the sofa. 'I've heard nothing all the time I've sat here tonight.'

I sit down opposite her and wait.

'The night my sister died, we sat together beside the pond. A summer drinks party was in full swing on the terrace here.' She inclines her head towards the French windows. 'A beautifully warm June evening. I'd borrowed one of her dresses and a pair of silver-heeled shoes. They nipped my toes terribly. A child, she said, dressing up in her clothes. She was waiting for Richard. He never told me why they were meeting that night. Hold these for me a moment, would you?' She hands me her stick and her bag, which is surprisingly heavy. She tugs each finger in turn of her cream cotton gloves and pulls them off.

She holds out her left hand and turns it towards the light coming from the lamp, the large centre stone glows.

'This was her engagement ring. Edward said I should wear it to the party. I'd taken it from her dressing table. I knew she would be angry. She was an indulgent older sister, spoiled me dreadfully, but there were limits.'

She looks up into my face.

'We argued over it. Helena tried to pull it from my finger. Who can blame her? I pushed her away, perhaps too roughly, I was not used to alcohol then. My heel caught in my hem and she toppled backwards somehow. I don't know quite what happened, but we fell, I on top of her and most awkwardly. The crack of her head on the edge of the metal seat was sickening.'

I recall the newspaper's grizzly report was of a blunt head trauma, the victim probably semi-conscious for a few minutes before she died. I'm shivering. I should say something, but words fail to come.

'You may think it couldn't get any worse, but it does. You can't imagine my horror when I realised how badly injured she was. We had just struggled, fallen . . .' She stares beyond me at the empty room. 'Never did I intend to harm her.'

She looks at me again, her dark eyes meet mine, but I have no clue to what she is thinking. This whole thing is so dreadful I can't think of anything adequate to say.

'Had I stayed with her she would not have lived. Even so, I should have been there with her for those last minutes. It is, perhaps more than anything else, the thing that has troubled me most over the decades. I heard the rear gate, you see. Richard was approaching from the loke as arranged. He was training as a doctor and was almost qualified by then. He would know what to do and how to help her. I panicked and ran, hid at the back of the long border. I watched him comfort her. He was still holding her when Edward discovered them there. I'm sure she was quite dead by then.'

She begins to pull on her gloves. 'I told Edward what had happened. Such a mistake! Of all people to confide in, but I was young, so foolish and, of course, thought myself in love. He held it over me for the rest of his life. I have never spoken to another living soul about it until now.'

I'm horrified at all she has told me, repulsed at what she has done. But, at the same time, I feel for this old woman. Her mistake that evening has defined her life since then. I can't help but feel a little sorry for her.

'I understand why Richard should have known, but why tell me?'

'I suspect Richard knew what had happened.'

She looks at me again, then back down at her gloves as she slowly pushes each of her fingers into the cream material and smooths the fabric.

'Helena was conscious, he tells me, for a minute or two. I asked him once if she was able to speak. He did not reply for some time. When he did respond it was to say her last words were to ask him to take care of me.'

My intake of breath is so sharp she glances up and smiles.

'Quite shocking, is it not, Katherine?'

I can only nod, not sure what to say. Did Richard know all along what Alice Havers had done? He had always looked out for her, as far as I could tell. I wish I had known him longer, had got to know him better.

'Edward told Oliver Lyle's father what happened. He was the family solicitor back then, a good one, unlike his son. Edward quite deliberately left me open to blackmail. Even after his death he had to be in control. Oliver Lyle is a greedy man. I let him swindle me over the land sales. Then, of course, I had him; if his dealings become public knowledge his career would be finished, he would not only lose his reputation but his liberty as well.'

A smile flickers on her lips. How much sense this would make to Mr Whittle if he knew.

'I don't think Lyle will keep my secret if the police arrest him, which they surely will. He argued with Richard over the land sales lately. Richard had realised what had gone on and was not prepared to be discrete, despite my begging him to leave well alone.'

'Did Shirley let you know Mr Whittle has spoken to the police?'

'She did. I understand Whittle is quite nervous of Lyle, that he runs around doing his bidding. Both of them are loathsome individuals!'

'With Mr Whittle's testimony, it will be easy to prove the fraud, the under-valuing of the land.'

We sit quietly for a moment. The house is sill, only the gurgle in the radiators, the plinking of the pipes as the heating starts up for the day.

'After all this time, it's unlikely they'll prove anything against you.'

She smiles. 'Is that your legal advice? There comes a time when, to be frank, keeping the secret was more burden than telling it. It is important you know about Helena, you will perhaps understand this house the better for it.'

'No more secrets?'

'Perhaps that is it.' She takes my arm. 'Do the police know what happened to Richard?' Her voice is so low I barely catch her words.

'They're waiting on post-mortem results. Mr Whittle and Shirley have reached their own conclusions, as I assume you have heard?'

She nods and reaches for her stick.

'He had been quite under the weather of late, dizzy at times. He may have just been taken badly, of course.'

'Let's hope so.'

She places the stick on the floor beside her feet and holds her free hand towards me.

'If you wouldn't mind giving me a pull, Katherine, or I may never manage to get to my feet again.'

She leans heavily on my arm as she stands. Mark is in the doorway smoking a cigarette. I stare back at him as he takes a long drag before heading back into the hall, closing the kitchen door behind him. Mrs Havers waves her stick forwards and we slowly move round the chairs and head for the door.

'The guilt I have carried all these years. Allowing an innocent man to take the blame. Cowardly in the extreme. It's so difficult to live with one's self with so much self-loathing. I wear Helena's ring every day without fail. It's a constant reminder of what I have done and what I have lost. But I always remember, as if it were ever possible to forget. I hope you will understand and not despise me, too much.'

We cross the hall, her gait is easier now, she's leaning less heavily as we reach the front door.

'I'm an only child so it is difficult to fully understand your loss in that sense, but every day I see that sibling bond in the twins. They're sleeping together now in Tom's bed.'

She pulls open the front door with an ease I have to admire. She takes my arm again as we head down the front steps. The taxi driver stares at us as we crunch across the gravel, he opens the driver's door, jumps out and opens the rear passenger door.

She lowers herself into the taxi. The driver shuffles his feet in the gravel, a hint for me to move. He can't close the door until I step away.

'Richard continued to visit me after I left Haverscroft. He knew what a time of it I'd had: being married to Edward, losing my boys and not ever really knowing what happened to them that day in the loke. Richard knew how Edward had taunted me, and of course, we had both lost Helena. I like to think our friendship went some way to making up for my atrocious behaviour. I wish only I had told him the truth, that we had spoken of what happened to my sister. Perhaps, he may, in time, have forgiven me.'

She puts her bag on her lap, and holds the stick in her hand.

'Please visit me, Katherine, if you can.'

She sits very straight, looks me full in the face. It's impossible to read her dark brown eyes. 'If you feel it's your duty to speak with the police, then you must. I would not want you to have any of this on your conscience. My only request is you speak with no one else on the subject. I could not bear people to gossip.'

I step back from the taxi. She seems very small as she stares back at me. The driver closes the passenger door. He hurries into the driver's seat, slams his door, the engine revs. I knock on her window. She fumbles, panicky, unable to operate the electric button. Her lips move as she bangs her stick against the back of the driver's headrest. I step closer to the car as the window slides down and catch a hint of powder and perfume.

'If Edward didn't want Helena and didn't love you, why would he stop you from leaving?'

She reaches her hand through the open window. I take it in mine and hold it tightly.

'Control, he always had to be in control.' Her face is creased with concern. 'Edward is at his most dangerous when one tries to leave. Go at once, don't delay.'

I force a smile and hope it will reassure her, at least a little. 'It'll be okay now. There's a plan, as you say. Everyone knows what needs to be done. Go home, don't worry.'

She nods, I release her hand and step back from the taxi.

'Please let me know when you and your family are safely away from here. I shall not rest until I have that news directly from you, Katherine.'

CHAPTER 35

TUESDAY 2ND NOVEMBER, 6:11AM

I DROP A second can of dog food into Sophie's purple rucksack as Mark comes back into the kitchen.

'What are you doing?'

'Packing. We need to leave.'

'Right now? What the hell's wrong with getting some sleep first?'

I'm shaking my head as he speaks, moving about the room, grabbing Sophie's pencil case, dragging Tom's school bag from beneath the table. No way is he going to delay me and the children getting out of here. We can't leave soon enough.

'I'll take them to Shirley's for breakfast and she can take them to school. I'll sleep then at Alan's.'

'Are you nuts?'

'No more than Jennifer.' I stop moving and look at him. 'Or Shirley, George, anyone but you. Come with us? We can go straight to Alan's if you'd rather.'

'The dishwasher guy's here sometime between eight and ten.' Mark stares at me. 'It's broken down, remember?'

I don't know what to say. I don't give a damn about the bloody dishwasher. It was such a relief yesterday morning when I walked away from this house. I don't want to spend a moment longer here than I have to and Mark will try and change my mind if we delay, I know he will.

'And the mechanic, he's coming about the car. He reckons he can tow it to his place, work on it there, if the back axle will stand it. It can't be moved otherwise; the battery and engine have been stripped out.'

Mark stops speaking, we stare in silence at one another. Riley barks and barks, I glance at the back door.

'He doesn't like being outside.'

'He's a dog, Kate. He's absolutely fine out there.'

I look at Mark and start shoving Tom's schoolbooks into his bag. 'We're going, with or without you. I'd rather you came.'

My throat is thick, my voice waving. I thought I'd decided what I wanted to do, that I'd tell Mark calmly we were done. Stupid of me. I head for the back door, Mark is quick, beside me, grabs my wrist as I reach for the doorknob.

'You're very concerned about a dog you didn't want. His fingers press into my flesh, I glare up at him, jerk my arm away.

'It's not what you think, Kate. Nothing's going on with Cassie. There's no one else.'

I stare into tired eyes. Stubble, at least a day's growth, shadows his jaw and can't disguise the hollowness in his cheeks. I want to reach up, touch his face, feel the warmth of his skin. I want to believe him, but I need a lot more than this. Too much has gone on and for too long. How can I be sure of anything he says?

'What then?'

Riley's howling, a weird thin sound I've never heard before.

'The sale of the London house fell through back in the summer.' Mark stops speaking, his eyes on mine. 'It didn't complete until . . . I'm so bloody tired.' He runs his hand through the front of his hair. 'I don't know what day of the fucking week it is!'

'Tuesday. It's Tuesday morning.'

'Yesterday afternoon then. It completed when you were at the police station.'

I stare at him, his words not making sense.

'What the hell are you on about, Mark?'

'I've been staying at the London place trying to sell it.'

'Not at Charles's?'

He shakes his head and stares at the floor.

'Mother said it was making it all worse not telling you, but it got so bad . . .'

Riley howls, I glance at the door, back at Mark.

'You weren't good when it first fell through. The doctor said you were to have no stress at all. I thought it'd just be a few days, a couple of weeks at the most, so there was no need to bother you with it.'

'How did we buy Haverscroft then?'

'I got a bridging loan. I've been taking every case going to make ends meet. Believe me when I say I don't want to be Blackstone's junior on the Southampton trial.'

'Are we okay now?' I can't believe all he's saying, all the deception to keep me in the dark.

'Just about. Mother loaned me some money.'

'We owe Jennifer money?' I'm utterly furious. He knows I would never want to be in debt to Jennifer. Never.

He holds up his hands. 'Just a loan, that's all.'

'You should've told me all this, not gone behind my back! Why didn't you delay buying Haverscroft like any rational person would? Are you entirely insane?'

I can't do the maths, my brain refuses to compute the

figures. A bridging loan for God knows how many thousands of pounds and for months. Mark knows I would never have agreed to taking such a massive financial risk. I ball my fists, hold my arms straight at my sides to stop myself lashing out at him.

'I can't explain it. I just can't. I tried explaining it to Mother . . . Once we saw this house that first day, I just had to have it.'

All their whispered conversations, Mark's snappy short temper, Jennifer's angry face I'd taken to be directed at me, the nutty, needy wife. No way did I ever suspect it was over money.

'Lyle offered to buy the place two, three weeks ago. Not a bad price considering the state of the roof, but I'm pretty sure he's got wind of a planning application I put in a few weeks back.'

'Planning? For what?' I'm astounded.

'A care home, possibly a small hotel.'

'Is there no end to this secret life of yours?' I glance at the backdoor, Riley's quiet at last. 'When did you think I might need to know any of this?' How can I have been so naive, so blind to all that's gone on?

'I couldn't tell you. You would've wanted to know why I was selling after I'd dragged you all out here. And that would lead to the bridging loan and there was no end in sight for it at the time. The chimney had just come down – you had enough on your plate. You can't imagine the stress, Kate. I couldn't tell you and risk making you ill again.'

So all his suggestions about taking my meds, did he really just want me to be okay? I need time to think, this is all going too fast. I play for time.

'Mrs Havers isn't going like it.'

'I don't give a damn what she thinks.'

'Sell it, let Lyle have it, Mark. Just get rid of the place.'

He shakes his head. 'He needs to up his offer. The house is worth far more if the planning goes through.'

'You're as bad as Mrs Havers, really you are!' I throw up my hands, Mark flinches, jerks backwards. Any other time, I might laugh, but I just can't. I just can't believe what Mark's done and without a word to me. I fold my arms, my hands tucked beneath my elbows.

'I'm truly sorry I hit you, Mark. I shouldn't have then, but I should now. It's been hideous here on my own. I thought . . . I thought I was going mad.' I turn my back on him, my voice cracking. I won't let him see me cry. 'You let me think that. You knew I was worried about it and you just let it go on.'

His silence is like a weight pressing against my back.

'I'm sorry, Kate.'

Sorry isn't enough, not now. It's too late. I take a breath. I'm exhausted. I need to focus. Get me and the children out of this house.

'At least you didn't go for the kitchen-roll tube.' His voice is falsely bright and jovial, but I'm in no mood for humour.

'What on earth are you on about?' I sound hard, cold, but at least my voice is steady. His feet shuffle on the floor tiles, I sense him closer at my back.

'Mother ranted one day about me holding stuff back from you and hit me around the ear with an empty kitchen-roll tube. I don't remember her ever striking me as a child. You'd have been hysterical with laughter if you'd been there.'

He wants me to turn around, tell him it's all okay now. I

stare across the room at the black glass of the window. After so much does he really think it's just a case of forgive and forget? He must be the mad one, not me.

'I'm still angry about Blackstone, but not at you, Kate, not any more. We shouldn't have got to such a bad place where something like that could happen. Mother's never spoken to you about Dad, has she?'

He moves to stand beside the table, hands leaning on the back of a kitchen chair. I can see him out of the corner of my eye, his face turned towards me.

'She won't, but I lived through it all. All the rows when he was home. All the time he was away working, Mother beside herself. She was unwell for a while . . .'

Riley's barking again. What on earth's the matter with him?

'She thinks the world of you and the twins, Kate. I know you don't think so, but she does. She just can't show stuff like that, not like you do.'

'We should fetch Riley in.' I just want to be away from here, leave all of this behind.

'I want us to be a family, Kate, change things like we agreed before we moved here. I want to have more time with you and the kids.'

I look at him. He straightens up, face full of doubt, waiting for my response. Silence stretches out, only Riley barking outside. He steps towards me, stops.

'I got you something.'

He digs in the back pocket of his jeans, holds out his fist, uncurls his fingers. In the palm of his hand is a tiny, clear plastic box. A stylus. 'I think it's the right one.'

I stare at it for a long time, look up into his face. 'The

kids and I are leaving, Mark. You agreed we can stay at the Rectory, right?'

'You don't actually believe we've got all this weird stuff going on, do you? I'll go along with Alan's thing if it helps.'

'If Jennifer says leave, would you?'

Mark looks startled, my voice, sharp, angry. He's still holding out his hand, his fingers close about the plastic box.

'Why can't you believe *me* when I say we should leave, that the children aren't safe here?'

He shrugs.

I slam my palm on the table, the sound loud in the silent house. 'Can't you see why it matters? Isn't what I say important? You need to trust me on this. Come with us for no reason other than I'm asking you to.'

I turn away, walk towards the sink, stare out into the darkness. Rage boils in the pit of my stomach. I'm too tired to do this right now but I can't let it pass. My eyes burn, the silence behind me thick and heavy. I wish the bloody dog would stop barking, just for a second.

'Say something, for God's sake, Mark.'

A face, bone-white, eye sockets sunken and dark, looms at me from the black kitchen window. I cry out, recoil from the glass, stumble backwards. The face, vanishes.

'What's wrong?' says Mark.

I step further away from the window, still staring at the glass. Only the glare of the kitchen strip lights and our reflections wink back.

'There's someone out there,' I say, glancing at Mark. 'Someone's in the garden.'

CHAPTER 36

TUESDAY 2ND NOVEMBER, 6:32AM

'I DIDN'T SEE anything. Do you want me to take a look?' Mark's staring at me, hesitating, holding back. Boiling anger dissolves to cold fear. I know what I saw.

Riley barks and barks and barks. I nod.

'I'll get the bloody dog in while I'm out there.' Irritation is palpable in his voice. The face, I'm sure I recognised it, the photos in the attic. Was it . . . ? I can't say it to myself, let alone out loud to my husband.

The bang is huge. An explosion of sound vibrating through the building, rattling the mugs and plates on the table.

I stare at Mark, see astonishment turn to concern.

'What the hell?' he says.

I don't wait to reply, I run to the kitchen door. 'The twins,' I call back to him as I wrench the door open and dash into the hall. The far window is alive with flicking yellow light.

Mark pulls up beside me. 'What the fuck?'

'Mummy?'

Sophie's on the landing peeping over the bannister, Tom beside her.

'Quickly, kids, into the kitchen!' I shout.

Mark drags the front door open, the gagging stink of hot fuel and sharp tang of smoke sucks in on an icy blast of air. He steps across the threshold, I follow. We stand together for what seems like an age but can only be a fraction of a second. He edges forward, stops on the top step, his hand held out to shield his face from the heat of jumping, eager flames.

'How . . . ?' he says.

I glance back at the landing. 'Get dressed, kids, anything, fast as you can. We need to get out.'

The Armstrong Siddeley's bonnet has crumpled into the base of one of the giant urns, strappy leaves and soil spew across the steps and gravel.

'The tank was drained, the engine stripped out . . .' Mark glances over his shoulder at me.

'Forget it, we have to go, get the kids out, Mark. Now!'

Flames flare up the front of the house. Flaking paintwork, crumbling facia boards, rotten sash-windows lap up the fire. My heart is racing, how much time do we have before the whole house goes up?

'Hey!' Mark sprints down the front steps, crosses the drive onto the lawn. I peer through choking black smoke, scan the dark garden. A figure stands in front of the bank of yews. At this distance it's impossible to make out who it is. A man though, judging by height and build. The face at the kitchen window?

'Mark!'

My husband's not listening, can't hear me over the roar of the fire and the crunch of his feet on gravel. I make to follow him, glance back. The hall is empty. Utterly still and silent. My chest tightens.

'Kids, let's go.'

No response.

'Kids? Come on!'

I run across the hall, smoke stings my eyes, scratches the

back of my throat. The landing's empty. I sprint upstairs.

'Tom, Sophie? Come on. Let's go.'

Tendrils of smoke creep from the office, the room shivering with yellow light. My guts churn with fear. Where are they? I run along the landing, slam the bathroom and office doors, head back to Tom's room. The usual chaos of toys, clothes and clutter. No Tom. I snatch up his inhaler from the bedside table and shove it into my coat pocket.

'Kids, we need to get out!' Panic in my voice.

Sophie's room: crumpled covers, pink bubbles of the lava lamp lethargically rising, falling. Where the hell are the twins?

'Tom, Sophie?'

Our room: an empty bed. Crashing somewhere overhead, a whooshing wheezing sound like the house gasps for air. The fire is moving fast. I'm shaking, panic racing through me.

The spare room door is wide open, the corner of the bed and top of the fireplace visible in the moonlight. Smoke hasn't reached it, the room strangely quiet and calm. The twins won't go in there. I head to the stairs and stop at the top of the flight.

'Tom, Sophie? Are you downstairs? Please, kids! Answer me!'

I look again at the spare room, bright with moonlight, nothing moves. I have to be sure.

I jog the length of dark landing.

'Tom, Sophie?'

I slow, walk the last few steps. The air is thick and frigid, cloying on my tongue. Cigarettes, a strong, stale odour of cologne. My heart thunders in my chest, silence hissing in my ears. More of the room comes into view, the bed, fireplace, dressing table. I can't see the twins.

'Tom, Sophie?'

My voice is halting, unsure, my mouth dry from heat and smoke. I'm close enough to reach out and touch the door. My fingers are trembling as I lunge for the small brass knob. Moonlight glints off the metal, the door swings towards me, slams shut.

'No!' I hammer on pot-marked paint. 'No!'

I kick the door, rattled the knob.

'Tom, Sophie? Are you in there? Try and open up from your side.'

I pound my fist against wood, rattle, shake the door in its frame. Nothing gives way.

I drop to my knees and pull the tiny metal key from the lock, put my lips to the keyhole.

'Tom, Sophie, I need you to help me. Are you in there?'

Silence.

'Kids?'

I glance over my shoulder, heavy rapid footsteps on the stairs. Mark stops at the top of the flight, sees me, runs to where I kneel.

'What the hell are you doing?'

'The door's jammed. The twins must be in there.'

Smoke fills the far end of the landing, a billowing wall of grey creeping towards us.

'We haven't got much time, Kate. The fire's almost on the stairs.'

Mark pushes me away from the door, rattles the doorknob, steps back and kicks his foot against the brass.

'Stop! For God's sake, stop it.' I tug at his arm. 'If you smash the lock we've no way in.'

Mark boots the bottom of the door. Hard blunt blows. He

grabs, twists the handle again and again. I glance behind me, there's smoke at the top of the stairs.

'Why would the kids be in there? It's the last place they'd go,' says Mark.

Cold penetrates to my bones, my hands, numb. Our breath fogs between us. Mark sees it. An explosion, splintering glass, flame gushes from the office. Smoke smarts my eyes as I stare into Mark's face.

'He has them. I know he does.'

'What? Don't be absurd. I'm getting something to smash the door in.' Mark turns towards the landing, I grab his wrist.

'Wait, let me try. We should stay together.'

Mark glances towards smoke curling along the runner, a curt nod. 'Make it fast, Kate.'

I square up to the door, take a breath, reach out, take hold of icy, dented metal. Turn the doorknob. Metal slides under my palm.

The door stays shut.

'Kate . . .'

'Wait!' I say.

'Have you heard them in there?' Mark hammers his fist on the door. 'Tom, Sophie!'

Mark's voice booms in my ear. I hear his rising panic, close my eyes, force myself to breathe slowly, in, out, in, out, in, out.

A slow, gentle twist of my wrist. The doorknob turns, the mechanism clicks. The door swings away from me. Mark presses us forward, we tumble into the room.

It's weirdly quiet, no smoke, no sounds of the fire, no crashing timbers. The undercurrent of stale cigarettes is here.

Mark strides past me, looks about the room, at me. 'Not here, Kate. Come on!'

I can't believe it. I was so sure . . .

Mark heads for the door. I pull up the corner of the duvet. No one under the bed.

'We need to get out, Kate!'

A cough, muffled, barely audible. I look towards the French windows, grab the chaise longue, pull it away from the doors. There's no one behind it.

'Mum!'

Sophie, her voice shaking and unsure. I spin around, look at Mark, scan the room. Huddled in the footwell of the dressing table are the twins. Tom's coughing, crying, Sophie shaking, her face, pale as paper. Relief crashes over me. I drop to my hands and knees, grab them, help them scramble out. I try to smile, to hide how terrified I've been for them, and still am for us all.

'What are you doing in here? We need to get out,' I say, trying to keep the anxiety from my voice.

'The shouty man . . .'

Sophie speaks so softly I barely hear her. Tom's nodding for all he's worth.

'Here. Take a puff,' I say, handing my son his inhaler.

'Come on,' says Mark, heading for the door.

The slam rips through the room, rattles the mirrors on the dressing table. The glass in the middle mirror cracks, a jagged section topples forward, smashes into thousands of glittering shards that scatter the table top and floor. Mark stands stock still in front of the door. He snatches at the doorknob, tugs, yanks it. It won't open. I know it won't.

'What the fuck's going on!'

'I told you, Mummy, the scary man!' Sophie's breath is hot against my cheek. Tom wheezes, coughs, hangs on so tightly to my wrist I feel his bones on mine.

Mark turns to face us. Words fail me. No time to explain.

Freezing cold air like a thousand icy fingers jabs my skin. Mark feels it too, I see it in his face, in his confusion, his eyes searching mine for an explanation.

Laughter, a low, dreadful sound fogging my brain, strangling my thoughts.

Sophie dives under the dressing table, Tom scrambling at her heels. They crouch at the very back, pressing against black wood and each other, hands over their ears, eyes scrunched shut.

I grab Mark's hand, shake it.

'Mark! Mark, listen to me. Block him, don't let him in.'

My husband's face is at once terrified, confused, contorting as the laughter grows. I hurry to the dressing table, crouch before the footwell.

'Kids, listen to me. Block him out.'

I grab Sophie's upper arm. She jerks away, huddles closer to Tom. I glance back at Mark, his head in his hands, smoke curling around his ankles, seeping in from beneath the floorboards and door.

The laughter grows louder, stronger in my head. Can't think. I screw my eyes shut. Don't listen to him. Think, Katie, think.

Only one thing comes to mind.

'Sing a song of sixpence a pocket full of rye . . .'

My voice is weak, high, reedy. I gulp in air, smoke catches my throat. I cough and cough, a sourness of burning in my nostrils, on my tongue. I open my eyes, look at my cowering, terrified children. Try again.

'Sing a song of sixpence a pocket full of rye, Four and twenty blackbirds . . .'

I tug Sophie's arm again, she peeps at me between matted strands of hair. 'Sing with me.'

'Sing a song of sixpence a pocket full of rye.'

My voice steadies. Sophie, then Tom's voices blend with mine, grow louder, stronger as we sing. The children fix their eyes on mine. I smile, keep singing.

'As loud as you can. Concentrate on the words, don't let him in.'

The children nod in unison. Mark's halting baritone joins with the song.

'Don't stop,' I say, pulling the twins from beneath the dressing table.

'Strip the bed,' I shout to Mark. 'Throw the mattress out of the French windows.'

Three quick strides and Mark's opened the windows, kicking at the rotten balcony. Metal groans, bits fall, hit the terrace with a dull clang.

Our voices chime together, louder, stronger.

'When the pie was opened the birds began to sing.'

'Sophie, help me pull off the sheets,' I say, throwing the duvet to the floor.

Tom wheezes. Coughs. His skin's grey, lips blue-white. I pull him towards the chaise longue.

'Sit,' I tell him, pulling the inhaler from his fingers, holding it to his lips. 'Take it slowly.'

Tom's eyes find mine as he inhales. I smile, hope I look calm, reassuring, no hint that my heart feels it might burst from my chest.

'I'm so cold, Mum.'

I take off my coat, wrap it around my son.

'Keep singing in your head, Tom. Try not to breath in too much smoke. We'll be out of here in no time.'

Tom's nodding, a half smile. I kiss the top of his head.

'Help me with the mattress,' says Mark, pushing the chaise longue with Tom on it to one side.

We drag the mattress from the bed, pummel it through the window.

'Down came a blackbird and pecked off her nose.'

Sophie sings so loudly she's shouting out each word.

'Don't step on what's left of the balcony, Kate. It won't take any weight.'

We hurl the mattress over the narrow balcony. It lands amongst the pots on the terrace.

'I'll knot the sheets,' I say.

Mark flings the duvet and pillows out after the mattress.

We tie the fabric to the leg of the dressing table, dangle the end out of the window. 'It's a bit short but it'll do,' I say. 'Take Tom, Mark. I'll hang onto the sheet up here and make sure it takes your weight.'

Sophie presses at my side, singing at the top of her voice. Mark takes hold of the sheets, Tom piggybacking, his arms tight about his father's neck.

'Follow Daddy and Tom, Sophie.'

'You're coming?' Sophie's eyes are huge in her white face, her lips moving with the song.

'Straight after you, Sophie. As soon as you're down, take Tom and Riley and run to Mrs Cooper's in the village, okay?'

The smoke seeping through the floorboards and under the door is getting thicker. The fire's reached this floor. I hang onto the sheet. It jerks as Mark, bit by bit, makes his way to the ground.

Sophie screams, eyes fixed on the room behind me. I force myself to keep looking at my daughter's face, not to turn round, not to look at the space behind me.

She moves fast, her backward step a reflex. I grab her wrist, my fingertips slipping against her skin as she falls. The balcony shudders, metal groans, tilts towards the terrace.

'Sophie!'

I'm snatching at air, flaking rust, flaying rose stems. Sophie slides on her back, hits the lip of the collapsing balcony. For an instant, she seems to stop moving, her fingers finding the edge of the metal. Mark's on the ground, arms outstretched, bending, cowering beneath the torrent of falling debris.

Snapping, cracking metal. The balcony ripping away from brickwork, falling, jerking though thick rose branches. Sophie looks up at me as she lies on the listing balcony floor, her eyes terrified. The balcony hits the terrace. Silence. Mark's calling Sophie. He rips rose branches to one side. The balcony landed flat on the terrace. Sophie lies inside it, covered in dust. My daughter's eyes are wide open, fixed on mine, not moving.

Tom's screaming. An unending noise splitting frosty air. He stands on the terrace steps clutching my jacket to his face. Mark's calling Sophie's name over and over. *Answer him, Sophie. Please, please, answer him.* He reaches her, leaning over, scooping her into his arms, half drags, half carries her to where Tom stands. He sits her with her brother, her back to the terrace wall. Her skinny arms around his neck clutch him tight.

'She's alright, Kate. She's alright!'

Mark stands, looks up to where I kneel at the edge of the

room. He's not looking at me. His eyes skid past me, focus on the room at my back. The stink of cigarettes overpowers the stench of the fire. The cold is as deep as a meat safe. Mark's running across the terrace, stops beside the broken balcony.

'Jump, Kate.'

Most of the mattress is buried beneath the balcony. Mark grabs a corner, tries, fails to pull it free. I glance at the ground, how many metres to a landing of smashed tiles, jagged metal, broken pots? Mark drags the duvet and pillows, covers the space beneath here. I can't jump. Won't jump.

I look across the terrace to where the twins stand huddled together. Sophie, then Tom start to sing. They're safe. Whatever happens, my children are out of this place.

I keep my back to the room, edge towards the sheet. Cold penetrates my hoody, my tee-shirt, burns into my skin. Laughter rings in my head, a warning growing louder, stronger. Impossible to keep it out. A shadow, deepening about me, as if someone stands at my back, leaning over me, blocking the light. I'm shaking, fear as much as cold. I grasp the sheet in both hands. I have no choice but to turn around.

I take a breath, steady myself, concentrate on the sound of my children's voices. I close my eyes, swing my legs over the edge, lower myself, elbows on the floorboards.

I won't listen to you. You can't harm me. I won't let you take my family from me.

I open my eyes. The room is a storm of swirling smoke, dust and amongst it all, a deeper darkness. It moves between me and the dressing table. One section of mirror remains, the ancient pitted glass dark, clouded. For an instant I fancy I see something, a curve of a lip, but then there's nothing. Only dust and smoke.

I push myself backwards. My feet find the fabric, rough brickwork. I lower myself slowly, the sheet taut, hand over numb hand, bouncing my feet off the walls, finding a foothold on a broken rose stem, an old stretch of wire. Mark has my ankles, my calves, his hands around my waist as my feet find the ground. He pulls me to him, holds me so tight he crushes the air from me.

'I'm sorry, so sorry, Kate.'

His body is at once warm and solid, but shaking violently. Over his shoulder, I stare at an empty terrace.

'Where are the twins?'

Mark takes my hand, we run to the terrace steps.

'They raced off to get the dog before I could stop them.'

We clear the steps, head for the front of the house.

'Lyle's done this.'

'Lyle?'

'I couldn't catch him earlier, but it was definitely him. I got a really good look.'

'Where did he go to?'

'He ran off towards the village.'

Fear burns like acid in my gut. I'm running flat out, lungs bursting. We round the corner to the front of the building. Sparks shoot into a star-filled sky. Flames spew from windows, roar through the roof. Frost smothers the lawn and driveway, sparkling in the light from the flames.

'Tom! Sophie?'

The garden, lawn and driveway are deserted. I stop, stare up at the burning building, Mark pulls up beside me.

'They'll be heading to Shirley's,' I say.

Would Oliver Lyle harm my children? If Mark's right about the house . . .

'Stay here, I'll check the kennel,' says Mark.

The scream is behind me, a deep, long, low howl that doesn't stop, gets louder as I turn to the sound. After the bright firelight I can't see, my eyes adjust, the dark garden comes into focus. A tall, dark figure runs from the lawn, crosses the drive, comes straight at me. I throw up my hands, cry out.

His shoulder smashes into mine, spins me around, knocks me to the gravel. He sprints to the house, charges up the front steps.

'Stop!' I shout, jumping to my feet.

The man turns to face us, stares through choking, thick black smoke. Oliver Lyle's eyes hold mine for an instant, cold hatred makes me gasp. He turns away, turns to the house, steps through the dark, gaping hole of the open front door.

'The guy's crazy,' says Mark, staring after Lyle. 'No way's anyone getting out of there.'

Barking cuts across the roar of the burning building.

'Riley!' I look about the garden, trying to fix where the sound comes from. The horizon is a pale white line towards the lane and village, dawn bleeding into the darkness.

'Come on,' I say, sprinting up the drive.

I hear them, our children, their voices shouting, Riley barking, barking, barking.

We turn the bend in the drive, Mark takes my hand, pulls me along so fast my feet barely touch the gravel.

The twins stand at the head of the drive, Riley a bundle in Tom's arms, Sophie waving insanely, beckoning us to hurry. She stumbles forward, flings herself at me. I hug her. Hug Tom.

'Come on!' shouts Mark, taking Tom's hand.

Towards the village is a widening band of bright sky. Frozen mist hangs across the fields, ghostly white in the strengthening daylight. Mark, the twins and Riley have reached the turn in the lane, they stop and stare back at me.

'Come on, Mummy!' says Tom.

I look at the house, at Haverscroft. Rafters glow like red-hot ribs. Can a broken soul heal? Can it mend? Perhaps, once the fire burns out, whatever was left here will be at peace. Alan Wynn might know. But right now, my family are waiting. And we've waited far too long. I run to join them.

ACKNOWLEDGEMENTS

A BOOK DOES not come into being by its author's efforts alone. I owe a huge amount of gratitude to all who helped shape Haverscroft in its various stages of growth. Particular thanks go to – Jane Appleton, you are a star, Phil Johnson for your never ending energy and enthusiasm and Emily Robertshaw for being Mrs Havers' unwavering champion.

Lynsey White, the very best writing tutor and friend. Reading each faltering chapter with your morning coffee went above and beyond. Without your faith and encouragement, Haverscroft would never have been.

Andrew McDonnell, fellow Salt 2019 author and Public House tutor, for your calm and constant advice – and the introduction to Salt.

And to Team Salt, Chris, Jen and Emma, thank you for loving my story enough to make it one of your own. #SaltAt20

NEW FICTION FROM SALT

ELEANOR ANSTRUTHER
A Perfect Explanation (978-1-78463-164-2)

NEIL CAMPBELL
Lanyards (978-1-78463-170-3)

MARK CAREW
Magnus (978-1-78463-204-5)

ANDREW COWAN
Your Fault (978-1-78463-180-2)

AMANTHI HARRIS
Beautiful Place (978-1-78463-193-2)

S. A. HARRIS
Haverscroft (978-1-78463-200-7)

CHRISTINA JAMES
Chasing Hares (978-1-78463-189-5)

RECENT FICTION FROM SALT

SAMUEL FISHER
The Chameleon (978-1-78463-124-6)

BEE LEWIS
Liminal (978-1-78463-138-3)

VESNA MAIN
Temptation: A User's Guide (978-1-78463-128-4)

ALISON MOORE
Missing (978-1-78463-140-6)

S. J. NAUDÉ
The Third Reel (978-1-78463-150-5)

HANNAH VINCENT
The Weaning (978-1-78463-120-8)

PHIL WHITAKER
You (978-1-78463-144-4)

RECENT FICTION FROM SALT

XAN BROOKS
The Clocks in This House All Tell Different Times
(978-1-78463-093-5)

MICKEY J C ORRIGAN
Project XX (978-1-78463-097-3)

MARIE GAMESON
The Giddy Career of Mr Gadd (deceased)
(978-1-78463-118-5)

LESLEY GLAISTER
The Squeeze (978-1-78463-116-1)

NAOMI HAMILL
How To Be a Kosovan Bride (978-1-78463-095-9)

CHRISTINA JAMES
Fair of Face (978-1-78463-108-6)

NEW POETRY FROM SALT

DAVID BRIGGS
Cracked Skull Cinema (978-1-78463-207-6)

MICHAEL BROWN
Where Grown Men Go (978-1-78463-208-3)

PETER DANIELS
My Tin Watermelon (978-1-78463-209-0)

MATTHEW HAIGH
Death Magazine (978-1-78463-206-9)

ANDREW McDONNELL
The Somnambulist Cookbook (978-1-78463-199-4)

ELEANOR REES
The Well at Winter Solstice (978-1-78463-184-0)

TONY WILLIAMS
Hawthorn City (978-1-78463-212-0)

This book has been typeset by
SALT PUBLISHING LIMITED
using Neacademia, a font designed by Sergei Egorov
for the Rosetta Type Foundry in the Czech Republic. It
is manufactured using Holmen Book Cream 70gsm, a
Forest Stewardship Council™ certified paper from the
Hallsta Paper Mill in Sweden. It was printed and bound
by Clays Limited in Bungay, Suffolk, Great Britain.

CROMER
GREAT BRITAIN
MMXIX